HIDDEN PROMISES

GEORGINA MAKALANI

ISBN: 978-0-6487227-1-7

Also by Georgina Makalani

The Magics of Rei-Een:
The Hidden Princess
Hidden Promises
The Hidden Phoenix

The Raven Crown Series:
Raven's Dawn
The Caged Raven
Raven's Edge

Other Stories:
The Mark of Oldra

The Legend of Iski Flare (Novella series):
The Legend Begins
Red Wolves
The Riddle of Daralis
The Last Child
The Tree Maiden
Reflections
The Beast

Short Stories:
Stuffed Frogs and Spinning Teacups
Searcher
The Silence (in Glimpses)

For the TWG

1

Remi walked with a determined gait through the front entrance of the prison. His anger at the magics burned across his skin. He couldn't believe their audacity to attack the centre of the Empire and the emperor himself. He tried not to think about Lis. As angry as he was that she had hidden her true nature from him, it was more disappointment he felt when he thought of her. He had cared for her so much, and he hadn't even guessed she was magic. It caused him to question the world he lived in.

He shook his head and refocused on his visit. He had made numerous visits to the prison since the attack, but he had yet to learn anything. One of them knew what had happened to his brother, and today he was going to get that information out of them, no matter what it took.

He strode along the cool, lengthy corridor, the pale, windowless stone wall to his right and the cells to his left. Each cell was separated from the next by a thick stone wall, but the only thing between the cells and the corridor was a wall of thick iron bars. Each cell, only just big enough for a man to lie down in, contained a single magic.

He noted that they all sat in the same position, backs against a side wall and staring silently at the floor. In the fifth cell along the corridor, the magic sat against the back wall of the cell and stared directly at Remi. When Remi stopped, the man grinned.

'I will start here,' Remi said, holding up his hand to stop the soldier walking behind him. He wanted to go into the cell, take the man by the scruff and demand answers, but the memory of what they had threatened Lis with was too close. As was what they had done to U'shi. Remi didn't know what the man might do in close quarters. He could always stop the magic with his sharp sword, but dead men gave little information.

The hunter had tried talking to them, but he hadn't managed to get any information. Remi needed to get something tangible from these men soon, or his father would have them killed no matter what he could learn from them.

'I can tell you nothing else about your princess,' the man said, standing slowly and swaying a little. They had been detained for several days and been offered nothing other than a little water. Yet Remi wondered what they could do for themselves if the need arose.

'Can you add nothing more to the fact that you want her dead?' he asked, although he wasn't really sure he wanted to hear anything else. Lis had not been what he had thought she was, and he hadn't seen her since the night he had discovered that. He still wasn't sure if he wanted to see her or not. Several times he had found himself walking towards her little palace, then turning away again.

'It is a fact you are already aware of. It is what we need to further our cause.'

'Your cause,' Remi said slowly. 'And where did my brother fit into that?'

The man shrugged, although he didn't look away. He knew something about Ta-Sho; Remi could see it clearly on his face.

'Did you meet with the crown prince?' Remi asked, trying hard to stand still. A nervousness he hadn't felt previously made his legs itch, and he wanted desperately to move from foot to foot.

'I am meeting with him now,' the man said, a friendly smile

surprising Remi.

'Did you meet my brother?' Remi asked firmly. He had no time or patience for games.

'I did not have the pleasure.'

'But you know who killed him.' Remi didn't ask, for he knew the answer.

The man shrugged again, as though it was not important, and Remi's hand closed around the handle of his sword.

'What makes you think it was one of us?' the magic asked.

'He was killed with fire.'

'Magic fire? Or did his lover simply touch a torch to his fine clothes?'

Remi reached out quickly, pushing the sword between the bars. He was fast, but the magic was faster, stepping back just out of reach. Remi desperately wanted to enter the cell, but he didn't know what this man might do, and he still had questions. If he frustrated Remi any further, he might kill the prisoner before he got the answers he needed.

'Do you have any idea what might have happened to him?' Remi asked, keeping his voice level despite the anger building in his chest.

'I might,' the man said, turning from the bars and sitting down on the floor. 'But you wouldn't believe me.'

'I might,' Remi said as the hunter appeared beside him.

The magic assumed the same position as the others and stared at the floor. Remi took a slow breath, trying to calm the frustrations threatening to burst through his skin. These men had the answers he had been looking for, yet he didn't know how to get that information from them.

One of them knew what had happened, or maybe more of them knew. For all he was aware, several men could have been responsible for his brother's death. He had made such a suggestion himself before, when his father had been sure there was one man— one normal man. But that wasn't the case. There was clearly magic; even Lis had sensed it.

'What else might she sense?' he murmured to himself.

The man looked up then. His face was serious, and Remi waited for him to grin, but it didn't come. They wanted her dead. How was their need to destroy Lis connected to Ta-Sho, and how could he get them to tell him the truth?

Remi indicated for the hunter to leave him with a quick sideways motion of his head. He gave Remi a hard look before he nodded and, taking the other soldier with him, left Remi with the magics.

Remi moved along to the next cell, where the man leaned against the wall just as the others did. He didn't know what skills these people had or what they might do with it, and there was a nervous energy around the prison in holding them there.

'Why did you need the crown prince dead?' Remi asked. 'How did his death benefit your cause?'

The man looked up at him slowly, but he shook his head.

'Is the man who killed him here?'

The man continued to stare at Remi but said nothing. If the killer was amongst the group, Remi doubted any of them would give him up. 'How did you get into the royal residence?' he asked.

'When?' the man in the previous cell asked. Remi wondered if this man was their leader.

As Remi looked back towards him, the man in the cell before him stood slowly. Like the man who had spoken, he never took his eyes from Remi.

'What exactly do you want to know?' the man in the previous cell asked, a tiredness to his voice.

'I want to know what happened to my brother. I want to know how you managed to work your way across the Palace Isle without our hunters knowing you were here.'

'Someone knew we were. Did you not feel our magic?'

Remi could still feel the background hum. Although he could sense the magic when they used it, now it was as though he knew the magic was there yet couldn't sense it. He sighed before he could stop himself.

'We just want a chance to live.'

'You want more than that, or you would have moved away to where you would be safe. Instead you attack our palace, the hidden princess, the emperor and empress—and before that, someone killed the crown prince.'

'We want what is ours,' the man said, and then no more.

Remi spent the next hour moving between the cells trying to determine what they knew. The only one to talk was the man in the fifth cell, and he wasn't making enough sense for Remi, nor was he addressing what Remi wanted to know. He wouldn't discuss Lis or anything pertaining to Ta-Sho's death.

Did they not know what had happened to him, or why he had been killed? They were fairly clear about what their future was meant to be, and Remi could only guess Ta-Sho had stood in the way of that. He needed to find another way to get the information from them. But he also had to be careful not to provoke their magic. If a fire bearer was determined to burn through Remi, he might not be able to stop it. He was always quick with his sword, but he might not get the chance to use it within the small confines of this part of the prison.

Remi left the prison with the same determined step as when he'd entered it, only now he didn't know where he was going or how he could get at the knowledge he needed. The man in the sixth cell had intrigued him—he'd been the only other one to look up from the floor—but only the magic in the fifth cell had talked. Remi wondered if they had another way of communicating or if it was enough that the occupants of every cell could hear his conversation.

He stopped and looked about. Again, he was making his way towards the hidden princess.

Healer Yang lay back in the afternoon sunshine and tried not to sigh. He hadn't wanted to leave Lis's side, but he needed some fresh air. When another healer had come to check on his progress with the princess, he had made comment on Yang's lack of skill. But it was her own doing. Lis wouldn't allow the healing to take.

She was sure the crown prince was going to kill her in his own way, and she wanted to die on her own terms. The prince had been nowhere near them since he had tried to kill her.

It was fear of what she was, Yang thought, *rather than a hatred of her, as Lis seemed so convinced was the truth.*

She didn't want to be where she was, as a hidden princess. She had only used her magic because she needed to, yet she was hurt by the prince's sudden change towards her because of it.

Prince Remi had been too familiar, Yang decided. It was not the way for a prince to behave. He had wanted to be close to her. He had visited at all hours, sneaking in to watch over her sleeping, taking breakfast with them to ensure she ate.

A single soft cloud moved across the sky. If he concentrated, he could pretend that there were no walls around him, that he was lying out somewhere free, like the little island Lis had grown up on.

'I told you she was not to be left alone,' the hunter Hui Te-Sze snapped as he pushed open the gate with a bang. Yang stayed exactly where he was.

'Sir,' the guard said, a nervous edge to his voice.

'I know what she can do,' he continued.

'Do you?' Yang asked.

The hunter leaned over him, blocking his view of the sky and dragging him back to the world he lived in. 'She can escape.'

'She can barely move, and despite her illness…' Yang wasn't sure how else to describe it. 'She is with the tutors.'

'And who allowed them entry?'

'The empress,' Princess Wei-Song said, although the world thought her only a maid. Her mother had done so much to keep her safe from a world that feared magic.

The hunter sighed.

'Why are you not watching over her then, *healer*? Is it not your job to ensure she is healthy?'

'She has given up,' he murmured, climbing to his feet. He was not surprised but still disappointed when the man smirked. 'There is little I can do. She will be dead soon enough and you can go hunt someone else.'

The princess by the door pulled her lips into a hard line. She too had tried to console Lis. She had suggested teaching her or testing her to see what else she could do, but Lis wouldn't risk her prince any further. Yang had tested himself a little more and, despite the increased number of guards around their little piece of the world, he was quite enjoying his lessons with Wei-Song.

But today the tutors had come in force, at the behest of their empress. No matter the rumours, for they were only rumours, their hidden princess had not enough time to be trained.

Yang took a deep breath before he entered the little room. She knelt leaning over the table, and the air felt sickly and heavy. He tried not to breathe in, wondering if everyone could sense the putrefaction of his princess or if it was only his magic that allowed it.

She created her characters with a perfect hand. Her fingers closed around the brush, but he knew the scars that remained. She maintained her focus, and Wei-Song gave him a not very subtle look.

'How fares the lesson?' he asked, trying to mask his concerns.

'How is the sun?' she asked without looking up. He could hear the exhaustion and pain in her voice and wondered briefly if the tutors could hear it also.

'Sunny,' he said, and she looked up with a small smile. 'I could beg for you to come outside.' He knew he would have to beg her to leave the room and the guards to allow it, and so far the hunter was having none of it. He had considered asking the crown prince, but he wasn't very keen on seeing the man again. The prince was the one who had destroyed her, not those with magic trying to prevent a prophecy. A prophecy that seemed would not come to fruition.

The surprising aspect of the situation was the lack of people who knew just what she was. Yang had hoped it was the prince who kept her secret, but it was more likely the empress. Although he had no idea how she had managed to convince the prince to keep it quiet. The guards who surrounded her certainly knew what she was, and they didn't look at her with the same level of hatred the prince had that night.

The emperor had recovered and assumed that his soldiers had taken the magics down. It also appeared, from what Wei-Song told him, that the emperor was determined an end to the fighting had occurred. They knew differently. Yang could still feel the hum of magic, and he wondered if the prince could also sense it. Although the prince hadn't been able to sense the Hidden.

He sighed as she turned her attention back to her work. She moved gracefully, fluidly. Yang knew she had a skill he did not, and he wondered if that was why the crown prince kept her alive. But when would she have the chance to use her skills?

'You are sighing again,' she said without pausing in her work.

'I try not to.'

'And yet you do.'

'What would you like me to do?' he asked, bowing low.

She huffed and shook her head. 'Don't pretend I am something other than what I am.'

Tutor Jichun muttered something under his breath.

'Is it wrong?' she asked, real concern on her face, and Yang wondered if she could magic whatever was needed.

'You are perfect,' the tutor hummed. 'The empress wishes to take your classes tomorrow. She has asked us to clear the schedule for her, although I don't know what she would teach.'

'Do you not think she has the ability?' Wei-Song asked, and Yang couldn't hide his smile. She was so protective of her mother. He wondered how many times she had hidden with her before she could hide more openly as a maid.

He also had an idea of why the empress wanted time with the hidden princess. For she was just as keen as Wei-Song to learn what Lis could do. She was going to be disappointed, he thought as he watched Lis's gentle strokes over the paper. She put the brush down with a shaky hand and he stepped forward.

'I think you should rest.'

'I agree,' the tutor added before she had the chance to retort.

She bowed to them both and moved to the back of the room where a narrow bed sat against the wall. Yang sighed before he could stop himself. The room, this little palace, was not fit for a hidden princess. Particularly one who had saved the royal family.

'Prepare the tea,' he said to the maid and then glanced up, remembering who she was. She bowed, clearly in character for the tutor, but he would pay for the comment later. The three of them had become an odd little family of sorts.

The tutors bowed and took their leave. When the door shut behind them, it was as though Lis's strength evaporated. She slumped in the bed, and he raced forward to help her lie down. 'You do too much,' he murmured.

'You would tell me I don't do enough,' she whispered, her eyes heavy.

'You certainly appear as though you can do all that is required.'

'Lucky I have you and your tea,' she said with her eyes still closed. 'Don't look at me that way.'

He poked his tongue out despite her eyes remaining closed. She giggled, and the sound warmed his heart.

He had tried to cheat her a little. When she would sit up and drink her tea, he would pour a little of his energy into her. He had learnt how to be subtle. In a way, it was like when he tried to heal, the will of it making the magic ebb from him to her. He worked in a similar way as she slept of a night.

She shook her head when he helped her to sit up as Wei-Song appeared with the tea.

'I know what you try to do,' she whispered, giving him a sideways glance as she took the cup.

Yang tried to concentrate with the sound of movement in the yard, and then the prince stood in the doorway.

Lis continued in her slow movement as though he wasn't there, but Yang could feel the tension in her muscles. Wei-Song stood slowly between them, allowing Lis to take the full weight of the cup. Yang smiled. Wei-Song was fierce, and he had a good idea she would win any fight with the crown prince.

As Prince Remi remained silent, Lis gently touched Wei-Song on the arm, and he could feel the strength it took for her to do it. The girl sighed and walked out into the garden. Lis handed the cup to Yang, but he remained where he was.

'What else could he do to me?' she asked, her voice cracking in her throat despite the tea.

'You are sure?'

She nodded once, her eyes never rising from her hands. He bowed low and, with the cup still in his hand, followed Wei-Song out into the garden. The sunshine he had enjoyed so much not so long ago felt harsh and unkind.

His fate was entwined with hers, and he could not let the prince kill her further.

2

Lis looked far worse than Remi had imagined, far worse than the last time he had seen her, and he still wasn't sure what he thought he could gain by seeing her now. His mother suggested too often that he visit, and yet it had not been so long ago that she had warned him away. Reminding him of the traditions, and that he was ruining what semblance of the world they had left.

Although that seemed to lie about him in tatters now. After the magic and the men and the power she had. It scared him, honestly scared him, and he didn't know what to do with that other than kill her.

She looked so close to death now that he wondered if it was the magic that did that to her. She was slumped forward in the bed, her eyes dark, her skin sallow and her cheeks hollowed out.

Has it been so long?

She pushed the covers back and swung her legs over the edge of the bed. She looked so thin, and a strange dark spot covered her belly, as though an evil leached from her. He wondered what good the healer did.

She noticed him looking and waved her hand, although it took obvious effort to do so. 'I am nothing,' she said, her voice thin and strained.

'Do you mean it is nothing?'

'I know what I say.' Her voice was just as quiet, but it carried a strength behind it, a vehemence that surprised him.

He stepped forward and she flinched. He stopped, clenching his fists by his side. He had left his sword with the hunter, who was not happy about it, but he didn't think he could face her with it again. He didn't know how she would react, and he wasn't sure what he might do.

She pushed herself up onto shaky legs and fell forward rather than knelt, bowing low before him.

'Forgive me for not greeting you properly, Your Highness. If I had known you were coming…' She looked around the little room and then back to the floor before her. 'I would have prepared an appropriate greeting.'

'You never prepared anything for my previous visits,' Remi said, unsure how his voice sounded so level.

'Breakfast was Mu-Phi's domain,' she said, her head still focused on the floor before her. 'Tutor Na would be disappointed in my training. I shall endeavour to do better.'

'I am sure you study hard,' he said, taking another small step forward. Her body tensed, readying to move out of the way, and it burnt in his chest that she feared him. But then she didn't appear to have the strength to escape him. He bent forward to help her up and then remembered the power she did have. He straightened, leaving her on the floor. She might not be what she appeared.

'You may get up,' he said.

She shook her head, staying where she was.

'I am sure you rise when my mother commands it.'

'If you command me, I will obey,' she said, putting her hand flat on the floor and gathering her dress in her other hand.

He watched bewildered for a moment before she pushed back to her toes, lifting slowly from the ground. She shook a little and put out a hand, more for balance than anything else, and he took it to steady her without thinking.

She gasped, overbalancing as she pulled away from him. He

reached out again, pulling her close and breathing in the strange scent that surrounded her. She shook wildly in his arms, her hand moving to her stomach, and when he chanced to look at her face, he could only see fear as the tears welled and spilled over quickly.

'You are stronger than this,' he said.

She shook her head. And he released her onto the bed, lowering her carefully. Her arms wrapped around her middle, where he noticed the dark stain had grown.

'What has happened to you?' He knelt before her, pulling her hands from her dress and trying to ignore the shaking.

She shook her head.

'Healer Yang,' he cried out, and she cowered from him, trying desperately to pull from his hold.

The man appeared quickly but paused a step from them, a dark expression on his face. Remi knew the man blamed him for this mess.

'Why have you not healed her?'

'She can't be healed,' he said, his voice clipped.

'Because of the magic?'

She tried again to pull from him, but there was no strength there at all.

'Because of you,' the healer said. 'Because she does not want to be healed.'

Remi looked at her, the fear still evident on her face.

'You don't want to live?' he asked.

She shook her head.

'Why?'

'If I am not worthy of a quick death, then I must endure a slow one.'

'You have done this to yourself,' he scolded, releasing her hands, and she pulled herself away from him as far across the little bed as she could. 'This is not where a hidden princess should be.'

A strange cackle filled the room from the woman who had seemed so sure of herself not so long ago. 'Hidden,' she laughed.

She made to touch her hands together, and Yang shook his head. She clapped them together with what little strength she had and then laughed again. 'I can't hide,' she said. Her bottom lip quivered as dark tears ran down her cheeks.

'Lis,' Yang chided gently.

Remi looked between the two of them, then reached forward and gently touched a finger to her cheek. It was as though she cried blood. Yang shook his head and left the room.

'What have you done?' he asked.

'What you wanted of me,' she whispered, the seriousness back in her voice.

'I don't want this.'

'You need a new princess,' she said, allowing her tired body to slide down to lie flat across the bed.

'I have one.'

'You don't want her. The people don't need her.'

'I heard there was a prophecy that she would unite the empire.'

'From a mad man with fire in his hands. I am sorry, Remi.'

His skin prickled when he heard his name. She had never used it before. She closed her eyes, and panic filled his chest.

'I won't let you do this,' he commanded.

She huffed and remained still. He watched her for too long, the light dimming around them until the girl appeared with a lamp. He wrapped the covers around Lis, worried that she would not make it through the night.

He had done this. But then he didn't know what he should do. He couldn't discuss with his parents what she was, for he knew what would happen then. She might have saved them, but she was still one with magic.

She sighed in her sleep and then groaned, rolling slightly, and he moved from his stiff knees to sit on the edge of the bed. Yang watched him from the corner of the room, and he waved the man forward. Yang shook his head. 'It is your turn,' he whispered and stepped back into the shadows.

Remi lay down beside her and gently brushed the hair from her face. The tutor had reported that she was unwell but still completing her studies. His mother didn't appear concerned, but then he didn't know if she knew what had occurred between them.

He gently rested his hand on her shoulder. He wanted to pull her into his arms as he had before, to have her cling to him as though he were a lifeline rather than the enemy he had become. 'I didn't hear the fizzle,' he murmured close to her ear. As his sword had penetrated her skin, he hadn't felt or heard anything. But then if she was Hidden, perhaps no one would.

'Fly,' she murmured. 'Remi, fly.' And she rolled into him a little more.

Lis woke warm and comfortable for the first time in what seemed like an age. Her body felt a little less stiff as she stretched. Yang had spent too much time trying to help her. Although she had tried to tell him she was not worth the effort, he wouldn't leave her side. In part because he too had learnt he was Hidden. Able to hide his true skill away from the hunters. He certainly seemed to be embracing it. After healing the empress of the darkness they had thought the priestesses had put on her, he had dedicated his time to healing Lis. She smiled at the thought of his warm embrace. He was usually close, but not usually wrapped around her body, and it was comfortable.

A hand rested on her foot, and she glanced towards the end of the bed where he sat, his hand on her leg, his back resting against the wall, sleeping soundly. That meant someone else was at her back. And although she had become friends, in a way, with Wei-Song, Lis knew it wasn't her.

A deep voice murmured something and sighed against her skin. A wave of energy like what Yang had passed to her flowed over the arms wrapped around her. Did he understand what skill he had?

'Your Highness,' Wei-Song whispered over her. 'Do you want your morning tea?'

'Do you ever sleep?' Lis asked, trying to sound light.

'Not yet,' the prince murmured as he rolled over onto his back.

Lis turned and looked him over; he was calm in his sleep, his brow less furrowed. He looked like the man she had begun to like when he would visit her room in the residence and make sure she ate her breakfast.

Wei-Song looked at him with a mix of annoyance and curiosity. A brother she didn't know, one who didn't even know of her existence, let alone who she really was.

'You murmured in your sleep,' she said, handing Lis the cup as she sat slowly, pulling her leg from Yang's grasp and leaning against the wall.

'I'm surprised I got any, surrounded as I was.' She sipped at the small cup. The tea was bitter, but she drank it without complaint. Yang would have ensured it had something in it to help her heal.

'You were cocooned in their care,' she said. 'What did you dream of?'

'I don't remember,' Lis lied. She was sure she'd been flying again, Remi's arms tight around her, and she wondered if that was because of what he did for her. She had also dreamt of the fire and destruction, but it hadn't left her feeling dry and burnt as it had before.

'He has embraced what he is,' Wei-Song whispered, looking over at Yang sleeping awkwardly. 'You need to do the same,' she said with a friendly smile.

Lis sighed and opened her mouth to say something else, but Wei-Song bowed low and turned.

Lis realised the prince was awake, lying still, his eyes blinking into the morning light.

'You look better,' he said.

She bowed her head to him but couldn't speak. What could she say to him? She didn't know where to start, and she was scared that he still feared her.

He surprised her by taking her hand in his and examining the marks his sword had caused across the skin. They were red and angry, but they had healed over. He ran a finger across her palm and she shivered at the touch, pulling away from him. He let her go with a sigh.

'Your Highness,' she managed, her voice feeling raw, and Yang murmured something in his sleep.

'You called me Remi last night,' he said, a smile playing on his lips. She felt a relief with it, but she bowed again.

'I beg your forgiveness,' she said.

'There is no need,' he said. The smile slipped, and he rolled away from her off the bed.

Fear washed over her again. 'I understand that you cannot forgive me,' she said as Yang stirred.

The prince looked at him before running his hand over his hair. He looked about, perhaps for the maid, then walked to the kettle on the end of the table. He poured himself a cup and sat down. She watched him closely, unsure of why he was here and what he might do.

She had a vague memory of him the day before, the overwhelming pain of his presence, and she put her hand to her stomach.

'Does it hurt you?' he asked, his voice level and his eyes kind.

She shook her head. 'I feel much better this morning,' she said.

'As you do most mornings,' Yang murmured, 'before you undo all I do.'

Yang leaned back against the wall, his eyes still closed and his hand reaching out for her. She smiled at him and leaned back beside him. 'You have to let me go,' she whispered, reaching out for his hand.

'You are determined to die?' the prince asked.

She nodded without opening her eyes. 'I have nothing left.'

'You have your position, your duty.'

She heard Wei-Song laugh, but when Lis opened her eyes she was gone.

'How will you appear as an emperor,' she asked him gently, 'when you can't even look at me? Would you have me hidden away forever?'

He shook his head.

'There are other expectations of this duty, one of which is producing your heir.' She sighed and closed her eyes again. He might return to the very old custom of concubines. She nodded slowly to herself at the idea. He could find a way to make her live this pain every day.

'What do you see?' he asked, too close, and she opened her eyes to find him before her again.

'A way for you to have what you want.'

He sat slowly on the edge of the bed, and the healer blinked opened sleepy eyes. 'You work too hard,' she said, squeezing his hand. 'Sleep.'

He nodded and drifted away again. She felt so clear this morning; he had given her too much.

The prince looked at her hand and then back to her face. 'Tell me,' he murmured, 'will you have another man's child and sell it as mine?'

She looked at him closely for a moment, confused at where his words had come from. 'You would take another. The emperors of old would take concubines to ensure their line would continue. You could not take a child of mine to be heir.'

'What?' he stammered.

'Magic,' she whispered, leaning forward. 'You could not risk what it might do.'

His face set in an angry scowl, and she pulled back from him.

He called for the guard. The noise jolted Yang awake, and Lis regretted the move when she looked at his tired eyes.

The hunter appeared carrying a sword, and Lis wished she could disappear back into the wall.

'Prepare a group,' he said. 'We travel to the baths.'

The hunter looked at her with narrowed eyes. 'She will hide,' he sneered.

'I can't,' she threw back.

He sucked in an angry breath but left the house to do as he was bid.

'Are you to drown me?' she asked.

'I want to help you,' he snapped, standing up, and Yang looked between them.

'It could help,' he murmured as he looked at her more closely, his hand on her cheek. 'You look a little better.'

'You did too much for me,' she said, leaning into him.

'Now,' the prince called from the door.

Lis moved to the edge of the bed and stood. She felt a little less wobbly than she had the previous day, but Yang was quickly beneath her arm, holding her up.

'Prepare fresh clothes,' the prince called into the darkness. Lis wondered if Wei-Song was there or already hiding. 'Come,' he said, motioning towards the door, and Lis wondered what he had planned.

The journey was hard on her body, with the sedan chair jolting her back and forth. She worried for Yang; he had pushed too much of his own energy on her. She was carried through the gate and the litter put down.

She stepped out onto the gravel path and winced, for she hadn't any shoes. The prince had her up in his arms, pressed against his body, and she tensed. When he carried her through to the royal baths, she was surprised that she was still able to use them. But as they neared the deep pool, the fear that he would drown her overwhelmed her, and she fought his hold.

'You give the impression you want to die,' he murmured as he put her down carefully. She stepped away from him, the tiles slippery beneath her feet. 'But you don't.'

'You don't know me,' she murmured.

'No,' he said, with a real sadness, 'but I want to help you.'

Lis could only stare.

'Now get in the water.'

She looked between the water and him, unsure how or what she should do next. She looked back towards the door and longed for Yang to help her.

'Get in the water,' he said, his voice firmer as he stepped towards her.

She stepped back but slipped, and he caught her easily.

'This is not right,' she murmured. 'People will talk.'

He laughed, and she relaxed a little at the sound. 'I have already seen you, and you sound like my mother. No one knows we are here. No one will say anything.'

Lis looked back to the door. *The hunter might,* she thought.

She nodded slowly and started to remove her clothing, but the sash was tight, and her fingers wouldn't work as they should. He stepped forward and helped. She stood before him with her arms by her sides and wondered at the fast beat of her heart. She had been annoyed the last time that he hadn't really looked at her. Now he stared openly.

'You are so thin,' he murmured, running his hand across the hollow at her shoulder. She tried not to shiver under his touch as she wondered what else he would do to torture her. For he seemed to be doing so much better at it than she had done to herself. He reached for her stomach, and she glanced down at the black mark that spread its wispy fingers across her flesh. The wound was still evident at the centre of it, although not as deep as it had been.

Yang had worked hard to try and heal her. But she had allowed the rot to take hold. If she survived this, she doubted children would be possible. She blinked back sudden tears.

'What have you done?' he whispered.

'You are the one who pushed a sword into me,' she said, standing taller. 'You are the one who wants me dead. Why do you all try so hard to prevent it—or is that part of the game?'

He shook his head slowly and took her arm to guide her towards the water.

She moved carefully down the steps and then stepped off into the middle. She allowed the water to cover her head, and the warmth surrounded her. She floated for a moment before breaking the surface.

When she looked up, he watched her with serious eyes. Yang stood beside him looking concerned. She turned her back on them both and sat upon a step.

She rested her head against the tile and then sat up. She could only think of the magic man who had attacked her on her first visit, and it was as though she was waiting for the same fate. She stood again and made to climb out, but Yang smiled when she looked up.

'It looks better,' he said.

She scowled and continued to climb.

'What are you doing?' the prince asked.

'You wanted me in the water. I have been in the water.'

'I thought you might relax.'

'I cannot,' she said. 'Why do you do this?' she asked, suddenly unable to prevent the anger washing over her. She stood naked before her crown prince. 'Do you hate me so much that I must suffer for the rest of my days? If you cannot do as you must, perhaps I should talk with the emperor so he can do what you can't.'

'What do you think—'

'Please, just kill me,' she blurted, frustrated that her voice wobbled as it did. 'I am not strong enough to bear the torture.'

He shook his head slowly, and she stepped back into the middle of the pool. She sank a little, but she had to work at staying under. Her body betrayed her, trying to rise to the surface, and then there was movement before her in the dark water as strong hands pulled her up.

'Don't do this to me,' Yang admonished. 'I am getting a bad reputation as a healer, and if you die, it will be ruined.'

He was fully dressed and struggling, starting to sink. A strong hand grabbed him from behind. The prince stood on the steps, wet to his knees as he tried to lift the sodden healer out. Once out beside the pool, Yang started to shiver.

'What have you done?' Lis asked.

'What I am trained to do.'

'Can you even swim?'

'You are the worst friend I have,' he whispered, and the tears flowed before she could stop them.

Wei-Song appeared and stopped for a moment before rushing forward with a large towel, which she draped around Lis's shoulders. 'I'll get another,' she murmured, then raced back out of the room.

'You would think the royal family would be prepared,' Lis muttered, looking about the space before pulling at the blanket around her. She leaned over her friend, but the prince put his arms around her to stop her movement.

'The maid will bring more,' he said.

'But he needs it now.'

'Not as much as you do,' he said, still holding her tight.

Yang lifted himself onto an elbow and nodded. 'He is right,' he said with a sigh, the shiver still working over his body. The water was warm and the room was warm, but he continued to shiver.

'You were too tired for this,' she murmured. 'Did you spend the night trying to heal me again?'

'I will not have you talk of this anymore,' the prince said, his voice angry. As he let her go and stepped away, he too shivered a little, and she realised just how wet he was.

'Why am I here?' she asked.

'I thought it would help.'

'Help what?' She stood and pulled the blanket around her.

'Your mind,' he snapped.

'As though you could heal the magic?' she asked, wondering if such a thing were possible and why they hadn't tried it before the killing started.

He sighed. 'I cannot let you die,' he murmured, looking at the ground as though acknowledging defeat. 'I couldn't kill you, and I can't watch you let my confusion and hatred consume you.'

She blinked in the face of his honesty, vaguely aware of Wei-Song wrapping the healer in a blanket.

'You do hate me,' she said, then covered her mouth. She bowed a little. 'As you should.'

'I don't hate you,' he said. 'I…'

'You are scared of me,' she said, looking down. 'I would never harm you.'

'I know that, but you do when you allow yourself to… when you try to…'

Lis sighed and knelt carefully on the tiles. She held her hands out to the prince, trying to hide her body from him. 'What do you want me to do?'

'Allow the healer to heal,' he said. 'And…'

She waited, her hands still outstretched as he knelt before her.

'Where has the strong woman gone?'

'Which one?' Lis asked, pulling her arms in close to her chest.

'The one who would laugh with me over breakfast. The one who dreamt of fire.'

Wei-Song stepped forward. 'I will watch over her,' she said, getting between them and helping Lis to her feet.

'I shall send for Mu-Phi,' he said.

Lis nodded once, and the princess with her arms around her guided her back to the door. 'I will watch over her,' she repeated.

3

The empress swept into the room, holding her hands out to Wei-Song just as Lis caught her eye and shook her head.

She clapped them together instead and smiled at Lis, who had sticks in her hand and food raised to her mouth. 'You look much better,' she said, then glanced at Mu-Phi, who was kneeling by the table to ensure enough food was placed in her bowl.

'She has strict instructions,' Lis said.

'So it seems,' the empress mused, sitting slowly opposite her at the small table. 'Remi assures me this is a safe place,' she added, looking around the small space.

Lis nodded as she stuffed food into her mouth. She was actually much hungrier than she'd realised. Had it been so long since she had eaten properly? Once she had allowed the healing to take hold, it had not taken long for her body to happily accept her decision and the food she shovelled into it.

Yang still sat close, watching her more closely than the prince, who had visited again that morning but still could not quite look her in the eye.

'He helps,' the empress said, indicating the healer with a tip of her head. 'The Imperial Healer has concerns with his ability, but I see you are stronger.'

Lis nodded again. 'He does too much,' she said, before pushing another mouthful in.

'I had a plan for the day, but I'm not sure it is the best idea.' The empress glanced at Yang, but Lis knew it was for Mu-Phi's sake. She was a spy and they all knew it. 'I would much rather we just sit together.'

'Have they found you somewhere suitable?' Lis asked.

The empress nodded absently. 'Although the world looks different with the residence gone.'

'I can imagine,' Lis said.

'You have been moved too often,' the empress added.

'Always by necessity,' Lis said. 'I'm not sure what I imagined for my time here at the Palace Isle, but this isn't it.'

The empress smiled and reached across to take her hand. Lis noticed Wei-Song shift uncomfortably in the far corner of the room.

'Perhaps now that the prince has sent Mu-Phi to watch over me, Wei-Song could return to you?' Lis offered.

The empress smiled, but Wei-Song shook her head. 'She thinks you are in greater need,' the empress said, her voice a little sad.

'We will cope. There are people everywhere, in case something were to happen.'

'Do you think you are in danger?' The empress leaned forward, concern heavy on her voice.

'I think the prince still worries he is in danger.'

'That is not the case,' Mu-Phi said sharply.

'Really?' the empress asked, her previous relaxed demeanour evaporating. 'You know my son's mind so well?'

'He is only worried for the safety of the princess,' Mu-Phi said without blinking, and the empress turned to Lis and raised her eyebrows.

'They are friends,' Lis whispered loudly across the table. 'She knows the mind of the prince better than most; far better than I could presume to know,' she added, wondering if he'd spent his night wrapped around her, and an odd thought arose.

'What is it?' the empress asked.

Lis shook her head. The previous morning, she had woken feeling heat and energy flow through her, but not just from the healer. The prince had imparted something on her as well, and she wondered if he'd done it willingly or if his magic had leaked in some way, aware of the void in her. She had been well aware of the magic, but it was only now dawning on her just what it might mean.

Wei-Song stepped forward from the shadows.

There was much the empress was aware of and more she would willingly protect them from. But Lis was hesitant to share what she suspected of the empress's son. And Mu-Phi's presence wasn't the only reason.

'There are some things I would like to discuss with you,' the empress said. 'Do you think we could dismiss the staff for an afternoon?'

'Do I have the power to do such a thing?'

Mu-Phi opened her mouth to complain, but then she stepped back, bowed and left.

Wei-Song took the chance to step forward and take her mother's hand before she followed. Lis looked to Yang, wondering if he would find an excuse to stay. He smiled and bowed to them both. 'It would appear too strange if we did not all go. I will take the opportunity to visit with the healers.'

Lis smiled and allowed him to leave.

'There is something you are not telling me,' the empress said softly. 'I know this has been more difficult than it should be. I know what you are and the risk to you. I also know my son had concerns that you had not shared with him that you were a hunter; and yet I understand what he is now willing to do to protect you.'

Lis gave her a small smile. 'He is unsure of me,' she said. 'He may understand better than you think what I really am.'

'He cares for you,' the empress said, leaning across the table and taking her hands. 'Even if he discovered the truth, he wouldn't hurt you.'

Lis shook her head.

'He has risked much for you and ensures you are safe.'

'I can't let my guard down with Mu-Phi.'

'She has protected you before.'

'She didn't know what I was then.'

'And now she does?' the empress asked, the concern etched deeply across her face.

Lis opened her mouth to say something and then closed it again. 'He must trust her very deeply,' she whispered, more hurt by the idea than she had been by the sword he pushed into her.

'I want to see what you can do,' the empress whispered across the table, a childish grin on her face, any concern gone.

Lis shook her head.

'I know you have something very special in you, and I think the prophecy might be right.'

Lis looked around her, worried who might hear her and what that might mean for the empress herself. 'I don't have the strength,' she whispered.

'For the magic or what is to come? I know you have the latter. It is why I chose you.'

Her voice carried a strength that made Lis smile, to know that someone had such faith in her. And yet it caused a sharp, unexpected pain in her chest.

'I thought the priestess guided you.'

'I can't believe she would have selected you just so we would kill you. If such a vision had been granted to her, she could have ensured you returned silently to your little island and we would have heard no more. By putting you here, you have been exposed to magic you would not have been otherwise. You have the opportunity to train.'

'I would like that,' Lis said, 'but who would train me?'

The empress looked back briefly towards the door. 'Wei-Song is involved with a group.'

Lis looked down at her hands. The place Wei-Song had taken her to could be such a place, but was it safe? And would she be able to go and work with others? 'I can't leave here,' she said instead.

The empress sighed and nodded. 'The crown prince will not allow such a move, and I don't think he should know of the others.'

'Should he know about Wei-Song?'

The empress looked beyond Lis. 'I don't know how he would react to such news.'

'Neither do I,' Lis admitted. 'How can I train?' she asked, changing the subject. 'Mu-Phi will not leave my side. She may know what I am, but I won't be able to test it or learn more without giving away Wei-Song. I don't think the crown prince would be interested in encouraging my skills.'

'We have to find a way to keep him and Mu-Phi out of it.'

Lis stared at her across the table.

'Please, show me something,' the empress begged.

'I haven't been able to do anything,' Lis murmured. Her father had always talked of the first magic she had done as a baby, and it made him smile every time he told the story. Yet there was always a level of fear behind it. It was the moment he had known they could no longer stay on the Palace Isle.

Lis looked about and noticed a small vase of flowers on the table by the door. She leapt up and examined the arrangement. They were dying, with fraying brown edges on the leaves, but there was one bud that had not opened. She selected it and returned to the table. 'Could you hold this?' she asked the empress.

The empress nodded and took the bud. Lis closed her eyes and reached her hand forward. She could feel very little within it, as though it too was tired and burnt, but she tried to coax it forward. Willing it to show its beauty to the world. As the empress drew in a surprised breath, she opened her eyes and saw the pale flower in full bloom.

Lis leaned heavily on the table. 'That was hard,' she whispered.

'It was amazing. Have you done this before?'

Lis nodded. 'I have opened a whole field, and it felt so easy.'

'I didn't realise it would take you such time to recover from what you did for us in the throne room that night.'

Lis rubbed a hand over her stomach, wondering if she would ever fully heal from what the prince had done—and from what she had done to herself by preventing the healing from taking hold. She couldn't tell his mother that he knew what she was and had tried to kill her; he might just do it yet, and she didn't want to pull the empress between them.

'You worry for the magic you have,' the empress said kindly, putting the flower down on the table before taking Lis's hands and drawing them closer to her.

'A worry that the prince may run me through?' Lis nodded. 'I worry that I want him to. That I shouldn't be here, and that I may not be as healed as you would need me to be.'

'Need you to be?' the empress repeated. 'That we may need your magic?'

'That you may need me to produce an heir,' Lis whispered. She tried to pull her hands back from the empress, but the woman held tight.

'What makes you think you couldn't?' she asked. 'Or do you think the prince will not accept you if he discovers your magic?'

'I'm not sure why I have told you,' Lis admitted. 'He is a hunter and I am Hidden; it won't end well.' Lis stood quickly, feeling the effects of the magic, and she fell to her knees.

The empress sat down beside her, threw her arms around Lis and pulled her close. 'You ensured I was saved,' she said. 'I would want the same for you. I love you like a daughter.' She squeezed Lis tight. Lis returned the hold, feeling overwhelmed. 'To the people you will be my daughter, for I cannot share Wei-Song with them. Not yet.' She leant back. 'Perhaps when Remi is Emperor and you are Empress, the world will be a different place.'

Lis wiped quickly at the tears that wet her cheeks. She felt better supported than she had for some time. Yang had recently admitted he was her friend, and now she had someone who loved her for who she really was. 'Thank you,' she whispered.

'Perhaps you need some more rest,' the empress said, helping Lis to her feet and guiding her towards the bed. 'Although…'

Lis stopped. 'What is it?'

'I so want to know how you disappear.'

Lis laughed. 'Hide,' she said. 'I haven't been able to hide since that night in the throne room.' Her hand rested on her stomach again. The empress looked to it, her face clouded.

'Tell me how you do it.'

'I don't know. I think about hiding, I suppose, and then touch my hands together.' Lis did that as she spoke, and the empress's eyes went wide. 'Am I hidden?' She felt odd, different from when she'd hidden before.

The empress shook her head. 'I can see you, but…' She reached forward and touched Lis's shoulder. 'You are like a shadow.'

Lis looked over her hands, but she looked just as solid as she had before. She touched her hands together again, and the empress nodded as Lis returned to what she was. Then her knees buckled. The empress was under her arm and assisting her to bed.

'Rest,' she said. 'I will watch over you.'

'There are guards to ensure I cannot get away,' Lis murmured.

'There is no one to watch you sleep, and I know there are many who would insist there be someone by your side at all times. I am content to be that person.' The empress smiled kindly.

Lis closed her eyes and allowed the sleep pulling at her to take over. In the black silence that followed, she thought she heard Yang.

<h1 style="text-align:center">4</h1>

Remi marched along the outer wall of the Palace Isle and shook his head.

'She was determined there was something in the wall,' the soldier with him said.

'Why?' he asked, stopping abruptly, and the man nearly walked into the back of him.

'She could feel it,' he said with a shrug. 'The healer could feel something too.'

'Hmm,' Remi murmured, starting off again. He had not felt the buzz of background magic as much as he had before the attack that had levelled the royal residence. Had something changed that night? Other than the discovery that his future wife held a magic he could not sense, and very strong magic at that. The healer also worried him, although the man seemed determined that the princess and her health were his only concern.

He never left her side. Even when Remi visited of a night, the healer remained by the bed. In some ways, Remi wished he had the same loyalty to her, but her magic was so strong. He worried not only what she might do, but who else might hold the same power. Healer Yang may be one of those.

The soldier had stopped. It took Remi a moment to notice, and then he turned back.

'This is an entrance we have not tried,' he said.

Remi looked it over. He wanted to be in the prison, interrogating those with magic. It had been dangerous enough trying to keep them contained. Even separated, they'd still managed to use their magic no matter what the soldiers did, whether they bound their hands or gagged them. Remi was beginning to understand why they had simply killed them all during the war.

He belted on the door, taking his frustrations out on the greying wood.

'She's not like the others,' the man beside him said, and he stopped and turned to him.

The soldier stared him down as the door finally clicked and squealed open. The soldier on the other side took one look at the prince and bowed.

Remi pushed him out of the way and stepped inside. There was nothing—no buzz, no hint of magic. He nodded once and headed back out into the sunshine.

'I like her,' the soldier said as they continued on.

The city itself was quiet, and Remi wasn't going to engage the man in conversation. There were guards on the princess and, although he had a hunter nearby, he didn't want Hui Te-Sze around her. Yet the man made sure he was close. Remi might have been nervous, but he didn't want him stepping in and killing her just because he thought the prince should.

'Everything she has done is to please you,' the man continued, and Remi stopped.

'Are you another one of her men?' he asked, drawing out the last word.

The guard looked hurt for a moment before his features changed. Remi could feel the anger radiating from him. 'You don't listen very well, do you, Your Highness?' Without looking at the prince, he continued ahead of him.

Everyone seemed to be drawn to this girl. *This woman*, he thought as he imagined her slender body getting out of the pool. He stopped himself then, remembering the dark, rotting flesh on her stomach, the black veins spidering out across her skin.

He had done that to her. He had pushed his hatred on her. And despite his fears, he had wrapped himself around her that night, holding her close and wishing with everything he had that she would recover.

The soldier glanced back at him and then refocused ahead of him. 'Where to?' he asked.

Remi wanted to go to Lis, to check that she hadn't fallen back into her stubborn ways. She had eaten breakfast and looked brighter, and he had left very detailed instructions for Mu-Phi to ensure she improved.

'The prison,' he sighed. 'I don't think we will break them, but I'm enjoying trying.'

The smell of burnt flesh met them as they entered the prison gate, and the soldier ran ahead into the building. Remi looked around the destruction of the prison entrance. Swords and spears lay about, with several badly burnt bodies in the middle of the path. He only guessed they were soldiers from the remains of their armour.

A groan drew his attention to another soldier, leaning amidst the shadows of the wall. The hunter. His shoulder and neck were badly burned. The armour was peeled away, the gore exposed.

Remi stepped forward, and the man moaned. He dropped to his knees and pushed his fingers to the other side of the man's neck. A weak movement pulsed beneath his fingers. 'We need a healer!' he cried, but no one came.

He raced inside the prison to find a similar situation. Men charred and injured. The other guard who had run ahead was moving between bodies and cells.

'What has happened?' Remi called.

'They are gone,' the soldier called back. 'All of them have

burned their way out of their cells.'

Remi ran towards his voice to find the bars bent and broken. The straw that had lined the floor of most of the cells had been burnt to ash. He ran a hand over his face and through his hair, wisps of it falling from his neat bun and brushing against his face.

'We should have killed them,' the soldier said.

Remi nodded. He had wanted information. He had wanted answers as to who they were, what had happened to his brother, and why they were still so determined to kill Lis. But he wouldn't get those answers now, and more men had died.

'Get healers,' he said and turned on his heel.

'Your Highness,' the soldier said to Remi's back. 'Good luck with the emperor.'

Remi nodded rather than answered. He was just thankful his father didn't know the truth about Lis and the others like her. Although, as he headed out past the destruction of the prison, Remi wondered if perhaps he should.

As Remi ran towards the throne room and his father, his mind racing with what he would say and what he *should* say, he slowed and then stopped. Moving ahead of him through the crowd was Mu-Phi. She strolled along the street, her hands moving easily at her sides as she looked at the people and stalls around her. She continued on her way, unaware of him watching her.

He glanced back towards the way she would have come, from Lis's little palace tucked away in a corner of the island. The hidden princess was meant to be hidden and so no one had questioned her disappearance. Everyone assumed she had resumed her place, particularly after the royal residence was destroyed.

Remi looked that way, saddened by the gap it had left on the skyline. He returned his gaze to where Mu-Phi was walking to find she had disappeared into the crowd. Why would she leave Lis when he had given her such strict instructions not to?

He had to talk with the emperor first; then he could check on

Lis and ensure nothing was amiss. The healer at least would be with her.

He leapt up the steps two at a time and pushed into his father's study despite the guard trying to stand in his way. Two advisors stood before him. Remi slowed but continued walking into the room as they spoke.

'If he has found a way to protect us, then I have no issue with this. And of course, he is to be trusted.'

'But they cannot,' the other man added. The emperor nodded slowly and then looked up at his son.

'We are in conference,' he said.

'It is important,' Remi said, bowing low to the emperor.

'So is this,' the emperor said, and Remi maintained his lowered position.

'You are keeping those magics in check?' the first advisor asked, and Remi straightened with a sigh.

'What is it?' the emperor asked.

One of the advisors physically paled, and Remi knew he would pay for what he was about to say. 'There has been an incident at the prison.'

The emperor waited as one of the advisors let out a squeak.

'They have broken out. The guards have been seriously injured or killed—the prison is a mess.'

'Escaped,' one breathed.

'How could you let this happen?' the emperor asked, his voice dangerously level. 'You spend too much time fussing over the hidden princess when you have work to do. You are distracted.' He pointed a finger at Remi. 'You forget what you are.'

'I can't forget what I am,' Remi snapped, then bowed before his father with his head to the floor. 'Please forgive me. I thought I could contain them.'

'And they are now free to wreck destruction on the Empire again. I will have no more of it. Hunter or not, you are the crown prince first. You must focus on the Empire and its needs before anything else.'

'I do,' Remi started, but the emperor held up his hand.

'No more excuses. The next one we come across with magic, no matter their station or benefit to the empire, or even the information they may be able to impart, is to die.'

Remi touched his head to the floor again before his father.

'Go.'

Remi scrambled to his feet and raced from the room. He was fuming. His father wasn't going to listen to anything he might be able to share. And again, they would learn nothing that could help them in this fight. They would be left surrounded by those with magic they couldn't sense.

Perhaps Lis knew more than she had said. Maybe she knew others and… She had been just as shaken at the idea of what had happened and what they'd claimed she was. Or had she lied to him?

There had to be a way to track them down. He made it to the top of the steps when another advisor raced towards him, arms filled with books and reports.

'Have you set up an office with your father?' he asked.

Remi shook his head.

'I need to talk with you on a number of issues.'

'It will have to wait,' Remi said, starting down the steps.

'Can the people wait?' the advisor asked.

Remi stopped and returned to the top of the steps. 'I have a small palace towards the wall. Walk with me and discuss your issues, and I can tell my man where you can leave your reports.'

'Thank you, Your Highness,' the advisor said, bowing low and nearly losing half the reports in his arms.

Remi took some of the top ones from him and led the way. They were all the same sort of report, someone wanting something he either couldn't give or didn't think very important. He shuffled what he had in his hand and stopped. This report was from the Imperial Healer, and he flipped it open as they walked. The report mentioned Healer Yang, a young, talented healer who worked beyond his expectations with the hidden princess. Although the Imperial Healer wondered if there was not something unnatural occurring, as she was not recovering.

Remi stopped reading and turned to the advisor. 'I want to see the Imperial Healer,' he said. The man tried not to look frustrated as he pointed them in a different direction. Remi barely paid attention to where they walked as he followed.

The report then continued in a very different vein; the Imperial Healer was also worried for the empress. A long-term illness had taken its toll on her health, and she hadn't appeared to be recovering. Then she had started to improve dramatically in line with the destruction of the royal residence. The Imperial Healer wondered at the miracle. He expressed concern again that there was something unnatural working in the palace.

More likely to be the priestess, Remi thought.

As they walked through the healer's workrooms, he was overwhelmed by the spices and herbs that surrounded him. They almost blunted his senses, and he wondered if something could be done to prevent the hunters from hunting.

He followed the advisor through the main door into a smaller office, although large for the station of a healer. Remi pushed the reports he had in his hand into the already full arms of the advisor.

The Imperial Healer sat behind the desk, and Healer Yang sat on a stool to the side. Remi stopped and looked at him. 'What is going on?' he asked, his frustration preventing any appropriate form of greeting.

'You have received my report,' the Imperial Healer said, standing and bowing to Remi.

Remi nodded once.

'Your Highness, it appears that much has changed in the days since I wrote to you. I am assured by the empress that the hidden princess is much better than when I saw her myself. And we work to find a way to treat her better.' He indicated Yang. 'We shall work together.'

'Why are you not with the princess?' Remi asked, hoping his voice didn't sound as strained as the rest of him felt.

'She is with the empress,' Yang answered without looking up. 'I took the time to research what I need.' The Imperial Healer coughed, and Yang looked up at him before turning his attention to Remi. 'Forgive me, Your Highness, I concentrated too long on the princess.' He slipped from the stool to bow before the prince.

Remi waved him away.

'And your concerns for my mother?'

'After learning of the magics captured in the palace, I fear it was them that influenced your mother's health.'

Remi sighed. Could they have made her ill? Perhaps it was Lis who had been doing it.

He moved back through the healer's building, ignoring Yang still kneeling on the floor. The advisor bustled along beside him.

Instead of stopping at his own gate, he continued along the deserted road until he reached the small palace where he had hidden Lis. He pushed the gate open to see the soldiers still alert and filling the garden. The advisor hurried in beside him.

Remi marched through the soldiers dotting the courtyard towards the door and then stopped. The new maid sat on the step. She stared unseeing into the backs of the men surrounding them, and she looked sad.

He shooed the man away from him and sat beside her on the step. She didn't look up, only sniffed and wiped her hand across her nose. He smiled at the movement; there was something familiar in it.

'Do you want to talk about it?' he asked softly, and she jumped. 'I'm sorry,' he murmured.

She shook her head and looked down at her lap. 'I forget where I am sometimes,' she murmured.

'Is the princess giving you a hard time?' he asked with a lightness in his voice, because even though she had not been herself, he imagined she would be kind with anyone.

'Not intentionally,' she said.

He opened his mouth and then looked towards the door. 'Can I help?'

She shook her head.

'The princess tried to dismiss her,' Mu-Phi said, appearing before him.

Remi looked back at the new maid, not much younger than himself, and he felt a kinship to her, a connection he couldn't explain.

'I thought the empress missed her,' Lis said softly behind him. He turned, remaining where he was, and felt relieved that she still looked as well as she had that morning, if not better.

The advisor startled him, dropping the papers in his arms and falling to his knees. Lis laughed and stepped down beside him to help. Remi thought he heard her groan just a little as she dropped to her knees.

'What do you have here?' she asked.

'He was trying to get me to do some work,' Remi said. Then his mother emerged, and he stood and bowed with a smile.

'Not having much luck?' Lis asked the man. He nodded madly before he realised what he had done and refocused on picking up the papers.

'I do miss you,' the empress said, stepping forward and taking the maid by the hands. She smiled warmly. 'No one can replace you,' she said more softly, and the girl nodded slowly as she sniffed again. Then Remi's mother surprised them all by pulling the girl into her arms. 'Come with me,' she whispered.

The girl bowed down when released. 'I thank you,' she said, 'but I have work to do here. I will return when I know the princess is what she needs to be.'

'That is an odd thought,' Remi said, then turned red as he looked around the group. 'Forgive me,' he said, turning to them all in turn.

'I know how little you think of me,' Lis said, bowing her head to him. 'I am grateful for the thought, Wei-Song. You may return to the empress at any time,' she added, and the girl smiled at her.

'Your Highness,' the advisor said.

'Put them inside,' Remi said, motioning the door and feeling uncomfortable under Lis's gaze.

'Are you to teach me, or are you to move your office to my bedroom?' she asked.

The advisor baulked in the doorway.

'I would rather be close,' Remi said, and the advisor actually moaned. 'You could take them back with you,' he shot at the man.

'Not with all those magics out there,' the advisor muttered, walking into the palace.

'What magics?' Lis asked, and the young maid slipped effortlessly between Remi and Lis as though to protect her.

'I didn't want to mention it, but there has been a break-out at the prison.'

'How many?'

Remi shook his head.

'How many?' Lis repeated more forcefully.

'All of them,' he sighed.

She looked around the guards watching the walls and then back to the empress. 'When?' she asked.

'Not long,' he added.

She turned and raced inside, dragging the young maid with her, and the empress followed close behind. Remi found Lis rummaging through the papers as the advisor tried to stop her.

'What are you doing?'

'Looking for the information you are trying to hide from me.'

'Who hides from the other?' he asked, then instantly regretted his words as she stood tall and her face hardened. She stepped up to him. 'I will not do this.' Her voice was level and calm, and he was reminded of his mother—who, he noted with a quick glance, grinned. 'You either leave it alone or kill me now, but I will not have this held over my head.'

He nodded once and held out his hand for her to continue her search.

'There is no news,' the advisor said. 'It was only just discovered as I searched for the crown prince.'

She looked up at him and stepped back.

'Do you want your reports delivered here?' he asked the prince seriously.

'I don't want people coming and going,' the maid said, chewing her lip, and Remi was reminded of his brother. 'The hidden princess cannot be protected this way. Take your papers and your prince and find somewhere else.'

The man pulled his papers together without question and headed for the door.

'I'll be back,' Remi muttered as he followed the advisor.

He paused by the gate to ask the soldier to find another hunter or two to join the watch, and he waved at Mu-Phi to join him.

5

'This is not going to end well,' Lis murmured as she looked at the door.

'He does what he can,' the empress said, surprising Lis by taking her hand.

'I meant the magics,' Lis said. But as she thought of the prince, he confused her. He appeared to want to be around her, but she wasn't sure if it was to keep an eye on her or because there was some truth to the idea that he cared for her. There was still that fear at the back of her mind that he might suddenly decide it would be a good idea to run her through. 'I need to know what I can do.'

Wei-Song nodded, and the empress looked towards the door. 'Perhaps you should not be a part of this,' Wei-Song said, stepping forward and taking Lis's hand. 'If the crown prince returns and realises you knew what we were, what will he do?'

The empress sighed. 'You are too thoughtful,' she said, putting a hand to the girl's face. 'I shall leave you to do as you need, and I will return tomorrow.'

'Thank you,' Lis said, bowing before the empress. 'You have done so much for me. Is it safe to travel in the streets if they have escaped?'

'I would think they have run for now,' the empress said as she moved towards the door.

Lis followed and noted the increased number of men within the little walls of her world. The empress's guard stepped forward and bowed as one before her.

'Would you rather a sedan chair?'

The empress shook her head. 'I want to walk through the streets. It would reassure the people.'

They moved as one through the gate and, despite the number of men still filling the space, it appeared quieter without her there. One man glanced over his shoulder but then turned back quickly.

Lis stood on the step, watching the closed gate and wondering if the prince would listen to his sister and try to reduce the number of people coming and going. It was a far cry from when Lis had been first hidden away, and with such people visiting it wouldn't take long for those determined enough to find where she was.

She walked back inside her small home and took a deep breath. 'Teach me,' she said, and Wei-Song actually sighed. 'I thought this was what you wanted.'

'I do,' she said softly. 'Only it may not be as easy as you think. Everyone has different strengths, and I know little of you. Tell me what you can do, and we will see what else you may be able to achieve.'

'Could I learn different forms of magic?' Lis asked.

'I don't know. Do you want to wield fire?'

Lis looked at her palms, where the thin scars still ran across her hand from holding the prince's sword. She tried to imagine fire growing in her palm, but it didn't happen, not even a flicker of heat.

'I can hide,' she said. Then she twirled before the princess and her clothes changed. Her flowing pink silks turned to a simpler dress of blue, something more akin to what Wei-Song wore. Her hair too had changed; it hung loose and free down her back, the pins that had held it so meticulously in place now in her hand.

Wei-Song gave her a nod of approval. 'What did you show the empress?'

'Something I loved to do for Peng,' Lis said, then stopped.

'Can you show me?' Wei-Song asked. Her voice, soft and gentle, coaxed Lis from her memories before they could take hold.

She nodded and returned to the vase, but she had taken all she could from it. 'I need an unopened flower.'

Wei-Song walked out into the garden and returned quickly with a small branch from a tree in the garden. It barely had buds on it, but Lis held her hand out toward it and coaxed the flowers forward. She smiled as the pink buds bloomed, and then she continued to coax life from the branch. As though the flowers alone were not enough, small red leaves appeared before they turned a brilliant green.

'Impressive,' Wei-Song said.

'I haven't tried so much before,' Lis said, sitting at the table. The things she could do drained her more than they used to. 'When I was a baby, I opened a jade flower on the end of my mother's pin,' she said.

'You can coax things forward that have no will to come?'

'I like flowers,' Lis said with a shrug.

Wei-Song knelt at the table and poured tea into a cup before pushing it across to her. 'Tell me what else you have done,' she said.

'I breathed life into dying coals, but then I think anyone could do that.'

'Maybe you should rest some more. When do the tutors return?'

'Too soon,' Lis said with a sigh, sipping again at the cup.

'Can you hide?' Wei-Song asked.

'I tried, but it wasn't the same.' She touched her hands together and again felt the thready wispiness of earlier. She slumped down onto the table. 'It takes too much.'

'You are pushing her too hard,' Yang said from the doorway.

'She wants to learn. Have you heard about the prison?'

He nodded and moved forward to take Lis's wrist. 'You need more rest,' he said. 'Yesterday you were dying; only today have you decided not to. If you continue like this, you might not have the choice.'

'But they are coming,' she said, allowing him to help her stand from the table.

He guided her towards the bed, where she lay down without complaint.

'They are not coming yet,' he said.

She sighed and closed her eyes. She must have drifted into sleep, for the light had changed in the room when she opened her eyes. It slid across the floor from the windows, and a candle burned on the table where Wei-Song read. Mu-Phi worked over a pot, and she could smell the rice and something sweet. Yang sat on the end of the bed, also reading, squinting in the dim light. The world was quiet.

Lis heard the gate squeak open and close quietly. Then murmured voices in the yard. She sat up, too aware of who it might be, but then if they were coming it would be less polite.

Without looking up, Yang rested his hand on her leg beneath the covers. But she waited, watching the door.

When the silhouette of a man stood in the doorway, Lis pulled her legs from beneath Yang's hand to get his attention. The man stepped into the room, and Wei-Song stood and bowed. As Lis focused on his damaged face, her grip tightened on the covers.

'Your Highness,' Hui Te-Sze said, bowing towards her. His voice sounded just as rough and damaged as his skin. He sat uninvited at the table, and Mu-Phi stepped forward with rice wine. Lis wondered where it had been kept and whether she had hid it for the prince.

She slipped her legs from the bed and, when he looked her over, she realised she was still in the simple blue dress. She sat slowly at the table and studied his face.

'Why have you come so late?' she asked the hunter, watching

as he lifted the cup with a shaky hand. 'Mu-Phi, bring something for the man to eat,' she said. 'He looks as though he could use it.'

'You are too kind,' Hui Te-Sze said as Lis poured another cup of wine for him.

'You were at the prison,' she said. Mu-Phi sat a bowl down before her, and Lis pushed it across the table.

'I was not prepared,' he said, looking at the food but not attempting to eat.

'Are they hard to contain?'

He looked at her closely and nodded once.

'Can you stop them?' she asked.

'I thought you would want them freed,' he said, looking up at her.

'They want me dead.' Lis accepted the bowl Mu-Phi sat before her, but she didn't eat.

'But you are one of them.'

'I am sure there are men who don't have magic you have fought against or disagreed with,' she said, and the hunter continued to study her across the table. 'They are just men like most. They think their cause more important than those around them.'

He looked at the bowl and then back to her.

'Are you here to kill me?' she asked, picking up the chopsticks and moving the fish and rice around the bowl.

'I think all those with magic should die. They have done nothing but kill for the last twenty years.'

'Is it not time to find peace?' Lis asked. Yang moved around to lean against the bed, watching her almost as closely as the hunter.

'The magics don't want peace; they want control.'

'Not all of them,' Lis said. 'I don't.'

'You, princess, will have control when you are empress.'

'If I survive that long,' she said, smiling at him.

He huffed and pushed a piece of fish into his mouth. He chewed slowly, the motion clearly causing him pain, and he watched her.

'Yang,' she said, motioning him forward. He stood slowly and bowed low. She knew it was for the hunter, but it still made her uncomfortable. 'When the hunter has finished his meal, would you look him over? I worry that he has not received enough attention.'

'I have been with the healers all afternoon,' he murmured. 'It is luck only that I was able to walk here.'

'Healer Yang is very skilled,' Lis said, and he gave her a pained expression. 'I would like to show you that I mean you no harm.'

'Do you mean harm to others?' he asked.

She pressed her lips together and put her sticks down.

'Mu-Phi,' she called, not taking her eyes from him. 'Light the lamps.'

Hui Te-Sze put his hands up and then bowed his head. 'I can feel the heat of the candle enough, Your Highness.'

'Why are you here?' she asked, again, her voice more forceful.

'He thinks you are different. I needed to see it for myself.'

'And?'

'You must understand where I come from.'

She nodded. 'And will you run me through?'

He shook his head. 'Not yet,' he murmured, pushing more meat into his mouth.

Yang knelt beside her at the table and they ate in silence. When the hunter had finished, he stood, bowed low and, with a quick glance at Mu-Phi, he left.

Lis knew she was dreaming, for the world around her was hazy and hot. Her dreams all seemed to be hot since she had come to the Palace Isle. She was walking through a deserted city, but not one she knew. Although the buildings looked familiar, they were unknown. A group of girls walked by in two neat rows, veils covering their faces. She followed them.

No one accompanied them and no one watched over them, but as Lis struggled to keep up with the group, no one else was around to cause them any problems.

They moved beyond the tall buildings through a winding street with high walls. Red gates stood out along its length, but the girls continued. They came to a black, unmarked gate and disappeared inside. She followed to find them evenly spaced in a large courtyard, as though exercising; she pressed herself against the wall and waited.

When the group started to move, she sucked in a breath. The girl closest to her waved her hand, and a plant grew from the gravel at her feet. It grew taller as she continued to slowly move her hands up, blossoms and leaves sprouting along its length. Another made the wind howl around her. Each girl had a different skill; each could change the world around her or create in a different way.

Lis focused on one at the back of the group who stood still, looking over the others. She moved her hands, but nothing happened. Lis stepped closer. The girl touched her hands together, and Lis felt the hum of her magic. Then she realised she couldn't feel the others. There was nothing. But for this girl it faltered; she could feel it one moment and then not the next. The girl touched her hands together again, but nothing happened. She looked towards Lis as though seeing her.

The girl raised her veil, and Lis stopped. She looked just as Lis had as a child, as though she was a young Lis in a different world. She clapped her hands together loudly and disappeared. The others turned to her and then back to their own work. She clapped again and reappeared, a grin across her face. As Lis wondered why she couldn't see the girl when she hid, the girl raised her hands above her head and clapped again, only this time Lis heard the fizzle of her magic dying.

The other girls screamed as she dropped to the ground, and Lis screamed with them.

The courtyard disappeared as her own room slowly came into focus. Warm arms held her too tight, and she could feel the magic ebbing through her.

'That's not helping,' she murmured, and she looked up to see

Wei-Song shake her head.

The prince moved quickly from the bed and bowed.

'Forgive me, Your Highness,' Lis said quickly, turning and bowing back, and she winced at the movement.

He stepped forward and then froze. 'I thought you were getting better,' he said.

'As did I, but I fear my dream has…' She stopped and looked at the fear on Wei-Song's face. 'What has happened?'

The prince turned to the maid and then back to Lis.

'Why?'

Wei-Song shook her head again. She bowed and backed up.

Lis shook her head, trying to rid the sounds of screaming that still filled her senses.

'What is it?' the prince asked, leaning forward.

'A bad dream—nothing to concern you,' Lis said, then turned and took in the hurt on his face. 'Please forgive me.' She bowed again. Coughing to clear her throat, she motioned Mu-Phi forward who stood with a cup in her hands.

Lis looked to the prince first and let her hand drop. 'I was screaming,' she said, her throat still feeling raw. 'I'm sorry if I woke you.'

Wei-Song appeared beside her with a cup in her hand, and Lis gave her a warm smile as she took it. The prince turned an angry look on Mu-Phi, but she remained where she was.

'I'm sorry,' Lis said again.

'You weren't screaming,' Wei-Song whispered.

'It felt so real,' Lis said, turning to her.

Wei-Song nodded slowly, but her eyes were on Mu-Phi.

'What wasn't helping?' the prince asked.

'I felt trapped in my dream,' Lis said quickly.

'You woke feeling trapped,' he murmured. 'I take liberties I should not. I come to watch over you, but I cannot maintain the watch.'

Lis shook her head, unsure what he meant.

'I fall asleep too easily,' he said.

Lis handed the cup back to Wei-Song and slid from the bed. 'At least there are many others to watch for the magics. Will I be able to leave this palace at all, or am I to remain trapped here?'

'Trapped,' he said. 'Unless you wish to pray. Although the new high priestess has not requested you yet.'

Lis was unsure if he meant this in jest or if his words were true. There was a black gate somewhere on the Palace Isle, and she wanted to find it. Although she wasn't sure what it would mean for her if she did.

'Until we know where they have gone or what they plan, you must remain here where I know you are safe.'

'Am I safe?' she asked.

'Of course. The men...'

'What if they know what I am and want me dead like the other magics? I think you have proven that they can't be held if they don't want to be.'

'Will you run away again?' he asked, and she could hear the anger in his voice.

'I couldn't if I wanted to.' She clapped her hands together, more for effect than anything else. As she became a smoky, thready ghost of what she was, Mu-Phi sprang at her, and the prince put out his hand to stop her. Lis put her hands back together and then placed them before her. 'Oh, I feel very safe,' she said.

'She won't hurt you as long as you don't try to run.'

'I wasn't running; I was proving a point. For I have lost what I had, thanks to you and your sword. I couldn't run if I wanted to, because I can no longer hide.'

She didn't mean for the anger to be so clear in her voice, but she couldn't hide it. She'd had so little before, and now she had nothing. Again, Wei-Song shook her head, trying to give her a gentle reminder to hold herself together. But as Lis had no time to herself, it was getting harder to do that. Now she didn't even have her bed to herself. If it wasn't Yang trying to heal her in her sleep, it was the prince.

She looked at him closely then, wondering just what he had as a hunter. 'How do you know when there are other magics around?' she asked.

'I can sense them, like you do.'

She shook her head. 'Not like I do. What do you feel?'

'It is as though I can feel them, like the air becomes solid around them, reaching out to me.'

She nodded once. He was different, but there was still a form of magic there, and he didn't know it. They didn't sense the other hunters. Maybe some of them were Hidden, and maybe they had an idea of what they were. Although when Lis thought of Te-Sze with his burnt face, she doubted that he'd considered such a thing.

'Why do you ask?'

'I can feel you of a night,'

He blushed and she scowled. 'I can feel you hunting,' she snapped. Although that wasn't quite right, it was more like she could feel his energy flowing across to her. Like it was when Yang tried to heal her, and when Wei-Song helped her defeat the magics in the palace by lending her more energy.

She'd had the feeling before, only she was certain of it now. When she had woken not long ago, it had felt as though he was pushing it on her, which had only served to press her dream more harshly upon her.

She looked at Wei-Song, who stared for a moment and then looked at the floor. She understood. She knew what he was, and she was worried what might happen if she told him.

'I need to prepare for my day, Your Highness,' Lis said, trying to move beyond the wonder of what she had learnt.

He bowed stiffly and headed for the door.

'Perhaps Mu-Phi could use the break as well,' she called after him, and the woman stepped forward. 'Just until she remembers who she works for.'

'I know who I work for,' she said.

'And yet the rest of the world believe that it is me. I would prefer you did not run me through before the empress; she might find it upsetting.'

The crown prince looked at Lis for a long moment before turning to Mu-Phi. With a flick of his head, she followed him from the room. Lis sighed before she dropped to the cushion at the table.

'I know,' Wei-Song said, 'but you cannot say a word.'

'I don't,' Yang said, sitting beside her.

'He is magic,' she said.

'Who?'

Lis looked back towards the door.

Yang shook his head madly. 'He is a hunter—he can't be magic.'

'I can feel it,' Lis said. 'When he hunts, when he lies beside me of a night.'

Yang raised an eyebrow.

'He passes more energy to me than you do,' she said, and Yang bit his lip.

'He would rather die,' he murmured.

'Yes,' Wei-Song said. 'And he may take Lis with him.'

6

The priestess knelt before the image of the goddess Aga and closed her eyes. The world shifted in the darkness behind her lids as she tried to keep the smile from her face. She had been trained well and experienced visions for most of her life, hence the call to the priestesses. But since she had risen to the rank of high priestess, her world had changed dramatically.

In a way, it had hurt her to deny her skills and lie to the soldiers and the prince when she had claimed no knowledge of what the priestess had been or tried to do. The risk of discovery was very real, but she would gladly risk her own life rather than betray their secrets. The secret had to be maintained, to protect all the priestesses around the Empire.

At times of difficulty, she longed to be back on the Sacred Isle, where they were protected and secure, and where only pilgrims visited. But the priestesses were needed here, to keep an eye on the girl and the prophecy, and to ensure an end to it.

It had been known since the child's birth what she would become. In some ways, the priestess had thought there would be a simpler way to end this. She could have been killed as a child, and this could have ended before she grew. But the visions of others claimed that if this happened, she would be replaced by another, and another, until the prophecy was fulfilled. And yet, there continued to be those who tried to stop it.

The hidden princess was the key to the prophecy. And now that this girl was in that position, she had something to work with. The more the priestesses and the magics did, the more the world changed around them. The former high priestess had been determined that with the right influence, the girl would do as they wanted. But she was stronger than that—stronger than all of them, this priestess had realised when she'd watched over her. Yet the girl had shown no understanding of just how strong she was until the attack in the residence.

Now the royal family tried to hide her away, but it was clear where she was. The coming and going of soldiers and the crown prince, the tutors and the empress. The world knew the whereabouts of the hidden princess once more. She sighed. She wondered if she could influence where they put the girl and thus have better access to her, but she doubted the empress would allow such a thing again.

The little princess Wei-Song had been a surprise. The high priestess had felt her, sensed her magic and her family line. She wondered if the emperor knew that she lived, or if the crown prince even knew of her existence.

There were very few worshipers in the temple, but the man at the back tugged on her senses, so she turned slowly to look at him. He stepped forward, bowed low and held out a plate of orange slices. She took it from him and sat it at the feet of the goddess before her, then stood beside him for a moment.

'They will soon discover you are here,' she whispered.

'No one senses magic in the temples,' he murmured. She looked around, hoping no one had overheard him, then scowled at him.

'Why are you here?' she asked.

'I would like to offer my congratulations to your new position,' he said, giving her a shallow bow. 'I would ask if you have seen anything to benefit us.'

'Not yet,' she said. And she wouldn't want to tell him if she had. She had certainly seen a lot further, but it wasn't enough. It wasn't a future she could promise.

Another priestess appeared in the temple and looked over the man before he bowed again and left. She motioned to the new high priestess, who followed her back out into the private part of the temple.

'It is not safe for them to come here,' she whispered hoarsely as she slowed to walk.

'He knows it is safer than we would like anyone else to know,' the high priestess murmured, taking her place on the mat at the head of the group, their heads bent in prayer.

The girl opened her mouth to say something further, but the high priestess shook her head. The girl bowed low and retreated to her own place.

The high priestess watched her go, thinking it odd that she considered her a girl when they would have been close in age. But her skills and elevation to the position had given her more than she had hoped for. With the knowledge of the ages to come, she felt far older than her peers.

She had woken from a dream of the former high priestess dying, in which she had felt the magic push through her soul, burning her as it took hold. When she had raced from her bed into the temple to pray to the gods for guidance, the other priestesses had knelt before her. It was clear that she had been chosen, and she wasn't challenged. It was not a position she had expected, but it settled on her. And with the knowledge of her daily visions, she was the only one who could hold it.

As the images formed in her mind, she knew what she would tell the other priestesses and what she must keep to herself. She had wondered if the former priestess had kept so many secrets, but she now knew what her predecessor had, and the answer was already known.

The hidden princess became clear in her mind. She watched the crown prince with a nervousness that the high priestess understood. He was a hunter, and they both knew what he was capable of. Despite the secrets of the healers and the apparent skill of the man who remained at her side, the high priestess knew the crown prince had something to do with the princess's recent injury. It had been inflicted after the priestess had been killed and the magics captured.

She focused on the image of the hidden princess. It wasn't that the girl worried what he might do to her, she realised, but that she knew something of him that he didn't know himself. The little princess hid as a maid looked over him as well. Two hidden princesses. She allowed the idea to grow. What might that mean for them? Both hiding their magic, one hidden to be Empress and one hidden by the empress.

Wei-Song was determined to protect the hidden princess, even if it meant harming her own brother, and the priestess knew there was no way to turn her to their cause. She wondered if Lis understood what the priestesses were.

The past flashed before her. The colour was not as vibrant as with her visions of the present or future, allowing her to understand the difference. The former high priestess stood with her hands around the hidden princess's throat in a cell, and she could feel the crown prince growing closer. She had risked herself and the priestesses for the girl, and the new high priestess felt anger towards her predecessor. She would not make the same mistake.

Too many mistakes had been made in trying to end this. In trying to find a way for them to be what they were without fear. The prophecy may have indicated that she would allow magic to live again within the Empire, but it would be under the rule of others and they would be at constant risk. If they were able to govern themselves, the world would be very different. The former high priestess had endangered that.

One man had attempted to prevent her becoming the hidden princess by saving the prince, but that had gone horribly wrong. If he had survived, that silly, selfish girl would have been Empress. Or at least that was how it would have appeared, but destiny had a way of pushing through their efforts.

The death of the crown prince had been a blow. As soon as he had died, a number of the priestesses had seen a vision confirming that the new hidden princess was coming. His death had ensured the prophecy was closer to being fulfilled.

It was up to her to find the answers they needed to prevent the hidden princess becoming the empress who would destroy everything they worked for.

She breathed in the cool scent of the room. The white stone radiated a magic of its own that leant its power to her. She allowed her shoulders to relax, and her fingers started to numb. She emptied her mind, pushing out her fears and worries and anguish at the mess that had gone before.

She didn't reach or pull for an idea, an image or even a particular person.

The hidden princess appeared again, as though she stood directly before her. Her hair was wet as she stood in the rain, her dress similarly dishevelled. She looked upset as she shook her head. 'No,' she said, her voice soft and almost lost on the wind that blew around them.

The crown prince stood looking similarly battered by the weather, but he held out his sword. His hand shook with apparent anger, and tears flowed unchecked down his cheeks. 'You lie,' he screamed, a desperate, grating sound, and the priestess felt his heart break before he stepped forward.

The high priestess opened her eyes and smiled. Lis would be her own undoing. She just had to make sure what she had seen would happen.

7

Mu-Phi tried to keep her steps light as she followed Remi from the little palace. She couldn't understand why he couldn't see the danger, but she wasn't going to bring it up again. She had tried to watch over the princess, whom she knew had done all she could for Mu-Phi when she'd been injured. But Mu-Phi had spent her whole life learning of the dangers of magics, training to fight against such people, and now the prince wanted her to protect one of them.

It didn't matter who she was, or that he had only just found out. The hidden princess was a magic. She was dangerous, and Mu-Phi was certain she had bewitched him in some way. Mu-Phi stood by of a night watching Remi lie against the princess. His body relaxed against hers, his arm draped across her. If all was as it should be, he would be nowhere near her and have nothing at all to do with her. His brother had never visited with his hidden princess.

But she knew Remi had felt differently about her from the beginning. He had visited her when he shouldn't; he had been close to her palace, lingering by the baths or the temple. He cared too much and, now that he'd learnt what she was, it prevented him from doing what he should.

The hunter would have talked him around. He had nearly talked Remi into killing her that night. Yet even he appeared to have turned now, changing his mind as to what danger she presented. She was a magic—she was dangerous no matter what they thought.

'She can't go anywhere,' Remi muttered ahead of Mu-Phi, and she stopped. He turned back and gave her a sad smile. 'I know what you think,' he said, kindly. 'But no matter, we must remember who she is.'

'I haven't forgotten,' Mu-Phi snapped. When his features shifted to show his disapproval at her words, she forgot her earlier promise to herself and allowed her frustrations to show. 'I think you may have forgotten what she is.'

'Who she is,' he said.

'That doesn't matter given *what* she is.' Mu-Phi said clearly. 'You have to consider what it means, what it will mean going forward. You can't marry her; you can't make her Empress; she can't produce your heir.'

He blinked away his sudden surprise, but she saw it. 'What would you suggest? That we kill her and I find another? Or do you have another in mind? Because I think we might have broken enough traditions for my mother.'

'There were so many at the Choosing,' she tried.

'And their families would rather disappear than allow a daughter on this island at the moment. A crown prince dead, one hidden princess murdered and another injured.'

'By your hand. If you tell them what she is…'

He shook his head. 'I promised her.'

'Why?' she asked, allowing the exasperation to come through in her voice. 'Why would you promise that to such a woman?'

'She doesn't mean to hurt us,' he said.

'That doesn't mean she won't, or that she isn't lying.'

'Perhaps you should stay away,' he said, turning back in the direction he'd been walking. 'There is much you could be doing to help your Empire.'

'I won't leave you with her,' she said, tramping after him. 'You can try to reassign me, but where you go, I go.'

He sighed again but continued to walk.

'She will be the death of you,' Mu-Phi murmured, trying to keep up.

He stopped and spun on her so quickly she actually took a step back. 'Enough!' he boomed. 'Or you will have no choice where you go, and it will be far from here.'

She nodded once, hearing the sincerity and anger in his voice. She had pushed too far. But he had to know. She had lost one prince to magic, and she wouldn't lose another. She had not been where she was supposed to be when Ta-Sho was murdered. He had sent her out to discover information instead of watching over him. He had meant so much more to her than a prince to watch over. She had loved him, and she had thought he loved her in return. Despite the traditions and the bride hidden away in training, it was Mu-Phi he had pressed against in the night, her skin he had kissed as he whispered his love.

She remembered him painfully when she watched his younger brother with the magic. Ta-Sho was only marrying the hidden princess for tradition, and Mu-Phi knew he would have continued to hold her of a night. With the new crown prince, it was more than tradition driving him to this woman, and Mu-Phi was certain the girl would be the death of him.

Remi seethed at the open hostility of the woman behind him. He knew what she had been trained for. He had been involved in much of her training, despite her being his brother's guard. They had a friendship, a kinship in a way, and he had respected her. Although he knew what had gone on between them. He remembered the outrage at what U'shi had done, but it was her place to be faithful. As future Emperor, Ta-Sho could have done what he wanted. Not so long ago, emperors had taken concubines. Remi blushed at the idea. Lis had mentioned something similar recently, as though she couldn't face the idea of his touching her—or was it that she didn't think he would want her?

He could feel the heat building in his body thinking of her. Her scent, her soft breath when she slept. She was all he needed. And he had cared for her. He still cared for her, no matter what she was, and he had to keep her safe. He glanced at Mu-Phi as she came to walk beside him. He was sure she was thinking of the same thing, only she wasn't as keen to keep Lis safe.

It didn't matter what the world thought, and so far he had managed to keep it from everyone, including his parents. Although with the time his mother spent with Lis, he wondered if he could continue to keep it from her.

'What could I do then?' he wondered aloud.

'Where are we going?' Mu-Phi asked, and he stopped and looked around him. He hadn't been thinking very clearly at all when he had left Lis. But he had to find the magics. 'My father is not keen to release me to search out these men, no matter my skills.'

'You would send me?'

He shook his head. 'I think I need to go anyway, see what I can find. Someone must know something. If I take a small group, I could search the outer islands more thoroughly without drawing too much attention.'

'The people already know something is going on,' Mu-Phi said, nodding towards the space the residence had occupied.

'But they think we are taking care of it, that the hunters are doing their job and killing any magic they find.'

'You want me to stay,' she said, her voice heavy with disappointment.

'I do, but you may not keep her as safe as I hoped. The new maid appears to be very dedicated.'

'She doesn't look familiar to me at all. How long was she with your mother?'

'I don't know,' Remi said, thinking about the girl who seemed so familiar to him. 'Are you sure you don't know her?'

Mu-Phi nodded once.

He was torn. Mu-Phi was the best spy he had. She could protect Lis from any threat, but not from the threat she was herself.

'What do you want of me?' she asked, bowing before him.

He sighed. She hadn't done such a thing since he had agreed to train her.

'You don't trust me.'

'Can I?' he asked.

'Yes, Remi, you can. I might not agree with you, but I will carry out your orders.'

'Then stay. Watch the maid,' he added.

8

Lis was disappointed to see Mu-Phi re-enter the palace and move back to the kettle. She waited, but the prince didn't follow her in, and Mu-Phi didn't speak. Lis watched her for a moment, then glanced at Yang.

She had wanted the chance to learn more about what she might be able to do. But Wei-Song wanted her to rest, and Yang backed up Wei-Song. As it was, there had been very little time between the prince leaving and the maid returning.

Lis wasn't sure she would sleep as well with the girl around. Mu-Phi wanted her dead—it was clear on her face every time she looked at Lis—and yet the prince had agreed to allow her to live. He would not have sent Mu-Phi back in if he did not think Lis would be safe.

Lis had not mentioned again her idea of what the prince was. She glanced over at Wei-Song as she prepared her clothes for the day. *Does she resent him?* she wondered. He didn't know who she was, and yet she had been sent away and ordered to be murdered, all for being just as he was. And now he was in line for the throne. The only one left. Might the world change that much if he knew what he was?

She pulled the small stack of books closer and opened the first one, disappearing back into the history of the Empire and the main families who had helped build it. A cup appeared beside her and, as she reached for it, she looked up to find Mu-Phi leaning over her. She jumped back, knocking the books over and just missing the tea.

'I am sorry to startle you,' Mu-Phi whispered, bowing and stepping back.

'Why are you here?' Lis snapped, and the girl kept her eyes down. She pulled herself back together and blew out a long breath as she collected the books.

'He wants me here,' she said.

Lis gave no indication that she had heard her. Once she had straightened her books, Lis went back to the one she'd been reading. After a long moment, she asked, 'Are the tutors coming today?'

'Are you well enough?' Wei-Song asked.

Lis smiled at the girl for her concern and nodded.

'I have said they are to wait,' Yang murmured from his position on the floor, a pile of books beside him. He scanned through one, deposited it on the other side of him and selected another.

'I need some stimulation,' Lis said. 'There is so much to learn. Do you know how many times a day I have been told there is not enough time to teach me all I need?'

'Do you know how many books you consume a day compared to the average hidden princess?'

'How many average hidden princesses have you known?' Lis asked, putting down the book and turning to Yang.

'You already know how to read and write. The girls who were hidden away had no such skill. You can sew and embroider on the finest silks, you know your history, you understand the current political climate better than most. I doubt there is much left for them to teach you.'

Lis blinked at him, and he glanced up at her silence from the book in his hand.

'Am I wrong?' he asked.

'No,' Wei-Song chipped in.

'You think I am ready to be Empress?'

'I don't think they said that,' Mu-Phi murmured.

Lis motioned her forward and indicated she sit at the table with her. 'Because I have magic, or for another reason?'

Mu-Phi looked nervously towards the door and shook her head.

'He isn't here. I know you hold no friendship or respect for me. Be honest.'

'There is something in the way you hold yourself... No,' she added quietly, 'that's not quite it.'

Lis studied her across the table, disappointed that the friendship she had thought was forming between them had come to this.

'You aren't strong enough,' Mu-Phi blurted.

Wei-Song stepped forward, but Lis held up her hand and she stopped.

'You don't appear strong enough,' she tried again. 'You allow those around you to see your vulnerabilities,' she said more confidently. 'An empress would never do such a thing. You need to maintain a superiority.'

Lis looked at her closely. 'I don't think the current empress behaves like that.'

'You would never see her let down her guard.'

I have, Lis thought. 'Surely she would to some degree with her family,' Lis said instead.

'It is not done,' Mu-Phi said, getting up from the table and moving back to the corner.

'You don't think I should show my true self to the crown prince?'

'He knows what you are,' she said, her voice not as friendly as it had been.

'But should I not allow him to see *who* I am?' Lis asked, watching closely as the girl looked everywhere but at her.

'It does not matter. He does not love you. That is not what a royal marriage is.'

'He loves you, perhaps,' Lis said.

She shook her head and focused on the pot before her.

'I agree that he does not need to love me,' Lis said. 'But we are to work as partners.'

'He will be Emperor; you are just a symbol at his side.'

'A symbol,' Lis said slowly. 'An interesting idea. Do you think the current empress is aware of how unimportant she is?'

Mu-Phi opened her mouth and then closed it again.

'I wonder if U'shi would have thought such things,' Lis said, more to herself, as she returned to her book.

'That girl was spoilt and silly. She would never have been a match for the crown prince. She would have been what the people expected and nothing more.'

Lis allowed the book to drop as she stared at the girl. It was more than anger that carried her words.

'Do you blame her for the prince's death? Do you think she was more than she appeared to be?'

Mu-Phi shook her head and refocused on the pot before her.

'You would not have met the hidden princess,' Lis continued. 'She was one of the last to follow the traditions, to be truly hidden away. In the days when the streets were cleared and the prince stayed away.'

'I may have found a way to have a look at her.'

Lis raised her eyebrows in surprise. 'What did you think? She was very beautiful.'

'She was unfaithful,' Mu-Phi murmured.

'I am sure the first crown prince was true to her.'

Mu-Phi looked up suddenly. 'He was a good man,' she said before her focus returned to the pot.

Lis watched her for a moment longer and then glanced at Yang, who also watched the girl before he returned to his book.

'You have a way with princes, it would seem,' Lis said softly, her eyes on her page again.

'I am a servant to the crown,' Mu-Phi said softly, not looking up.

'I am sure you are,' Lis said.

The words on the page before her escaped her attention as she tried to determine just what about this girl had won her the attention of two princes. But then it didn't change anything of her own situation, other than the girl was still likely to run her through.

9

The wind blew through his hair, and he smiled at the smell of saltwater it carried. It had been far too long since he'd had the opportunity to travel. His father had been too strict about his staying and continuing the duties of a crown prince, but that wasn't who he was. He had allowed the advisors to pile his desk with papers and reports, yet there was something else always tugging at him. Something more important. And that was the magic returning to the Empire.

His father understood the threat now, but he insisted there were others who could do what Remi had done. Yet none of them were strong enough. The closest had nearly lost his life when they'd escaped from the prison. Remi only hoped the man didn't attempt anything with the hidden princess while he was gone.

Despite Mu-Phi's fears for him and what Lis was, he knew she would watch over her for him. He had not given her enough time after the death of his brother. He knew what they had been even if no one else did, least of all his father. But she was a dedicated soldier, and he knew she would do what had been asked of her.

The salt air was free of any hint of magic. Remi didn't know where to start looking for these men. He did know they were off the Palace Isle for the moment, if only to gather their forces and return. There were stories of small groups living on the outer islands, and he was determined to find them. The only problem was it would take too long to reach them.

They sailed hard with the wind, and the small boat, filled to capacity, hit the waves hard and threw them around. Remi's hand held tight to the railing to keep him standing at the bow, hoping he could find something of the magics out here. He was desperate to visit with General Long, to ask if he was aware of any such strongholds and why he had done as he had to protect his daughter. Remi knew the answer to the second question and had decided to leave the man alone, heading to the other end of the Empire, out beyond Third. They travelled out from the main islands, but Remi had already sent hunters to cover every island.

The knowledge of the Hidden and that they existed worried him even more, but then Lis was right—he hated to admit—they were not the problem. They were not the ones trying to take control. The visions and prophecy were a concern, for he still had no idea where they had come from. No single person could be tracked as having produced the prophecy; it had simply been reported.

On the far side of Third was a small school, and despite their distance from the shore he watched small children play on the sand that led to the water's edge. Their squeals of delight travelled to him across the water and made him smile. His father was right, he had to start thinking of these people as his own. He always had, only now the responsibility was greater. He wouldn't just be protecting them from magics; he would be watching over every aspect of their lives.

He focused on the horizon, where he could see nothing but water. They were headed for a small chain of islands that arced around the edge of the Empire. It often marked the edge of the world on maps, and it was somewhere he had never visited before, despite his travels. It wasn't until the following day that the first island came into view. The first one they passed was barely larger than the boat they travelled on, but he could see the hunger for dry land in the soldiers' eyes.

The next island in the chain was still a way off, and he thought for a moment he saw smoke as it grew closer. When they finally reached it and the men raced ashore, Remi soon discovered a cliff on the opposite side where the waves hit it at force and the water sprayed high into the air.

The island contained three small dwellings made of slats of wood with straw rooves. They hadn't been used in years, and the dust was thick on every surface. The weather-worn door hung from its hinges, and Remi could see through the palings to the yard outside. The garden had grown wild, and there was no food stored.

Remi wondered who had lived here last as he moved through the house, looking at the small tables and narrow beds. Was it a family? Where had they gone?

The men reluctantly got back onto the boat, sailing to the next island and then the next. They still found no sign of life, let alone magics. When they reached the next island, close to the centre of the small chain, they found what remained in a similar condition to the other islands. Despite their grumbles, the men were not keen to sail for another day or night to return to familiar waters, so Remi decided they should stay.

The island contained more buildings than they had seen on the others, with a few trees, and the whole thing was surrounded by a high fence. It was part of the reason Remi had thought there might be more to it than there appeared to be. But again, there was no sign of life, no food stores or wine. An empty island, as though those who had lived here had left. As the sun began to set, Remi found the remains of a small sailboat. It had been tied to what might have once been a pier, but both it and the boat were in ruins. When he looked more closely, he could see signs of burning, not just weather.

Could this have been one of the places the army destroyed in the magic war? Those who had lived here may have harboured magics and been driven away, run away or were killed by the likes of General Long and his hunters. Some of the larger islands closer to the main islands of the Empire had been abandoned during those years. Or not long after, when those with magic had been killed. Their families and those remaining in the village had left in fear of being associated with them. Even those who had tried to harbour magics had been killed, and some islands had lost every living soul.

Remi looked out over the sea towards his Empire and wondered for the first time if the magic war had been a good idea. If the killing of every magic had been the only way to save Rei-Een. Could there have been a different way? Could they have worked together as they always had?

What was it they had wanted that had led to this? Schools? A chance to be who they really were? Was that all Lis wanted? She had gone to such lengths to hide who she was, but that was fear her father had probably instilled in her. That she must hide who and what she was, or she would be killed.

Had she had tried to do that her whole life? Could she really not have known what power she had, what she was capable of, until that moment in the residence when she had tried to save them all? At least that was what she claimed.

He sighed. He wanted so much to believe her. To trust her. No matter what she was, something drew him to her. Something that made him want to protect her and watch over her.

Could she learn to be something else? Could she learn what power she truly had and what she could do with it? Remi remembered her sadness and desperation when she had tried to hide before him and instead appeared as smoke. She didn't have what she'd had, and he wasn't sure if that was because of what she had done—or what he had done when he had nearly killed her.

Would she heal? He wanted her to. He wanted her to be what she was, yet with that came uncertainty as to what she could truly become when her powers were restored. And once she had the ability to hide from him and run, would she do so at the first opportunity?

It was not something he could do anything about. The only certainty he had now was that he couldn't kill her. No matter what she was, what she would become or what threat she posed to him, he could only protect her.

He looked out into the ocean and breathed in the fresh, pure scent of the world. It had seemed like so long since he could take a breath without magic filling his senses. But he knew it was out there and, despite the comfort it gave him, it worried him that he couldn't sense it now.

He turned back for the house and found himself a quiet, dusty corner for the night.

The following morning, they sailed out for the next biggest island. One he knew had seen much during the war. A musty scent pervaded the air as they grew closer, and broken, burned cottages marred the hills. It seemed very real. Despite the years since the fighting, Remi wondered if he would still see blood on the grass.

Although the world had tried to reclaim the land, the horror that had occurred there was still evident. As he waded ashore, Remi could see the glint of white bones amidst the grass and stones. He entered a small cottage, or at least what remained of it. Scorch marks covered the walls, some of which had fallen down along with part of the roof, but he could see that was due to a lack of maintenance. Bones covered the floor. Some of them may have been pulled at by animals, but many remained where they had fallen. Remi wondered whether the animals wouldn't touch the magics.

He knew that, during the war, they had killed all those with magic, no matter who they were—yet he was surprised to see smaller bones, clearly children. He wondered what killing a child would do to a man. Women would have died as well. He felt a different war here. Perhaps it was his sword pushing into Lis that had changed his feelings about such a fight.

He could still see the determination and pain on her face as the metal pressed against her too-soft skin, the fear that flashed across her face as the sword actually pushed deeper inside her. Terror had washed over him in that moment, terror that he might have actually killed her. And when he had withdrawn the sword, the lack of a fizzle confused him. He wondered if he had been misled.

He worked his way to the top of the island, through the death and destruction and out to a place where he could look over the world. He turned slowly, taking in the whole island, and for a moment he could hear the battle: the death, the screaming and the swords.

He closed his eyes and took in a deep breath. The musty scent that had met him as he came ashore was thick, but it was tinged with something else. Almost a hum of magic, but not quite. Then it overwhelmed him, flooded through him, and he wondered if it was the ghosts of the island. The magic felt solid around him. He turned back for the village, looking over the calm movement of his soldiers searching cottages and hillsides. He wondered only briefly what they thought might have happened here when the first fireball fell from the sky.

'Magics!' he screamed, but it was redundant. The soldiers were already moving, swords flashing, shields deflecting fire. A strong wind blew up around him, knocking him from his feet. Thankfully, he had his sword already in his hand and used it to prevent himself from falling, the tip digging into the dirt. As the sand blew about his face and stung his eyes, he was sure he saw another child half buried before him.

By the time he regained his composure and moved down the hill towards the shouting, it was all over. Men lay tired but unharmed. He looked out towards the sea. The boat they had travelled on burned in the bay, and another ship sailed out and around it, disappearing quickly against the rough waves.

They were out here, and he had lost them. And for the moment, he couldn't follow. He watched them disappear into the horizon, then sank down into the grass. They hadn't fought like he had expected them to, and he wondered for a moment if they were survivors of the island rather than the magics he sought. Could they be different? Could there be magics who would be allies rather than enemies?

He shook his head, dispelling the idea, then looked again over the island.

'Someone get out to the boat and put out those flames,' he called. He could see movement on the ship. A couple men stripped their armour and took to the water. He only hoped they would be able to make it back to the Palace Isle. But then, he hadn't done what he had set out to do. He would need more if he was to face his father's displeasure at his leaving.

'What are we to do, sire?' a young soldier asked.

'They were hiding here somewhere. Find the place; find anything to give us an idea of who they are and what they want.'

The man bowed and disappeared. The faint hum of magic still surrounded him, and Remi wondered whether something or someone else was still here. Fire and air. The various skills of the magics were no longer spoken of, but many texts referred to them. His father had wanted them destroyed, wiped from the world along with any idea of magic. But they needed to know what they were fighting, and some of the earlier hunters had kept good records and kept those records safe. The only magic not recorded was of the Hidden, who had been only a rumour.

Remi now knew them to be true, only he knew nothing of what they could do. Lis had shown great strength, but he wasn't sure what she had done. In a way, it was like she had pushed the others back. Did she even know herself what she had done to save them?

He resolved to talk with her when he returned, to see what she could do, what she knew, and what she might be willing to share with him. He wasn't sure it would be everything, but she was all he had as a reference.

Remi walked back to his place at the top of the hill and then over to the other side. The water stretched on to the horizon, uninterrupted on this side of the island as well. He wondered what might be out there that hadn't been mapped. He slipped on the steep gravel path and reached out to the tree by the side, but the branch was rubbery, and he landed on his seat in the dirt. He looked at the branch in his hand and let it go. The tree sprang back to its original position, and he climbed to his feet to look over it. It wasn't natural at all. The bark, although appearing rough, was smooth, and the leaves were hard to pull off. Remi pulled it again and watched as it bent like bamboo. Behind it, a darkness opened in the hillside. Remi let the tree snap back and stepped back to the top of the hill.

'Fetch me a torch,' he called.

After some moments, a soldier appeared with a torch blazing in his hand. 'What have you found?'

'I'm not sure,' Remi said. Moving carefully over to the tree, he pulled it back. The man looked with raised eyebrows and, without hesitation, headed into the darkness with the torch held out before him.

10

The room lit up around them as strange shadows played out across the walls. It had been carved deep in the hill from the earth and, although simple, it appeared many had been living here for some time. Without his falling and finding the strange magicked tree, Remi knew this place would have remained hidden for some time.

The soldier with him reached for a pot on the table.

'Don't touch anything,' Remi said.

'They won't be back.'

'They may be. And if it looks as though we haven't found this place, they may feel safe to use it again.'

The man nodded and withdrew his hand. Remi circled the large table that sat in the middle of the room. Curtains hung from the cavern wall, behind which were shelves of food and stores. Bedding was rolled up along the other wall. Unlit lanterns dotted the space. He wondered if they lived here all the time or only used it to hide. At the back of the room, a small crawl space was cut into the rock.

'Wait here,' Remi ordered. He crawled into the darkness and discovered a narrow tunnel that ran deeper into the hillside. It was dimly lit, although he didn't understand how. It was tight, but Remi travelled quite quickly on his hands and knees. When the tunnel came to an abrupt end, he banged his head on the wall. As he sat back to rub his head, he realised the ceiling above him had been cut away.

He reached up and then stood. It was light in the shaft above him, and he noticed steps cut into the wall. He took a breath and climbed. It felt like a long time climbing, but it grew lighter the higher he got. Eventually, when he reached out, he felt wood. He pushed and found himself inside one of the abandoned cottages with a clear view across the sea towards the main islands of the Empire.

They saw us coming. He closed the hatch and started back down.

'Can you hear me?' he asked the darkness.

'Your Highness?' came the reply, and Remi smiled. They knew what they were doing. But how could they get so many out so quickly? he wondered as he made his way back to the room. Or were there not as many as they thought hiding in the dark?

'Any other crawl ways or trapdoors?' he asked once he was standing back inside the room.

The other man shook his head.

When they headed back out into the sunshine, Remi wondered how long he could remain locked away from the world if needed. He thought of Lis, locked away in her little palace, unable to even enjoy the garden due to the number of soldiers occupying it.

But then she wasn't in the dark; she was surrounded by friends. And it was for her own protection. Although he wondered if she considered the two maids and a healer as friends. Yang certainly was, and there was more to his friendship with her and the maid who had looked after his mother. She would do anything for Lis, Remi thought. Despite what she was—or did she not know?

He shook his head. There were bigger problems now. He had found proof magics were hiding in the Empire, only now he didn't know where. And they had been determined to kill the hidden princess. His hidden princess. He needed to get back to her to ensure she was safe.

'How is the boat?' he asked the first man he came across.

'Sailable, although our captain thinks it will be a slow trip.'

'We just need to get to the nearest island and find another. I want us back on the Palace Isle before nightfall.'

'I don't think…'

'I don't care what you think. You will make it happen.'

The man bowed and raced away. He had been gone too long already, and with little to show for it.

Lis woke to the sound of the gate, pushed the healer away from her feet and was out of bed when the door opened. Wei-Song sighed in her sleep. Lis was tempted to wake her, but she didn't want to draw attention to herself. She stood in the shadows and watched the dark shape of a man creep into her little home.

It was not what she had thought she would consider the little palace. In the last few days, with quiet reading and conversations with Yang and Wei-Song around so many issues—while Mu-Phi kept her opinions to herself—Lis had relaxed into her little world. The tutors had returned that day. The lessons were brief but, as Yang had said, they were starting to see that she knew far more than they had given her credit for, and so they had started to stretch her learning beyond what she'd thought they would.

The man reached her bed and leaned over Yang before looking about. Lis had wondered if the soldiers would allow someone in rather than protect her as the prince had promised. But then, someone determined to kill her might not move quite so quietly.

She squatted down by the table and breathed lightly into the coals beneath the kettle. They glowed red, lighting the room briefly. In the red glow, the prince turned her way, his face worried, his eyes wide.

'What has happened?' she asked, stepping forward.

His eyes stayed on the coals for a moment before he looked at her, real concern etched on his face. She wondered if he worried what she might do to him.

'What is it?' she asked again, the fear more evident in her voice than she wanted to show him.

He shook his head.

A gentle light lit the room as a candle sparked to life. Wei-Song stood with it in her hand. 'What did you find?' she asked him.

But he didn't take his eyes from Lis, who gulped under his intense stare. Yang murmured in his sleep, moving across the bed to lie where Lis had been, and the look on the prince's face changed to anger.

Lis was tempted to see if she could hide from him. And she wondered if Yang should as well. In the time she had been too ill to leave her bed, Wei-Song had taught him to hide, but he'd had little time to practice. He had grinned so broadly when he'd discovered what he could do, and he had immediately launched into all the places he would like to test it. The idea of it made her smile, but then there was the fear of what Mu-Phi might do if she learnt the healer was not a hunter, but a Hidden too.

Despite the efforts of Yang and Wei-Song to make things as easy as possible for Lis, she still didn't sleep as deeply as she needed, and although the mark on her stomach had healed and the creeping rot had vanished, she could still feel the cold steel inside her skin.

She had relaxed without the prince's constant visits. Although she missed him and his warm body of a night, she had felt a freedom she hadn't felt in some time.

Lis lifted the little kettle over the coals and handed it to Wei-Song. 'Fetch water,' she said, 'and wake that useless maid. Her prince is here and requires whatever it is she provides him.' She sat with a sigh at the table.

'I did not mean to wake you,' the prince said, standing tall and rigid and unmoving.

'But you did. What can I do for you?'

'I wanted to check that you were well. The magics…'

'What about the magics?' she asked, interrupting him. 'Did you find them?'

He shook his head. 'I found where they were, but I fear they have returned to the Palace Isle.'

'I haven't felt them,' Lis said quickly, looking beyond him at Wei-Song as she stepped forward with the kettle.

'They may not be close, but they may have had the time to plan.'

'They have been planning this for a long time. Where were they?' she asked.

'On a distant island.'

Lis allowed her head to drop into her arms. 'This is never going to end,' she murmured.

'We will not let them get close.'

'You haven't been able to stop them in the past,' she murmured.

'It is my objective to keep you alive,' he said, his voice carrying frustration.

She squeezed her eyes closed. 'Would it not be easier to let me die?'

'Why do you do that?' he asked.

'Consider what your life was before I came. What it would be if I were not here. I have to admit that my life was easier without you in it,' she added softly.

He sighed, but he didn't move.

'Your Highness,' Mu-Phi said, her voice still thick with sleep. 'What can I do for you?'

'I don't want her here,' Lis said, lifting her head slowly. 'She is not keeping me safe.'

'She has much practice; she is a strong soldier. She was on the guard that watched over the former crown prince,' Remi said.

'And she did not save him.'

Mu-Phi lunged at Lis, and as Wei-Song held out her hand, Lis held her own up, blocking the woman. Mu-Phi pushed against the barrier, face twisted in anger, arms swinging. A hot anger flooded over Lis.

'Do you share with this prince what you did the last?' she asked, not hiding the venom in her voice.

'No,' they both said in unison.

'So there was something.' Lis lowered her hand and allowed the shield to drop, causing Mu-Phi to overbalance. 'I don't care if you fill my courtyard with men—they may stand in the doorways and by the table and over my bed, if that gives you comfort—but I want her out.' Lis tried to keep her voice level, but she couldn't look at them.

The prince sat at the table opposite her and waved everyone else from the room. Wei-Song waited a moment before she dragged the poor healer with her.

Lis poured water into a cup. It sat between them as the prince's eyes studied her again.

'You have your strength back,' he said.

She nodded once.

'And will you run away?'

'Where would I run to?' she asked.

He sighed.

'I have already made my promises to you, but it is never enough. Are we to live the rest of our lives like this? Or is mine to be shortened, as you threaten me with each time I see you?'

'Do I?' he asked, reaching for the cup.

'What do you want?' she asked. 'What do you think I can give you?'

'That is an interesting question. I'm not sure I have an answer. Yet despite our differences, I would still like for you to remain as you are, the hidden princess. I think you will make an excellent empress.'

'A figurehead the people look to, with no real power.'

'Do you want power?' he asked, and she shook her head. 'What do you want?'

'No one asks that,' she said, pouring another cup and sipping at it slowly.

'I have asked.'

'Why is there so much training, learning the ways of the world and history, when you will see less of me as Empress than you would as Hidden Princess?'

'I think our traditions are changing,' he murmured.

'That does not answer the question.'

'My mother acts as advisor to my father. She has a say.'

'Is it heard?' Lis asked, then bit her lip. She knew far more of what his mother had sacrificed than he did, and yet she had betrayed the Empire by hiding her child away. Lis looked towards the door and wondered who else might know this secret. There were those who referred to Wei-Song as Princess; they knew her history. As did the priestess.

'What is it?' he asked. 'You appear as though…'

'As though what?' She looked back at him.

'That you have realised something, something that could mean danger.'

'We need to find the magics.'

'We?' he asked, a smile playing on his lips.

'Mu-Phi can be a soldier, so why can I not help find the magics?'

'It is not the same.'

'No. I am learning that your relationship with the girl is something very different,' Lis said quietly, looking into the cup in her hands.

'It is not what you think,' he said as he leaned forward.

'What do I think, Your Highness? Please do tell me.'

He sighed again. 'We are friends.'

'Like Healer Yang and I are friends. And yet you look at him as though you could run him through.'

'He sleeps in your bed.'

'On my bed, as you do.' She sighed. 'Does she not sleep in your bed?'

His face creased. 'You would think so little of me that I would take my brother's…'

'Your brother's what?' she asked. She looked away from him as the conversations she'd had with the girl about the former prince started to make sense. 'And yet the uproar at U'shi's behaviour…' she added quietly.

'No one knew. It would have tarnished him, and I could not have that. In days of old, the emperor would have taken many wives.'

Lis nodded. She knew the history. The change had come when one man had loved his wife more than his station. The desire for more sons to ensure the line continued was no longer needed; peace had come to the Empire. The laws had been changed so that the firstborn son would become the crown prince and the crown would pass to him. There was no competing, no question of succession.

'Did he love her?' she asked.

'I believe so,' he said softly.

Without the need for many wives, the advisors had devised a plan to ensure the empress was the best of all the maidens in the Empire.

'What did he know of the magics?'

Remi shook his head, and she stifled a yawn.

'You should rest,' he said, standing slowly from the table. 'I should not have disturbed you as I did, but I have just returned, and I wanted to be sure you were safe.'

She stood and bowed to him. As he reached the door, she said, 'I'm sorry.'

'For my brother?'

The question stung. She wasn't sure if he meant it as a sympathy, given what they had just been talking of, or if he was inferring she'd had something to do with his death as he had said before. And the tear surprised her.

'That you are stuck with me,' she whispered. 'That I have brought trouble for you and the Empire.' Her skin prickled, and she shivered. She bowed again, and when she raised her head he was gone.

11

'I don't think this is a good idea,' Wei-Song said earnestly.

'I know, but I have to try.'

'Lis, let me go,' Yang said.

'I know you are keen to try, but…'

'I can sense as well as you,' he countered.

'But you are unpractised at hiding, and it is more draining than you realise.'

He nodded reluctantly. 'And if the prince comes?'

'I don't think he will. And if anyone else comes, use your weight as a healer—claim I am sick or something.'

'Then the prince will come,' Yang whined.

'He is trying to find the magics, and I can help.'

'He will not appreciate it,' Wei-Song murmured. 'What if he sends Mu-Phi back?'

'I don't think he will. But in that case, I will be as quick as I can.'

'How do you propose to get out?' Wei-Song asked.

'There will be a change in the guards soon; I'll slide out with them.'

Yang groaned and turned away. They knew there was no way to talk her out of it, but it didn't stop their worrying. The gate squealed, and Lis touched her hands together and raced quickly across the lawn, trying to stay off the gravel paths. She glanced back at the doorway as she slipped through the gate, but she couldn't see either of them. And then she was standing in the street.

She walked behind the soldiers for a moment and then stopped. She felt more exposed than she'd expected, but she knew she had enough strength to hide from them all now. She only hoped she could find what she needed before the prince thought she had run away again.

It didn't seem to matter what they promised each other; there was still a lack of trust between them. She needed to focus on the magics, what they wanted and why they were after her. She sighed. She knew why they were after her—they wanted her dead. But she wasn't sure how that would help their cause. She closed her eyes and tried to concentrate on the magic, sensing the hum.

It was not as strong as it had been. She wondered how many magics had been on the Palace Isle and where they might be now. There had to be others working with them, although they wanted the power all for themselves. Who would work with magics if they wouldn't continue to collaborate once they came to power? It was too great a risk. She knew the history, that all those who harboured magics during the magic war had been killed, including women and children.

Lis walked slowly along the streets, breathing in the fresh air, her heart racing at the idea of being away from her little palace. She was still trapped, in a way, but it had been so long since she had been able to go out. The trip to the baths had been her last outing, and she still felt an odd nervousness at the idea. She had been too ill to prevent them. Yang did too much, risked too much for her, and she worried about him now more than she had. She stopped and looked back. She had left for good reason and planned to return, but if they found her missing it would be Yang who paid the price.

Hesitating, she thought she caught the scent of magic. She

followed the faint touch of it until she was standing outside the temple. She wasn't sure whether she should enter, but then she saw the hunter, Hui Te-Sze. His marked face made her shiver. She wondered if he had picked up the same faint scent or if he'd just happened to be walking by.

He walked right by her, his head tilted as though listening. She stepped into the temple and found it still and quiet. There was no hint of magic here. She walked down the steps and along the walls before the gods. What would they make of this? she wondered. What would they do if they could step from the walls?

She stopped where her mother's memorial had been. The memory of it hurt, as did that of her father. She had lost them both when she had been chosen as the hidden princess. No matter what she wanted or whether she ran away, she couldn't get to either of them.

The memorial to her mother had been destroyed in the royal residence, and Lis had not replaced it. She was disappointed in herself that she had not thought of her mother in some time, and that she hadn't considered replacing the shrine. It had been one of the many thoughtful things the crown prince had done for her, before he'd found out what she was.

Maybe he was disappointed in himself for having failed to sense her. Lis looked around the temple then. The former high priestess had felt something, although she hadn't been able to when they'd knelt before the gods together. Was she the only one who had an idea of what Lis was?

Lis turned again and saw the young priestess who had come to her room and helped her. She walked differently, gently in a way, as though not to disturb the gods, and there was a confidence about her that Lis hadn't seen except in the former high priestess.

'Grant me the wisdom,' the priestess murmured as she ran her hands over the images of the gods she passed. 'Give me the sight to see what is needed.'

Lis wondered what sight she sought. Could it be that she was the one who had the vision? Were the priestesses more than Lis thought they were? The priestess touched each god within the temple and then moved to the back, where another priestess stood.

Lis wasn't sure whether she could follow without them sensing her and working out that she was there. Desperate to know what they were doing, she inched forward, hoping her footsteps didn't echo.

The young priestess took her place at the head of the room. The others knelt facing her, and she them. They all closed their eyes and remained still. They were only praying, Lis thought. The actions of the former high priestess had her concerned about everyone, but she was sure not all priestesses were the same.

Lis crept out of the temple and back along the courtyard. She paused at the empty space that had been her last home and wondered for a moment what had happened to her mother's memorial. Had it been taken away with the rest of the broken wood? She wondered if they would rebuild the residence, and if the prince missed his height over the world.

Where did he stay now? Just at the thought, she saw the advisor hurrying along with his arms full of reports. There may be soldiers, but it was too easy for anyone wanting to harm them to discover where they were.

On a whim, she decided to follow him and see just where the prince was. He led her back towards her own palace, and she wondered if he had decided to make her table his desk again. It had been a difficult conversation during the night. She didn't know just what he wanted from her, or what he thought she could give him. At least he hadn't sent Mu-Phi back. Where had she been when the crown prince was murdered?

The little man moved quite quickly. Lis hurried to keep up with him and not lose him as he darted down an alleyway. Maybe he wasn't headed to the prince, but to sell secrets. Lis slowed a little as the hum of magic reached her, but then she recognised it as the prince's searching.

She entered the little gate with him, and the memory of another gate surged through her. Was there a black gate somewhere on the Palace Isle? Could she find it? Or could she ask about it?

The prince sat at the table, which was covered in reports, and the advisor stood in the doorway, his arms full. He coughed politely. The prince pointed without looking up.

'Is there any word?' he asked as the man dropped the pile on the edge of the table and then started to straighten up the reports. He moved some to the top of the pile, others into a second.

The prince looked up at him, and he shook his head.

'Where are they?'

'I don't know, Your Highness,' he murmured.

'Send Hui Te-Sze,' the prince said as he looked back to his notes.

'He is out searching.'

'I want a report,' the prince continued.

'There is one.' The advisor pointed to the top of the pile he had placed on the table. The prince dropped the one he'd been reading and reached for it.

He scanned the pages and then put it down. 'I don't understand,' he murmured.

'Can I help?' the advisor asked.

He shook his head and waved the man from the room. Then he tapped the report on his chin and put it down to collect another. 'There is nothing of any use to me here,' he murmured, discarding it and reaching for another.

Lis wondered exactly what he was looking for. She took a moment to look around the room. It was very similar to her own, and she wondered why he had chosen such a place. It was nothing like the opulence he'd had before. Lis was sure the empress was in a beautiful alternative, but then she realised the prince was not far from her own palace. Still watching over her.

She could hear the gentle hiss of an empty kettle over the coals, and she wondered if she should assist him in some way. The noise echoed in the small room.

'Mu-Phi?' he asked, and the girl appeared beside where Lis stood. She bit her lip to prevent a squeal. She would be run through this time.

He looked up and then ran his hand over his face. 'The water,' he said.

Mu-Phi nodded once but didn't move. 'Are you going to keep me here?'

'Where would you like to be?' he asked, picking up another report. 'I can send you back to your father.'

She shook her head and dropped to her knees. Lis watched her closely as the prince slowly raised his eyes from his reading.

'He would marry me off,' she whined.

'It is not such a bad idea,' the prince murmured, looking down again.

'It would be a betrayal to your brother,' she said, shuffling forward on her knees. 'Please, Remi, don't do this.'

He dropped the report and stared at her. Lis held her breath. They did have a relationship different to hers.

'We may be as close as siblings, but you must remember where we are and who you are.'

She dropped her head. 'Forgive me, Your Highness, but I cannot marry another.'

'Then what are you to do?'

'Serve you,' she said without hesitation. 'As I would have served your brother.'

He looked at her closely then.

'With my life,' she went on, dropping her head to the floor.

The crown prince sighed. He waved her from the room, and she backed up before disappearing into the yard and through the gate. The kettle continued to hiss. While the prince turned back to his reports, Lis hid the kettle, surprised that she could. She carried it through to the small rear courtyard with a pump and filled the bucket, then filled the kettle and returned it to the coals. As the steam blew softly across the table, he picked it up without thought and poured a cup.

Lis sat on the floor and leaned against the wall. As the light outside faded, she grew sleepy. She realised she had spent too long remaining hidden and she should consider returning to her own palace while she still could. The prince had barely raised his eyes from his reading, and she wondered what he learnt from all the reports. Did they tell him anything of where the magics were hiding?

She must have drifted, for she woke to a crackle of magic. She jumped, but again it was the prince, and she wondered if he searched all the time. In the dark room, he was still in the same position at the table, with the reports spread out before him as flames danced over his knuckles. Lis stared for a moment before she carefully climbed to her feet and tiptoed across the room towards him. If Mu-Phi saw this, what would she do? Despite her having just promised her life to her prince, Lis was sure it would not end as either of them expected.

She walked around him, studying the small flames dancing above the skin. It was beautiful and yet scary. He sighed and turned a page. She doubted he even knew what he had, and that scared her all the more. What might he do without thinking or knowing, and what might his father do to him?

'Stop,' she cried, and the room plunged into darkness.

'Mu-Phi?' he called, but she didn't answer. 'What has happened to the candles?' he murmured, and then a small flame lit up the room. He stretched and rubbed his eyes.

Lis stepped back. He was a fire bearer, and she hadn't sensed it. No one had. She had felt a magic around him when he sensed or hunted, but this was something very different. And she didn't know what to do with it. She had felt his magic flow across her as he slept, pushing on her at times, and yet... She studied him closely. Maybe he did know what he was. Maybe he was a different type of Hidden.

Lis needed to talk to Wei-Song. She had a better understanding of the magics of the world and what they could do. She might understand her brother. Perhaps there was a similarity between them. Then Mu-Phi was in the room, a pot in her hands. She put it on the table and uncovered it, and the prince forgot the reports.

'Is it that late?'

She nodded.

'Have you checked on the princess?'

She shook her head.

'I will go,' he murmured, pushing up from the table.

'You need to eat, and you need to rest. She is watched over.'

He produced a grumbling noise and pulled the pot closer.

'The healer does not...' She stopped as he raised angry eyes towards her. Then she bowed low and backed up from the room.

What exactly did he think Yang was? It was as though he did not want to be close to her, yet he also didn't want anyone else to be. Yang was her friend, the first true friend she'd had in some time, along with Wei-Song. Although there was always the feeling that Wei-Song needed something that Lis wasn't sure how to give.

She could feel the magic dragging on her. She needed to return before she couldn't. She tried to stifle a yawn and blinked back the tiredness threatening to overwhelm her. Then the prince was standing by his bed, blowing out the candle and climbing beneath the covers. Lis touched her hands together and became visible in the dark. She was exhausted, but now she could rest for a moment before trying to find her way home again.

She sat down against the bed, as Yang did when he read, and rested her head back. As she listened to the prince's soft breathing, she wondered how he would react if she climbed in beside him as he had done to her so often. But there was more to him than she was aware of, and she couldn't risk herself now.

She had drifted again, for when she opened her eyes the sun was starting to light the room. She stretched her hands above her head and, as she brought them down to touch together, a strong hand closed around her wrist. She looked up in fright as the prince looked down at her.

'What are you doing?' he asked.

'I wanted to learn what you know of the magics,' she murmured, feeling the heat of his hand around her. His grip was tight. Although she could touch her hands together, he would still have hold of her if she hid.

She tried to pull from his hold, but she couldn't. His grip remained tight, and his skin became warmer.

'Please don't burn me,' she whispered.

He released her instantly, and she scuttled across the floor away from him.

'Why would I burn you?' he asked, leaping from the bed and coming after her. She held her arms up in front of her face.

He squatted over her, taking her arms in his hands, trying to see her face. 'Why would I burn you?' he asked again.

She shook her head madly, trying to pull from him and wondering why she had thought this would be a good idea.

'Why?' he asked. His anger burned hot against her skin, and she cried out.

Mu-Phi appeared in the doorway just as Lis managed to put her hands together and hide. But as he straightened up, he maintained his hold on her. She was caught, his hands tight around her arm, and the sting was making her eyes water.

'Is everything alright, Your Highness?'

He nodded. 'I need to check on something.'

She bowed and backed from the room.

'Please,' Lis pleaded. He let her go and turned around to face her.

'Show yourself,' he said.

She touched her hands together, remembering that Wei-Song had said she would find a way to hide without the physical gesture. But she was yet to learn it.

He reached for her arm, but she pulled back from him.

'What did you learn?' he asked.

'Nothing,' she said quickly.

'You look like you found something more terrifying than the magics,' he said, his voice kinder as he stepped towards her. She backed up again and hit her back on the wall. A whimper escaped before she could stop it.

'Me,' he said, stopping. 'You find me more terrifying.'

She wanted to reassure him, but her mouth wouldn't work.

'I know I made a mistake,' he said, stepping towards her, and she wished she could disappear into the wall. 'But I wouldn't hurt you. I promised.'

She held out her arms then, the red raw burns evident on her wrists.

'Who did this?' he asked, reaching for her, and she withdrew again.

'Mu-Phi,' he called. When she appeared in the room, she took in Lis and her eyes hardened. 'Go for Healer Yang. Take no excuses from him.'

She nodded and disappeared.

'Please don't punish him for my mistake,' she said, her heart beating fast. 'I won't tell.'

'Won't tell what?' he asked, the confusion apparent on his face, and she wondered if he was toying with her or he really did not know what he had.

She gulped down her fear and shook her head. They maintained their stand until Yang rushed into the room. 'What have you done?' he started as he raced towards her.

'I haven't done anything. She was hidden,' the prince said. His voice carried an edge, but it wasn't the anger that had been there before.

Yang stood between them, and Lis held up her arms. 'Did he?' he whispered, and she nodded. Yang carefully placed his hands over the burn marks on her arms. They matched almost perfectly. She sucked in a ragged breath, remembering U'shi, burnt from the inside by a fire bearer, and she wondered what he might have done to her. Was he trying to discover what he was rather than looking for the magics? Why had she thought she could trust a man who had already tried to kill her?

'Shh,' Yang whispered. Lis looked up at him as he blurred before her. The hot tears spilled over her cheeks as his cooling hold soothed her somewhat. When he withdrew his hands, there was only a pinkish hue to the skin. But she couldn't maintain her strength, and she slipped down the wall.

Yang had her up in his arms and out the door before she could argue. As they moved through the gate, she felt the hiding cover her. 'What have you done?' she whispered.

'Shh,' he said quickly. They stopped, watching the prince race after them into the street and then stop. They moved away from him as he ran out and then back. She might get the chance to have some space from him. When they were close to her own palace, she grabbed at Yang's robes.

'He'll find us,' she whispered.

'He is going to find us anyway. We can't run, Lis.'

She nodded against him and allowed him to carry her home. As they entered the door, they reappeared, and Wei-Song rushed forward.

'How did you do that?' she asked him.

'You aren't that heavy,' he murmured, leaning forward and trying to catch his breath.

'You hid us both.'

'He knows where we will be.'

'He is a fire bearer,' Lis blurted.

Wei-Song shook her head.

'I saw it, and he burnt me,' Lis continued.

'I would have felt it. You would have felt it.'

'Then explain to me what he is,' Lis snapped.

'I can't,' Wei-Song said with a sigh.

The door burst open, and Yang staggered back as Lis squealed.

The crown prince stopped and looked over the group as Wei-Song stepped forward. Lis thought she might be trying to determine what he was, but she shook her head just a little.

'You promised me,' he said, his voice too loud, and Lis heard movement amongst the soldiers in the yard.

'As you promised me,' she said. This wasn't going to work. How had she thought this could ever be what it had been before? The air went out of her as she sank to the floor. Her mind raced, but she couldn't grab on to any form of solution. 'I don't know,' she murmured.

He stepped forward, and she tried to move back from him again. The same fear that he was going to burn right through her overwhelmed her. She could feel the burns on her arms flaring as she sucked in a breath.

'Lis,' Yang said, his voice loud and strong. It broke through the haze she was disappearing into. 'Don't,' he said.

She looked at her wrists, the pink marks turning red, her flesh looking bubbled and blistered, and the panic was too much.

Yang bent down quickly, pushing the prince out of the way as he grabbed her. 'Don't let this happen,' he whispered hoarsely.

She nodded, the tears running hot down her checks as she tried to focus on the cooling of his hands. 'I can't,' she whispered.

'What have you done?' Remi asked, leaning over her. She tried to pull away from them all.

'What have you done to her?' Wei-Song asked. Her voice was clear, so much like her mother's that it drew his attention.

He shook his head.

'What did you do when you touched her? What were you thinking?'

'She was trying to run away,' he murmured.

'In your room?'

He looked at Lis, then back to the woman he thought was a maid. He nodded and then shook his head. 'She was looking for magics.'

'I found one,' Lis said, then bit her lip as Wei-Song shook her head.

'You think I am a magic?' he asked, the hatred thick in his voice. 'You think I am one of them?'

Lis nodded slowly and held out her hands. Yang sat back with a sigh.

'You did that in your hysterical state,' he murmured, looking at her closely. 'If I were magic, someone would have known. The hunters I work with would have discovered me. My father would have killed me the moment it was felt.'

Wei-Song nodded slowly.

Lis stood, trying hard to push her fears deep down, hidden with her own magic. 'I don't know what you are,' she said, 'but I have felt the hum of magic around you since I met you.'

12

Remi turned and left the palace, pushing through the princess's guards who had started to gather at the doorway. The early morning light was just starting to turn from pink to orange, and he stood for a moment in the laneway watching the grey walls glow like the rooftops.

She had to be wrong. She had focused a fear in her mind, like when she wouldn't allow the healing to take effect. She had caused the burns herself and was going to blame him for them.

He shook his head. She had truly looked terrified. Was it all a ploy, a way to have him discredited? But in exposing him, despite the lies, it would expose her too. The risk to her was greater. Or was it?

He needed to find Hui Te-Sze, so he headed towards the centre of the island. Te-Sze had spent his days of late walking the island. He had covered nearly every inch, yet he'd found no sign of the magics. They were either very well hidden or not there. Remi couldn't understand why they would have given up so easily when they had wanted so desperately to kill Lis.

He walked, but he couldn't find the hunter. He saw others starting to move about for their day. Maids headed to the market; healers hurried about their business; a priestess stood in the morning sun with her eyes closed.

Remi's father would have him killed. If there was any chance he was magic, any chance he had been responsible for his brother's death, it would mean his own. Although his father hadn't believed the magics had returned, so no matter what had been done to Remi's brother, the emperor might not be as quick to believe his son was magic.

Did they all know what she was? Yang certainly did, for he'd been there when Remi had driven the sword into her. He shivered at the memory. Despite his feelings, he knew his instincts were right. She was dangerous. And then there was the little maid, the new one who had served his mother.

She had seemed to understand the accusations Lis threw at him, but she had shaken her head. He wasn't sure if it was because she knew he wouldn't believe her or because she didn't want Lis to speak up. Did that put his mother at risk?

He couldn't talk to his mother of such an issue. He couldn't ask her what she thought he was. Any sign that he was not what he claimed to be might put them both at risk. He stopped walking and looked around the quiet street he had found himself in. Lis had said she could sense him all along.

Was his hunting a form of magic they had not considered? Could it be they'd had magic all along but had not learnt what power they had? Why couldn't the other hunters sense him? They had discovered his hunting abilities at a young age; it was why he had been elevated and trained as he had. Whilst his brother had learnt the workings of the court and the Empire, Remi had learnt the secrets of hunting out those with magic.

Now he was trying to do both. He hadn't sensed the magic that had killed his brother, and he still had no idea what had occurred or who was responsible. He suddenly felt lost, as though he needed someone he could share his concerns with. Mu-Phi was not that person. She would blame Lis and endanger them both.

Why am I getting so worked up over this? She is wrong.

The hunter came around the corner and stopped, looking Remi

over.

'What have you found?' Remi asked, hoping Hui Te-Sze couldn't sense him as Lis claimed she could.

'There is no sign of them anywhere.' He shifted his head to the side, stretching out his scarred neck and wincing at the movement. 'I have covered every inch of this island.'

'What if they are Hidden?'

'I think your princess is right. I think there are different kinds of magics, and those out to kill her are the kind we can sense.'

Remi prickled at the idea of her being his princess. But the hunter's words gave him pause.

'You don't think all magics should be killed?'

The hunter shrugged. 'The world is not what I thought it was.'

Remi chewed his lip and nodded slowly.

'Do you need me, Your Highness?'

Remi shook his head. 'Only to ask what you know. And to report that the princess has been attacked again,' he added, then silently cursed himself. *What am I doing?*

'By whom?' the man asked slowly.

'She seems to think by me,' he said.

The hunter looked around the small street before nodding once and then continuing in the direction he'd been headed.

'You don't trust her,' Remi said, keeping pace with the man.

'If she thinks it was you, it is for good reason. Perhaps someone has impersonated you?'

'I was with her,' Remi said, and the hunter stopped.

'Tell me,' he whispered, and Remi felt the uncertainty of what this man would do.

'She thinks I have magic,' he blurted.

The hunter laughed. A loud, comfortable sound that reverberated from the walls surrounding them.

'She was marked.'

The hunter reigned in his laughter and looked over the prince. He sniffed at the air and walked around him. Remi tried not to sigh as the man gently touched a hand to his back, then to his chest as he rounded him.

'I don't sense anything.'

'Could she try to trick others into believing it?'

The hunter shook his head. 'I know what she is,' he said softly, 'but I trust her completely.'

'Completely?' Remi repeated.

The hunter nodded.

'And what did she do to gain this trust?' He couldn't keep the anger from his voice.

'You do not trust your hidden princess?'

'She is magic,' Remi said too loudly, then chewed his lip, worried someone over a wall somewhere might have heard.

'She is not like the others.' Te-Sze said.

'How can we be sure?'

'You really think that she would do this,' he said. It wasn't a question.

'Then explain to me what has happened!' The prince's frustrations ran over.

'I don't know that I can. There is too much I don't understand. What do we know of the Hidden? When did they appear? Are they connected to the Order of Huans that our hunters searched for during the war? Are any of them what we thought they were?'

'Are we sure of anything?'

The hunter shook his head. He winced a little, and Remi noticed how the tight skin at his neck caught on his armour.

Remi sucked in a deep breath and tried not to sigh. 'I'm lost,' he admitted. 'The people will look to me for answers, and I don't know what to give them.'

'Have you talked with your father?'

'He won't accept the danger, despite all that has occurred recently. He may not believe anything.'

'What do you believe?'

Remi shook his head. 'I can't have magic,' he murmured.

'I don't think you do. Perhaps it was part of her fears.'

'I thought you believed her.'

'I do, but I could be persuaded. You saw what she did to herself.'

'She appears scared all the time. Scared of the magics, of me, of herself in a way.'

'She knows she is an anomaly that should have been ended when her father learned what she was.' Te-Sze sighed. 'I understand why he didn't.'

Remi openly stared at the man.

'Would you have killed a child of your own if it was magic?'

'I would have said yes, but I'm not sure now.'

'I saw the hesitation when you knew what she was. I know you could not drive the sword through her, despite the magic,' Te-Sze said.

'I didn't hear the fizzle. But she certainly holds magic.'

'Are you worried she will hide again?'

'She found her way to my palace; she has already hidden.'

'But she didn't run away. She ran to you,' the man said with a sly smile.

'Not to me, but to the knowledge I might have.' Remi looked over his hands and sighed.

'What does she think you have?' the hunter asked quietly, moving him to the side of the walkway where they were poised to see if anyone was coming from either direction.

'She didn't... Fire,' he said, his voice barely a whisper. 'She said I burnt her.'

'There has been no evidence of this before?'

'Of course not,' Remi snapped. 'I can't do this. There has been a mistake.'

The hunter stared him down. Remi turned his back on the man and stalked off. He needed time to process this, to work out what she thought she had seen. Before he knew it, he was back at her palace.

'She's sleeping,' Wei-Song said, meeting him at the door, and again he felt a familiarity with the woman. 'And it took some time to calm her down.'

'What happened?' he asked.

She shook her head, just as she had when Lis had tried to talk before.

'Who are you?' he asked.

She opened her mouth and then closed it, her lips forming into an angry thin line. 'I am the one who watches over her,' she said firmly after what felt like an age.

'Will you always watch over her?'

'If she needs me to.'

He turned at the doorway but could not see into the room. 'I suppose Healer Yang is watching over her as well,' he murmured.

'She was very distressed,' Wei-Song said, looking towards the room.

'I wouldn't hurt her.'

'Don't keep saying that.' Her voice was calm as she turned back to stare him down. 'You do hurt her—you have hurt her. Even if you decide she should live long enough to be your empress, she will be broken long before then if you continue this way.'

'I can't find the magics,' he said. 'I can't find a way to stop this.'

'You are a hunter, are you not?'

He nodded mutely.

'Then hunt.' Her voice carried a vehemence he didn't expect, and he stepped back with the force of it to have the door shut in his face.

A guard looked towards him with the sound of the door, but he looked away again when he focused on the prince. Remi headed out into the alleyway beyond the gate. The hunter had searched the entire island, but they had to be here somewhere. He took off at a fast pace into the morning sun as the warm weather brought people out into the streets. He worked his way through narrow streets towards the outer wall, until he found himself in an unfamiliar part of the island.

He needed to get up higher, look over the whole island and get a feel for it; as he had done on the abandoned island. Only there was nowhere high enough, particularly now that the residence was gone. He smiled to himself, remembering the first day he had taken Lis to the hidden palace. When they had passed the temple, she had talked of climbing it. Only he didn't think the crown prince should be climbing the temple like a child. He needed to get up on the wall.

13

Lis found herself at the black gate. She knew she was dreaming again, but it felt real. The sun was hot on her skin, the air dry. She knew there was magic around her, but she couldn't quite sense it. Couldn't feel it like she had before, the hum of it across her skin. But she knew it was there all the same.

She pushed on the gate, and it swung slowly inwards. Beyond was a courtyard, weeds growing through the blocks that no longer looked as smooth and level as she was sure they once had. There wasn't a soul inside. As she stepped through the black gate into the still, desolate world on the other side, the gate swung shut behind her with a bang.

She swung back to look at it and then heard the voices of children. She looked back to find the courtyard as it once would have been, bright and fresh and filled with veiled children. The hidden princesses. She moved unseen between them, and they continued as though she weren't there. She studied each one, looking for herself again, but she couldn't determine which she was.

Children disappeared and reappeared in random patterns throughout the courtyard. One rubbed her hand together like she was making a fist but moved her fingertips over the heel of her thumb. The skin on skin made an odd, dry crackle sound, and then she held fire in her hand. Another swirled a finger to make the wind blow up around her. It pulled at her dress and lifted her long sleeves into the air. Her hair didn't move at all, and Lis stopped to watch in wonder. Another held out her hand, and rain fell from her palm to the stone below.

A fourth child stepped forward. When she held out her hand, a lone stem pushed its way between the stones and up towards her, where a flower opened. The one making it rain stopped and turned to her with a disappointed look.

'Another flower,' she said.

'I like flowers,' the first child responded, and Lis felt a familiarity.

'You won't be any good,' the child with the rain said.

'I am good,' she retorted.

'You can't do anything for the Empire with flowers.' The child's voice carried a singsong element to it, but Lis could hear the cruel intention behind it. The eyes of little Lis narrowed as the flower grew taller, branching out, its stems becoming thicker and darker.

The rain child poked her tongue out, and the vine suddenly reached out to wrap around her wrist, holding her tight. It wound tighter and tighter, working its way along her arm, and her hand began to turn blue.

'Enough,' a woman called across the courtyard, and silence descended. Lis turned to see a woman in white walking quickly towards them. She might have been a priestess, given the white, although she was nothing like the priestesses Lis knew.

'I said enough,' she said again, raising a finger and pointing it towards them. The vine withered and disappeared, and the girl grabbed at her arm where it had held her.

The other girl sighed, blowing out her veil. The woman pointed at her, and she dropped to her knees. She screamed, and Lis screamed with her, feeling the constricting power pull through her body. The child smacked her hands together, trying desperately to hide, but it wouldn't work. The constriction grew tighter until Lis thought she couldn't breathe, the scream dying in her throat. The child smacked ineffectually until she appeared to run out of air, at which point she dropped to the stone.

'You are all different,' the woman said. 'Embrace it. You must learn to work with others or there will be none of you left.'

The girl with the sore hand nodded slowly, still cradling her arm.

'Back to work,' the woman snapped, and the girl let her hand drop to her side, making rain fall from the other.

Lis stepped towards the child lying on the stone.

'Leave her,' the woman said, and Lis looked back towards her. She didn't appear to be looking at anyone but the child. Then she turned and left.

Another child across the yard waved her hand and a small cloud appeared above her, blocking out the sun. When she moved her hand slowly, the cloud floated across the sky to a point above the child lying on the stones, shielding her from the hot sun.

'She will punish you for disobeying,' the rainmaker said.

'I don't care. You shouldn't pick on her.'

'She is an easy target. She will never be anything of value. How can she protect the Empire with that skill?'

'There are rumours about her. You need to be careful.'

'I don't believe in rumours, only what I see. And I have far more power than she will ever have.'

The cloud-maker sighed. The other one clicked her fingers, wincing at the movement, and the little cloud rained on the unconscious girl. She didn't move. Lis stepped forward and put her hand on the girl's shoulder, and she sat up screaming. Lis screamed in surprise, then found herself back in her own bed.

The room was quiet and still. She had expected to find Yang curled on the end of the bed, but he wasn't there. Her chest tightened. Did he no longer have the energy to watch over her? She was so difficult, trying to be strong when she really wanted to leave this world behind. She thought she had found a direction again, but then the magics were free and the prince…

She stopped. She didn't know what to think of the prince. In some ways, it was a comfort that there was something so familiar about him. That they shared this skill and it put them at the same risk. But he didn't know what he had. She didn't either. And it might cause her more harm than good when he worked it out.

She threw her legs around and then realised there was something on the floor. She pulled her legs back up and reached down carefully in the dark to find someone lying on the floor. Yang murmured in his sleep, still watching over her, and she sighed with relief. She rolled back onto her back and stared up at the ceiling above her. Despite the darkness, she could trace the pattern of the wood and the fabric she knew so well.

Somewhere on this island was a place no one knew of. A place where the hidden princesses were trained. But they weren't just hidden—they were magic. Lis wondered if that was where the Hidden had started. Perhaps the training had been more than just for the Empire. Perhaps it had been to see who was stronger. Maybe they killed each other in their pursuit for the honour of Empress.

Who was the woman in white? Lis sat up again and then waited, hoping she hadn't woken anyone. She needed to find the black gate—she needed to find what was hidden inside. She might be able to learn just who these girls were and what they were taught. She might still be able to learn from them.

She was still tired from her outing the night before and the trouble it had caused. But she couldn't remain here any longer. She needed to know the secret, and she couldn't tell anyone she was going.

She touched her hands together and crawled to the end of the bed, where she carefully climbed over the edge so as not to disturb Yang. She twirled once to change into something more fitting for running through the night, thankful she could remain hidden. If something went wrong and she was discovered, she would be dressed in black and appear more like a young man.

Once in the yard, she paused as she realised she hadn't thought this through enough. But someone had placed a stool against the wall, so she ran towards it. Standing on it, she could reach the top of the wall. And despite the fact that she hadn't climbed anything since she was a child, she managed to pull and drag herself up and onto the narrow wall. Just as she did, a soldier sat on the stool, and she sighed with relief. She looked down into the dark street on the other side to find it was a little further than she'd thought.

Carefully climbing to her feet, she looked out over the world. She could only see a small part of it where the lanterns lit small fragments. She sat back down, took a deep breath and pushed herself off the wall.

Lis thought she made too much noise when she landed, but no one came running, and there was no sound from the soldiers inside her walled garden. She didn't know where she was, but she guessed it was towards the far northeast corner of the island. Far from the main crowds and possibly closer to where the original hidden princesses had been housed. She looked towards the direction where the prince was staying only briefly before heading the other way.

As a Hidden, she would see others if they were around, but they would be able to see her as well. She stopped suddenly, remembering the prince. He hadn't seen her when she was hidden, and she wondered again just what he was.

She shook her head and started along the narrow street, surrounded by the high walls. Now that she knew they weren't as thick as she had first thought and there were some lights glowing on the other side them, she realised she wasn't as isolated as she had thought. Although perhaps it was the tutors or the like that had been moved closer. Or more guards.

She stopped at a gate that looked dark in the night, but she was sure it was red when she drew closer. She placed her hand on it gently and felt the warmth of the wood. She continued on, running her hand over the rough stone walls and the dark gates that were dotted along them. And then there seemed to be nothing but stone wall. She looked around, wondering if she had reached the end of the street, but it stretched on ahead of her.

Then, on the left, she found an old gate. The paint was peeling away from the wood, and there was no plaque despite the grandeur of the gate. When she tried to push on it, it appeared to be stuck. She rattled the latch, but it turned loose in her hand. She stood back and looked up, wondering if there was a way to get over the wall, but she saw nothing. What could have been in such a place that they no longer allowed others inside?

She backed up again and stepped into the hard wall. After letting out a groan, she covered her mouth, then decided to move further along the wall to see if there was another gate or way in. It wasn't the black gate that she had been looking for, but it was something, and she felt a desperation to get inside.

She had reached the end of the street when she found another gate straight ahead of her. She looked up at the wall that surrounded the island and wondered if this was one of the exits to the walkway beneath it. Waiting quietly at the gate, she listened for soldiers or anything similar on the other side before she pushed it open. The moon appeared from behind a cloud, lighting the world around Lis to reveal the world she had seen in her dream. She quietly pushed the gate closed behind her. It was a different angle from what she had seen in her dream, but the world was just as it had been before the children appeared.

She moved slowly and carefully across the uneven stones, looking for any sign of life. There was none, and no sign or sense of magic. She wondered why this hadn't been turned into something else, such as a palace for some minister or advisor, or the like. There were no buildings within the large open space, and Lis wondered just what had been done here.

At the end of the courtyard stood a single gate, propped ajar. She walked quickly towards it. It was only once her hand was on the edge of it that she realised it was black. She gripped the wood hard and pulled the gate towards her.

The young priestess walked comfortably in the feet of her ancestor. Unlike her other dreams and visions, she was a part of this one, experiencing life as one of those in it rather than watching from a distance. But she knew it was something that had occurred long ago.

Her dress hung differently, the material heavier than what she usually wore. She felt pulled down and rooted in the unknown world. She walked amongst magical children, all of them with different powers, each determined to be the strongest.

They focused on their exercises, pushing flames from their hands or making it rain. The skills were as diverse as the children. She watched as one made a flower grow from between the stones, and the others laughed at her.

But there was something else about this child, something stronger than any of them realised.

As the taunting continued, the little flower turned into something much darker. It grew stronger, and the priestess could see the strength of the child in it as it wrapped around another child's arm. She wanted to watch what happened, to see if the child would go as far as the priestess felt she would. But her host stepped in and ended the situation.

There was so much more the priestess wanted to see, but she had no control here. She needed to find the hidden princess and what she was doing with her time. They were both linked to this place. They had a shared history, and the high priestess wondered if this view into the past was a way of seeing into the future.

She looked across the courtyard before she turned and headed away from the children. The black lacquered gate glinted in the hot sun, and she smiled. There was such a gate where she had trained on the Sacred Isle. In a little garden, tucked far away from the pilgrims.

14

Lis could see nothing in the darkness beyond the black gate, and she stepped slowly through the opened gateway. The moon had disappeared again, and she could only make out dark shapes against darker shapes. She knew that her little palace had once housed a hidden princess, but were her dreams a window to the past? Had they all lived together at some point? Or was there something else about the hidden princesses she didn't understand?

She tripped on something and stopped. Holding out her hands before her, she crept towards the closest large shadow, which she hoped was a building. She could feel no magic and yet, as in her dream, she could sense something. She knew it was there, but she couldn't feel it.

She reached a step as her hand found the round, smooth wooden edge of the building. Had anyone else been here? Did others assume that workers or the like lived in these far reaches of the island? She looked up to the wall that surrounded the island and wondered who watched from the watch towers and what they might have seen. She had been inside part of the wall, but she wondered if she would ever have the chance to walk the entire distance of it. And just what she might see from there.

In the shadows, she felt her way up the steps that appeared to run the length of the building. She ran her hand over the stonework until she reached another rounded pillar, which edged an opening. Sucking in a deep breath, she stepped inside, where the air was thick with dust and something else. A sadness washed over her, and she wondered if it was a remnant of the girls who had lived there.

Stepping forward slowly, and with her hand still on the post, Lis turned into the room and felt along the wall. The stone was the same as she had felt on the outside of the building. She bumped into a bench or table, the edge sharp in her thigh. It scraped across the floor, causing her to cringe, worried it might alert someone to her presence.

Feeling across the table, she found a candle sitting in a round holder. She felt around again but couldn't find anything else on the table. She picked up the candle and held the end up to her face, then breathed slowly onto it. When nothing happened, she shook her head. She hadn't really thought anything would. She had breathed life into coals before, but only when there was already heat there. She tried to visualise the flames that danced across the prince's knuckles and then breathed across the candle again. As she leaned back, the flame sparked to life and lit a small part of the world around her.

She was tempted to put it down for a moment, unsure whether she had managed to bring it to life. As she looked around, she realised she was no longer hidden, and she wasn't sure if she had done that herself or if using her skills to light the candle had changed something.

It didn't matter. If she found anyone else in the building, she would only have to blow out the candle to be hidden. She took a deep breath and turned to face the room. It was a long dormitory-style space with beds along the walls, each one heavily curtained with a wide step up to it. Before each bed was a small table. Lis looked down the room, which was much longer than she had first imagined. At least forty beds were lined along the wall. Did that mean there had been forty hidden princesses at any one time?

She closed her eyes and tried to remember how many girls she had seen in the courtyard in her dream, but she wasn't sure. Then she remembered looking along the line during her own Choosing. There had only been fifteen girls lined up before the royal family that day. There had been closer to forty when her sister had lined up as a child. If Lis had moved with the other young women into such a place to train for the crown prince, it may have been a very different life.

Spiderwebs and dust coated the once-fine fabrics on the beds and the surface of every table. Could this really have been what she thought it was? Had it been so long since it had been used? Was that why the gate was locked? Or was it only stuck?

So many little girls. Lis wondered if their families knew the truth of what they were and what had happened to them. Or had they been told stories of how they had somehow gone into service for the royal family? This was after the years of the concubines, so they wouldn't have provided any heirs for the royal line. Lis wondered absently if the laws might change if an empress could not produce a son.

She sighed. She was likely to be the first in a very long time. The room overwhelmed her, so she took the small candle and headed outside. The candle didn't light much beyond the steps on which she stood, and she wondered if she would have to walk every inch of this compound to discover its secrets.

She headed down the steps and across the rough-paved path. Weeds pushed up between the stones; the gravel had been lost to the ground long ago. A branch caught her unawares, and she jumped as it appeared out of the darkness. She put her hand to her chest. It was only a tree. If there had been a garden here, it had likely tried to take over. But then, Lis liked gardens and she had not been able to sit in her own. Not that it was hers. Mu-Phi had once mentioned that the whole of the Empire belonged to her—or at least it would when she was Empress—and Lis had laughed at the notion, certain the crown prince would not let it get to that stage. But she liked the idea of being free enough to travel wherever she wanted.

The path met more steps, and she found herself in a gazebo, surprisingly free of dust and cobwebs, overlooking dark water. She looked around more closely, worried there was someone here and she would soon be discovered walking through their garden.

She couldn't sense anything around her. Even in the water, there was no sign of fish or life. She turned and squinted back the way she had come. She had seen the grasses growing, and the tree, but now that she reached out, she couldn't sense any life.

She looked at the candle in her hand, the flame dancing at the end of it, and she wondered if this was in fact another dream. That she hadn't snuck out to explore the world, but instead was trapped trying to understand it in her sleep.

A cool breeze blew across her skin, and she sighed at the sensation. She was awake, she was sure of it.

She turned from the gazebo and found another building. It contained smaller self-contained rooms, each similar in size to what she now lived in. Perhaps they were for the tutors or staff; so many girls would need people to watch over them.

Lis walked along their length, counting five doors. More tutors than she had now, it seemed. She turned the handle of the last room and pushed her way in. Strange shadows filled the small space as faces stared at her from the walls. She dropped the candle in surprise, and it rolled along the floor, the flame still burning and making the shadows shift.

She stepped into the room and retrieved the candle. Looking around for where the base might be, she held it tight in her hand and raised it up to the nearest face.

Like the temple, these images were carved in the wall. As though someone would step from the stone. Unlike the temple, they were only faces. There were no gods here. She ran her hand over one, smooth and cool beneath her fingers. When she raised the candle to it, it appeared to be a young face. She stepped back and found that the faces covered every wall. There were hundreds of them, covering every inch, and for a moment Lis wondered if there were more here somewhere, not only in this room.

Some were younger and some were older, but every girl depicted in the stone was younger than Lis. Were they hidden princesses—were they the ones who had succeeded? She doubted it, for there wouldn't be so many empresses. Were these the ones who had failed, killed to enable the best of these girls to become what she was selected for?

The idea made Lis shiver as she wondered what may have happened to them. Each face was set on a flat stone, and she noticed a small mark at the corner of one of the carvings. She ran her fingertip over the small indentation, but it was a symbol she wasn't familiar with.

Holding the candle closer to each one, Lis worked her way around the room. Every face had a symbol of some sort. Some were similar to others, some different, and she wondered who would be able to tell her what they meant. Tutor Nizen, who had known the histories, had been executed for his affair with the former hidden princess; but he must have learnt what he had known from someone else.

Lis walked back out into the cool night air, relieved to be away from all the staring faces. It was as though the ghosts of these children still remained. She pushed into the next room, but it was narrower than she expected, containing a bed and table as the others had. She went to pull the door shut when she noticed something on the wall. An image had been painted on the stone in black; it might be ink, but she wasn't sure. It was a girl, and there was a sparkle about her eyes. A talented artist, Lis thought as she moved the candle around the ink to look at the brushstrokes.

Then she focused on the girl's face and stepped back, holding the candle out before her. It wasn't right, she thought. It was different from the other faces she had seen carved from the stone. She wished she could see more. The candle flickered as the little flame shone brighter, and Lis bit her lip.

It was an image of her. Maybe the girl she had seen in her dreams was someone who looked like her rather than was her, and this image was made after she had grown to look even more like Lis.

She ran a hand over her cheek and nose. But this looked so much like her, it reminded her of a portrait her sister had painted before they had known their lives would change, when she'd had Peng and her future had seemed set quite differently.

15

Remi had been on the wall all day, looking over the Palace Isle. There were walls, paths and gardens he had never seen in his life. He wondered what else may be hidden away within this place he had thought he knew so well. He had assumed too much about the buildings he didn't enter. That they were places of work or homes of servants. But once he was on the wall, he realised there were places that didn't appear to have seen life in a long time.

There were overgrown gardens, falling buildings, spaces void of life. Now, as he looked over these spaces in the dark, he wondered if they had been kept vacant, and whether his father would be willing to share that reason, if he knew it himself. For there were some buildings he was sure had not been lived in for hundreds of years.

Which also meant there were many more places the magics could be hiding that he hadn't thought to search. He would take the hunter the next day, and they would ensure they covered every inch of this island. There was a whole compound in this corner of the island that appeared to be nothing but overgrown garden.

He had found similarly abandoned spaces, but he had returned to look over this one. It was as though he couldn't quite focus on it even though it was there, and he wondered if the magics had something to do with that.

As he watched over it now in the dark, it seemed almost as though it absorbed any light, and he could see nothing but black from his vantage point on the wall. He had thought he had seen a small light at one point, but when he blinked it was gone. Was his mind playing tricks on him?

He couldn't find the magics, and there was no sign or hint of their magic from here. They were either well-hidden or had not returned to the Palace Isle as he had thought. But what were they planning? If they were as determined to destroy Lis as they had said, he was sure they would return soon.

Would the world be so very different when he was Emperor and she his empress? Would she have the say she wanted? Would she be the advisor his mother was to his father? She certainly had a better understanding of some of the world than he did. But beneath it all, Lis was magic. And yet he might be as well.

He shook the idea away and made his way along the wall, looking out at the ocean on one side and the city on the other. When he reached the watch house at the corner of the wall, he found he longed for the darkness again. Without a word to the watchmen in the tower, he nodded once and headed down the steps towards the base of the wall.

When he emerged in the narrow alleyway, he realised that on the other side of the strong, high wall before him was the compound he had seen. He sniffed at the air, but there was nothing. The wall was certainly higher than he'd imagined, and he knew there was no way over it. It couldn't have only been a garden. Surely at some point, a compound so large would have contained buildings and people. He didn't know his Empire as well as he'd thought.

Too much had changed in the world in too little time, and then it had changed again. Traditions had been lost to new ones, despite the importance his mother placed on them. They were the traditions of today, but they might not last. Remi knew Lis would be the last hidden princess. And whether she survived this or not, the next empress would be chosen very differently. He only wondered if he would survive to be a part of that process; and if he didn't, who might be Emperor?

The crown had been passed down through the family for so many generations, the idea of anyone taking it or usurping the throne was unheard of. Perhaps it would mean the end of the Empire if they didn't find a way to stop these magics.

Remi headed back towards his little palace and lamented the loss of the residence. Now would be the time to stand on his balcony and look over the world. But his father hadn't even considered rebuilding—not yet. If his brother had survived, he would have looked into the possibility and whether it was the right time. Remi was still too much of a hunter at heart. He wasn't the right man for the tasks expected of him.

A single candle burned in the middle of the table when he entered the palace. Mu-Phi was curled asleep on the small cot in the corner. The coals burned low, but there was some heat in the water as he poured it into a cup before climbing into bed. Unaware of just how late it was, he slipped easily into sleep.

Remi stood in the middle of a courtyard. The sun was hot on his skin, and small veiled girls ran around him. Hidden princesses. He looked up at the great wall of the Palace Isle to find no one there. They all ran around and squealed and then, when a woman in white appeared at a black gate, they lined up quietly in single file. As the woman nodded, they started to move through the gate, but they murmured amongst themselves and she shushed them.

Another girl stood off to the side; she hadn't joined the line. The other children turned back and looked at her as they moved through. The woman in white motioned towards her, but she turned away. Remi thought she was crying. He stepped forward, and she sank down to the ground.

'You must follow your sisters,' the woman said, her voice kind but firm.

She shook her head. 'I'm not worthy of this.'

'You were selected for a reason,' the woman said, looking around. Then she dropped down by the child, her voice soft. 'There is something very special about you. You are much stronger than you realise. You must find the strength or no matter your power, you will be lost.'

'Sister,' a firmer voice snapped from behind Remi, and he turned to see an older woman dressed just as the first.

'She needs some encouragement,' the first woman said to the older one.

'It is not our place to encourage; it is to teach. If she is worthy of the prince, she will endure all the tests.'

The younger woman nodded and hurried off.

The older one stepped forward, and Remi had to move to avoid her walking into him. Either he was hidden himself or he was dreaming. But given that no one had lived here for so long, he was sure it was a dream. Although it felt very real.

'You are special,' the older woman said. 'All of you are special in some way. It is why you were chosen. But you must harness your gifts, find your confidence, or another will triumph.'

The little girl nodded. Remi wondered just how old these children were and what kind of pressure they were placed under to meet the expectations of the crown prince and the Empire.

'I have dreamt of another prince,' the little girl said, wiping at her eyes. 'What if I am not meant for this one?'

The woman studied the child, and Remi wondered what she could mean.

'How do you know it was another prince?' she asked.

'I just knew,' the child answered. Despite the uncertainty in her voice, she looked the woman square in the eye. 'He had something very special.'

'Did he?' the woman asked, taking another step forward.

She nodded.

'Did he know he was special?'

The little girl shook her head. 'I had to show him, but he did not thank me for it.'

'Not everyone is willing to embrace their destiny.'

'I am,' the girl whispered. 'I know it is not here.'

The woman softened. 'There may be a future for you that we cannot control.'

'I understand,' she said, and she turned toward the gate, the woman guiding her without touching her. As they reached the black gate, the child looked back as though right at him, and then she was gone.

Remi woke in a sweat and sat up pulling at his clothes. The candle had been extinguished, so he sat in the dark. He wasn't sure where Mu-Phi was, and he longed for the morning light.

He knew it had only been a dream, possibly brought on by his long hours staring into that empty compound. Although the black gate was strange, for all the gates within the Palace Isle were red. In fact, he struggled to remember anything within the island that would have resembled it. There might have been a symbol on it, but he wasn't sure. And he was almost certain that despite it being a dream, the child had known he was there.

He pulled his shoes on in the dark, then raced back out of his little palace and along the narrow streets. There was no one around. Although he heard the occasional voice carried on the wind, he knew it was a soldier or the like. He wound his way along different paths until he was certain he was lost. He looked up and along the wall, trying to work his way to the far corner of the island. He wasn't far from it, but he couldn't find a way in.

Then he turned a corner to find himself surrounded by high walls. He moved along the wall, regretting that he had not brought a lantern, when the world lit up softly around him. He stopped and stared at the flames dancing across his hand. He swallowed down the sick feeling building in his stomach.

Lis had been right—he was something different.

A gate stood before him, grand but old. No markings were etched on it or hung above it, and Remi wondered if he had found the compound he'd been searching for. He tried the gate, but it wouldn't open. Shaking his head with frustration, he followed the wall and tried to ignore the light in his hand. Another gate appeared before him, slightly ajar.

When he pushed his way in, he realised he stood in the courtyard he had dreamed of. It was bigger than he'd expected. He marched across to the place he had seen the child. There was no sense of anyone here, nor any magic. Where she had squatted against the wall, a small flower pushed between the stones. What had the child thought was her future? Or what had she thought she couldn't offer the prince she'd been hidden away for?

The gate squeaked at the far end of the courtyard, and he was on his feet moving quickly towards it. Despite his uncertainties, he held his hand up to it. It was clearly black, although faded. There was no mark or symbol on it, and he wondered if it had been removed or covered over. He held his hand up to the wood, willing to see what had been there, when a pattern started to form. Silver symbols pushed their way to the surface. He stepped back as the world went dark around him.

He shook his hand, trying to get the flame back, when he noticed a light behind him. Someone was in this part of the compound. Despite the darkness, he moved forward quickly. Large buildings loomed over him like shadows as the ground crunched beneath his feet. He stopped. There was someone sitting against a building, and he moved quickly toward it.

Something caught in his throat, as though this was the child from his dream. There was something similar in the way she sat against the wall, something sad. As he grew closer, he realised it was a woman rather than a child, and with another step he recognised Lis. He stopped, watching her for a moment as she wiped her hand across her cheek. She held a candle in her hand. How had she found this place?

He stepped into the light of the candle, and she immediately blew it out.

'Please don't hide,' he said softly, wondering if she would be able to tell him what he was.

The candle flickered to life again, and she was on her feet. 'Why are you here?' she asked, wiping again at her face. He stepped forward.

Why was she crying? 'Why are you?' he retorted, his voice harsher than he intended.

'I dreamt of a black gate,' she murmured, 'and hidden princesses. What is this place?'

He shrugged. 'What happened in the dream?'

'It doesn't matter,' she said, making to walk past him. 'We should go.'

'What did you find?'

'I don't know.'

'You need to talk to me at some point.'

'I don't understand what I found,' she said, standing beside him and facing the opposite direction. He felt her sadness and confusion wash over him.

'Why can I sense you?' he asked suddenly, and she looked up at him. 'Why are you sad?'

She took his hand, surprising him, and led him back to the building she had been sitting against. She indicated a door with a tip of her head. He entered, then stopped as the candlelight made the faces shift before him.

'What is this?'

'I don't know.'

'Who are they?'

'I think they were hidden princesses.'

He held his hand up to the nearest face and peered at it closely, then at the next before he realised he had made fire dance across his skin again. He glanced towards Lis, but she just stared at the faces. His eye caught a mark on one of the plaques. 'Do you know what his means?'

He looked when she didn't answer, and she shook her head.

'There is something else,' she said.

He followed her out of the room and into the neighbouring one. It was a simple room with a cot, a desk, and when he turned, he caught the image of a woman on the wall. Holding up his hand, he recognised her for Lis.

'How?'

She shook her head and sniffed. 'I'm scared,' she murmured.

'Tell me of the dream.'

'Why?'

Remi took a deep breath and held out his hand, palm up. The fire moved around to sit in his palm and flicker like the candle flame. 'Because I have had a similar dream, of a veiled girl who dreamt of a prince.'

Lis studied him closely. 'Did you see the black gate?'

He nodded and then stepped forward. 'Bring the candle,' he said, racing ahead of her back towards the gate.

16

The high priestess opened her eyes and looked over the others bent in meditation before her. She breathed out slowly. The vision she had experienced was unsettling. It contained information she hadn't been aware of, and she wasn't clear if it was something that had happened or was to come. She filled her lungs with the calming air that surrounded her, taking in the vibes produced by the other priestesses in meditation and the magic that hummed through the walls of the temple.

She needed to be sure, and the only way for her to be sure was to visit with the hidden princess. There was no way, given the current circumstances, that the princess would come to her. She was likely keen to get out of her little palace, but her wariness and the recent attacks would not help.

The high priestess would have to go to her, and she would need to go today. The empress had not summoned her of late either, and it was time she put herself forward in her new position.

She had visited and assisted with the hidden princess before; she would be able to do that again. She had heard that the healer never left her side, which could be a problem, for she may not be willing to talk in front of him.

But she would have to try. She could build on the relationship that had formed before. Although she was a very different person now. The high priestess rose from her kneeling position and walked into the main part of the temple. She bowed her head to a few of the worshipers, and without a thought she was in the street. She could possibly work out where the hidden princess was hidden, but it would be better to get permission.

She needed to talk with the empress, who was the key to the hidden princess even if it was the crown prince who had taken control of who could visit. It should be as it had always been.

The empress looked up at her with surprise when she entered the room. Likely in part because she had not been summoned.

'I wish to visit with the hidden princess,' she said, without invitation to speak.

'Do you?' the empress asked, slowly standing from her small throne. 'And why is that?'

'It is time,' she said. 'Her training has been halted. The following years will disappear, and I am sure you hope she can be all she can be.'

'I would think her spiritual training would continue, as mine did.' The empress stepped forward. 'Only your high priestess had her own agenda.'

'I am High Priestess now. And the world is different,' she said with the authority of her position clear in her voice.

The empress remained unmoving.

'I have visited with the hidden princess before and talked with her at length. It may be that she could use a friend,' she said kindly.

The empress sucked in a deep breath. And when she let it out, she nodded almost imperceivably. The priestess gave a shallow bow in thanks and left the room. She needed to see this girl far more than she needed to appease the empress.

If there were any fears of the priestesses, the soldiers and the hunters would have turned over the temples. But they respected the gods too much for such a venture, so the priestesses were safe.

She walked quickly and then slowed her pace. She had not been told where the princess was, so she was unsure what they would think of her if she were to appear in her rooms. Then, as though the gods had placed him before her, the crown prince walked towards her. His mind was clearly somewhere else, for he didn't appear to see anyone around him.

She stepped forward quickly, blocking his path. He stopped, looked her over and stepped back.

'Your mother has granted me permission to visit with the hidden princess. But I'm afraid that I don't know where she stays,' she said, without introduction or addressing him as she should.

He chewed his lip as he considered her.

'I am not what the other was,' she said softly. She looked down in what she hoped was a disappointed manner, but she was sure she was stronger already than the high priestess who had gone before her.

He sighed and turned. 'I shall escort you,' he said, but there was a hesitancy in his voice, an uncertainty as to who she really was. They walked in silence, but there were times when she looked over and found him watching her as they walked. He shook his head as they continued.

She was surprised by the distance from the centre of the island and how close she was to the history of the hidden princesses. The gate was just the same as any other when they pushed through it. Although the number of soldiers filling the garden was not. *Does he not trust her?* she wondered.

The girl herself looked at her with anger when she made it into the small palace. And then her look softened as she recognised the priestess for the woman she had been before.

Healer Yang sat close while the little princess hovered in the background. The other maid had been removed, it appeared. It may have been that she was elsewhere, but the priestess had felt hatred in the girl once she'd found out what the hidden princess was. Although there had also been something else she couldn't quite put her finger on.

'Your maid has healed after the attack so long ago?'

The princess nodded once and gracefully folded the artwork she was working on, calling the other princess forward as though she were the maid. She cleared the table quickly.

The priestess wondered for a moment what the princess might be doing that she didn't want her to see. But then it could simply be that she wanted to be a good host.

'You have little room here,' she said, looking about and taking in the small space.

'I don't need much.'

'Your maid remains with you.'

Lis nodded once.

The healer looked her over and then nodded. 'I need to visit with the healers,' he said, and after bowing again he left the room. The prince remained by the door, but the princess didn't even look his way. *What do they have?* the priestess wondered.

'Your prince has forgiven you,' she murmured, leaning in closer.

'For what?' Lis asked, and the man stepped into the room.

'I heard of difficulties,' the priestess whispered.

They then looked at each other.

'I may have been misinformed,' she said.

'So it seems,' the prince said, coming in and sitting beside his princess at the table.

'I had heard that you had re-entered the hidden palace,' the high priestess said.

'I have, in a way.'

'The magics are still out there,' the prince continued for her. 'We need to keep her hidden. The public think her back in the palace.'

'Will no one see you here?'

'I don't go out,' the princess said.

She was stronger than the priestess expected. More confident in herself. She may not get what she wanted from the girl. 'Are you having any trouble since the attack?'

The girl shook her head.

'No strange dreams or sleepless nights?'

The princess shook her head again and looked to the prince. 'What are you searching for?' she asked when she turned back.

'I have had a strange dream of you as a child.' The priestess risked part of the truth to try and draw her out.

The woman opposite her leaned forward and drew a deep breath.

'It was somewhere unknown to me. With a black gate.'

'Do you have visions?' the prince asked.

'Why do you ask? Have you had a vision?'

The prince scowled at her, and she wondered just what they may have experienced that she wasn't aware of.

The princess put a hand on his arm. He jumped at the touch, and she withdrew her hand again quickly. 'I have had a similar dream,' she admitted.

'Of a black gate?'

Lis shook her head then. 'There are no black gates.'

'Perhaps the dream meant something else,' the priestess said. 'I am glad you are safe and well. Could I call again?'

The princess looked to her prince.

'She has much to do,' he said.

'I would like to try to replace the old priestess, to teach you what I can of the gods.'

Lis nodded once, and the priestess pushed up from the table and left them. She may have had the same dream, she thought, heading back to the temple. And with some more time, she may tell her just what that was.

17

Lis looked at the prince as the priestess left the little palace. 'What do you think she wants?'

'I don't know, but I don't think it is as simple as she says.'

'She wanted to know if we dreamt of the black gate,' she said.

'What do you think it means that she has had the same dream?'

'I don't think it was the same—not exactly the same. We have dreamt different things from that same place.'

'What do you think the message on the gate meant?'

'Only the chosen may enter,' Lis said, remembering the faded symbols on the black paint. 'I would think it had something to do with the Choosing and the princesses in training.'

'Although,' he added, 'they weren't really chosen, were they? They were training to be chosen.'

'Did they have to have some skill to enter the yard?'

'What did you see in your dream that you haven't told me?' he asked.

She wanted to trust him. And after the night they'd had and the magic he had used, she had promised to help him. 'They had magic.'

'Who did?'

'The hidden princesses.'

'But there was no magic in the royal line. Why would they

allow some with magic to enter as hidden princesses?'

Lis shook her head. 'Not some of them—all of them.'

The prince fixed her with a hard stare. 'I didn't see a single child with magic,' he murmured.

'You did; you just didn't see them use it. What did you see?'

He shook his head. 'Do you think the women in white were priestesses?'

'Or teachers. I don't know who can do what anymore,' Lis said softly.

'Teaching them magic?'

'Perhaps. You still haven't told me what the children were doing.'

'There was one girl—she didn't want to go through the gates with the others. I think they had teased her. The woman, whoever she might have been, told her she was strong. And it was as though she knew her future, and it didn't connect with the time they were in.'

'What do you mean?' Lis prompted.

'She said she was meant to help another prince.'

Lis smiled at the idea. 'Like this hidden princess is helping you?'

He shrugged then. She felt the new connection that had been forming between them falter. She wasn't sure what it was that they had, other than a dream that had led them to the same place, a hidden world they hadn't known existed.

'You think you are that hidden princess,' he said.

'She looked familiar, but it was the painting on the wall that unnerved me the most.'

'She did look like you,' he said quietly. 'I don't know what any of this means. Who would have the history to tell us exactly what went on, and how do we ask?'

Lis shook her head. 'Tutor Nizen talked to me of the histories of the hidden princesses, although nothing about the compound or palace or whatever the place is, nor the fact that they had magic.

What if no one knew what they could do?'

'But they were chosen from the Empire.'

'What if...' She trailed off, unsure how to tell him what she thought.

'What do you think?' he asked gently. She looked up into his earnest face.

'What if everyone had magic—they just had to be taught to use it?'

'But we can sense them,' he stammered.

'Not all of them. And why is that? Why can I detect some that you cannot? Why could I feel magic in that place, but not sense it?'

The prince studied his own hands for a moment. 'How could you sense it if there was nothing there?'

'I knew there was magic there. I knew magic hummed in the walls, I just couldn't feel it humming.'

'I had no such sense. Perhaps you look for it everywhere.'

She tried not to sigh.

'This is because you know it is everywhere,' he added, his eyes falling back to his own hands. 'What do I do with this?'

'You haven't told Mu-Phi?'

He shook his head without looking up.

She chewed her lip. This had impacted them both. They had dreamed of the same place; they were both in the same danger. 'The magics are coming.'

He nodded then and rose slowly to his feet. Lis looked around the empty room wondering why Wei-Song would have allowed them to be alone together for so long. But then perhaps she hadn't gone too far.

'I would like a better look at this, in the daytime,' the prince said.

'Should you take someone with you?'

'You don't think I will be safe?'

'You don't know who might follow.'

'I don't want anyone else knowing what we have found. If the priestess has dreamed of the black gate, maybe she is searching for it also.'

'She may be able to understand more of it than we could,' Lis suggested.

'She may not share that knowledge.'

'Do you think they are all like the former high priestess and could do what they did to your mother?'

'And to you,' he said softly.

She looked up at him, wondering what he had seen.

He shook his head.

'Tell me,' she said.

'When you were first found and we had you secured in the prison, I had gone to my father. When I returned, the priestess was with you, and it appeared as though she used magic on you.'

Lis's hand went to her throat. She only realised she had made the movement when his eyes settled on it, and he raised his eyebrows.

'You knew what she was,' he said.

'Not exactly, but I knew she had some magic. She also thought I did, although she couldn't sense it, and it appeared to confuse her somewhat. As though she knew it to be true but couldn't see it for herself.'

'Perhaps because you are a Hidden.'

'I don't know any more. I wish I could see the palace in the daytime.'

'You could come with me.'

She laughed before she thought about it. 'You would let me out? What if I ran away?'

'What if you were able to hide us both?'

She stood quickly. Yang had managed to hide her when the prince had burnt her, to get some distance between them. Yet it was not something she had tried herself, other than with the kettle. It might be something she could do, but she wished she had more opportunity to train with Wei-Song. Despite the truce that had developed between them since he had discovered her in the night, she still wasn't sure how long it might last or what might scare him enough to change his mind and run her through.

'Lis?' he asked, standing beside her. 'Could you?'

'I don't know,' she murmured. *Am I strong enough?*

He waited while she looked at him.

'I would have to hold...' She drifted off as the uncertainty of what they were washed over her again.

He held out his hand without hesitation, and she sucked in a deep breath as she took it. She hadn't practiced hiding without the physical gesture, and she wasn't sure if she could do it. She closed her eyes and blew out her breath slowly, calming her heart rate and thinking as she did when she hid.

'Oh,' the prince murmured.

She opened her eyes to find the two of them a shade of what they had been. She clutched his hand tighter. 'I don't know how long it will last,' she murmured.

'You can see me?' he asked, waving a hand in front of her face. She laughed.

'I can. I just hope no one else can.'

They made their way out slowly and quietly into the garden. The small stool was still against the fence and Lis pointed it out, but as they were required to hold on to each other, she wasn't sure how she would manage to get over it.

The prince stepped up and then pulled her up to stand beside him. As they pressed together on the narrow stool, she sensed his excitement, yet all she felt was worry. Being taller than her, he managed to climb using one arm and unseen footholds in the wall. Once he was lying on top of the wall, he pulled Lis towards him.

As they moved around each other, Lis was sure her skirt caught on the rough stone. She should have thought this through a little more; she should have changed. Only it was too late now, and she would need to let go of the prince to do anything about it. They were perched at the top of the wall, so chances were if they appeared suddenly, they would both die before the soldiers realised who they were killing.

Then they were jumping down, and she heard the rip of material.

She pulled him against the wall, pressing her back to it. She looked up, hoping the material wasn't fluttering in the stonework. But it appeared to have only torn. It had seemed so loud to her. She could only hope the guards hadn't heard it.

He opened his mouth, and she pressed a finger against his lips. He scowled for a moment before nodding, and she pulled her finger back. They headed quickly towards the other compound. Lis only hoped that when they reached it, they would discover that no one else had found it and she could do something with the material that was dragging along the road behind her.

18

Lis pushed the gate closed and was surprised by the squeal of the hinges and the echo of the latch throughout the courtyard. The prince still held her hand tight, pulling her towards the black gate as she tried to take in the space around her. So much had happened here, and she was desperate to see if she too could make magic happen.

She pulled him to a stop and held her hand over the weeds growing through the pavers. They thickened until a lone narrow blade worked its way towards her hand. Just before it reached her, it bloomed into a bright yellow flower. The prince dropped her hand and reached for it. As he did, he must have realised his mistake, for he stopped and looked at his hand. Then he turned.

'I haven't moved,' she whispered. Then she wished herself visible again.

'What have you done?' he said, his voice heavy.

She shook her head and let her hand drop. The disappointment washed over her. She hadn't created the flower for herself, but still.

'Your skirt,' he said, stepping forward.

'I caught it on the wall,' she murmured, looking down at the tattered mess. It was far worse than she realised. 'I can change,' she added. Lis closed her eyes and turned on the spot. When she opened her eyes, he was grinning at her.

'Aren't you supposed to be concerned by what I can do?'

'Despite my earlier fears, you can make the flowers grow and change your dress.'

She looked down over herself and smoothed out the simple material. Again, she had dressed similarly to the maids. There was less material to catch on the world around her.

'I thought you worried about what I can do.'

'I would have thought you were more worried about what *I* can do,' he murmured.

Lis ran her hand over her wrist, and he watched the movement. She knew the discovery of his power had hurt him as much as it had hurt her. She turned towards the black gate, which Lis thought was brighter than it had been before. The silver-painted symbols sparkled in the sunlight. But when they reached the door, the symbols were gone.

She ran her hand over the rough wood. Then she looked at the prince. 'How could they disappear?'

'They were gone when I was here before. Somehow, they came to the surface as I looked for them in the light,' he said, indicating the back of his hand.

'Can you do it again?'

He shook his head. 'I was just trying to see. I can see the gate now, and there is nothing there.'

Lis thought he was wrong. She placed her hand over where she thought the symbols had been, longing to see them. She felt the wood move beneath her fingers. A strange sensation, as though something moved through the wood just for her.

When she lifted her hand away, she took a step back.

'That is not what it said before,' he breathed.

She shook her head. 'Could it give different messages depending on the person passing through the gate?'

'If you think you are the little girl, maybe it is for you. Maybe your prince needs your help.'

Lis sighed, looking over the characters again. 'Help him to

learn.'

'Perhaps it is an old message, for those who were here before.'

'And who were they?' he asked.

'The hidden princesses,' she said, turning a frustrated look on him.

'Who train their whole lives to serve the crown prince.'

'You think this is intended for one of them to help the prince learn? What does he need help with?'

'I'm sure I know more than you,' he said with a laugh.

'Not about magic,' she added.

'But not much more. You might have it, but we don't know what others have, nor what I can do with mine.'

'Perhaps this is the place to learn,' she offered.

He looked up at the expanse of the wall looming over them that surrounded the island.

'Can they see us?' Lis asked.

He stepped back into the open courtyard and looked up at the tower, then waved his arms above his head. There was no movement on the wall. He drew his sword, and a cold sick feeling washed over Lis as he held it out, the bright blade catching the sun. Despite the feeling it provoked in her, it didn't appear to draw any attention on the wall. Either there was no one to watch over the city here, or they couldn't see him. He slipped the sword back into the sheath and held up his hands again.

Lis followed his gaze up to the wall. Nothing.

'It must be protected in some way,' she suggested.

'I saw only overgrown garden when I was on the wall. How could it appear that way? I couldn't even see the buildings and the pond.'

'I don't know,' she said. 'I thought we were here to look around.' She strode off ahead of him towards the run-down, faded buildings. She shook her head and focused on the weeds sparsely growing through the gravel. The sight of his sword still made her shiver.

Despite the daylight, the room of the large building was almost as dark as it had been by candlelight, and the beds appeared to be smaller. There were no belongings, nothing to indicate children had lived here at all, let alone children of privilege.

Lis headed back out into the garden and onto the small gazebo that overlooked the pond. The water was dark and oily, as though it had stood still for too long. She wondered how they would have had it flowing when the girls had lived here and whether it had been cut off or blocked when they no longer needed to use the palace.

She looked across at the smaller building with the doors all lined up. Had they had teachers who had stayed here, or were they the women in white? Were they to assist or just ensure the children were safe? Who was the little princess they had been so drawn to?

She moved to the first door, the one she had entered before, and it looked just as it had. She leafed through some papers on the desk, but they were blank, perhaps faded by age. Although she wondered at their age, whether they would have used wooden slips. Maybe someone had used this place not so long ago. But the bed was still covered in dust, and she doubted anyone had entered other than herself in a very long time.

The next room was similar. Just as covered in dust, and the small desk was covered in so many papers and scrolls that it was hard to know where to start. But there was something that caught her eye as she pushed the documents around the desk, something with a royal seal on it.

It appeared somewhat brighter than the papers around it, as though it had been hidden here long after the papers had been left. She held it in her hand, almost too scared to have it. Then she headed back out into the sunshine to find the prince.

'Your Highness,' she called softly, too afraid to alert others to their presence. Where would he go? Or had he hidden?

She startled when he called back.

She found him in the room with the ink painting on the wall. He looked over it with his nose only inches from the wall, then turned to look at her and back, as though comparing them.

'What is that?' he asked.

She shook her head and held it out.

'A royal seal,' he murmured. 'What does it say?'

'I haven't opened it.'

He let his hand drop and looked at her seriously.

'I can't,' she whispered.

He pulled open the seal, opening the paper carefully, and Lis could see it was older than she had thought. He stared at it for too long before he looked back to her.

'What does it say?'

'Nothing.'

She stepped forward and took it from him. 'Why would it say nothing?'

But as she opened it, she realised it had no characters painted on the inside at all. She held it up to the sun and gasped. 'Look,' she said, pointing to a faint watermark in the paper.

'What is that?'

'It is like the symbols on the faces,' she said, moving into the room on the end and then stopping. The night before, it had been filled with stone faces—now it contained blank white walls. 'How is that possible?' she stammered. She ran her hand over a wall. It was as smooth as the temple walls, and she wondered again if the priestesses were involved in this in some way. The square blocks seemed to close in on her, in the same way the faces had the previous evening. There were no marks, nothing.

'Maybe this is a message to leave,' the prince offered, following her into the room.

'The faces disappearing?'

'No, the sealed letter. Although I don't understand where they might have gone. Unless they were not here in the first place.' Lis turned to him angrily and he held up his hands. 'What if they weren't really here? What if they were magicked here?'

'Just for me, and now they are gone? You are suggesting someone knows we are here,' she said.

'Or they know we have been. I saw a light last night; that is why I came to you.'

'You saw my candle. Do you think someone else might have seen it?'

He nodded. 'Although that would mean they too were up high.'

'You just thought we were safe from view.'

'I'm not sure of anything. I need to get up there.'

Lis nodded once and looked around the room one last time. She came out to where the prince had been standing, to look at herself painted on the wall.

'I need your help to get out unseen,' he said.

She nodded, and they walked back to the gate. As they walked, she thought about the other gate, how it was locked and she hadn't yet seen the other side of it.

'I want you to stay here,' he said.

'Then how can I help you?'

'You could look out to ensure no one is coming.'

Lis nodded once and hid immediately. She watched the uncertainty cross his face before she stepped out of the gate and into the street beyond. There was no one, and no sound of anyone coming. 'Wait a moment,' she said before heading down the street a little further. By the time she reached the other gate to the hidden princess compound, there was still no sign of anyone.

She rushed back to find the prince watching the gate intently. Was he worried she would run away again? He took a step forward, and she unhid. He took a step back again.

'It is safe,' she said. 'There is no one around.'

He nodded and headed towards the gate.

'Do you want me to wait outside the gate for you?'

'No, I'll be as quick as I can. I have been harassing those on the wall enough that they would let me do what I like as long as it leaves them alone. I need you to be visible here. So I can be sure to see you.'

Lis nodded once and turned on the spot, making her dress bright yellow. 'Will this help?'

He smiled, and she smiled with him. 'We need to be sure,' he said.

He disappeared through the gate, and then she wandered to the middle of the space. Holding her hand out, she drew the grasses forward, taller and taller. They blew gently in the wind. Marking out the square stones they grew between, she drew them up to waist height. Then she walked through them, running her hands over the soft tips. It felt like forever since she had been outside in the air, with the world growing around her. The air smelt different when the grasses grew, as though they brought the sweetness with them.

She suddenly wanted to fill the world with green, and she pulled on everything she had. The stones cracked, and the grass pushed them out of the way rather than just through the gaps between them. She stretched out her hands, and the world started to shake. She dropped her hands, letting the pull of the new growth stop, and stared at the sudden change around her. She had stopped before too much had grown, but the stones had been pushed not only out of the way but beneath the ground; short grass covered the entire space around her. She wondered if she could have transformed the entire courtyard.

She gulped down the strange feeling filling her chest. Just how much power did she have? And how useful would it be to turn the Palace Isle to countryside?

She looked up at the wall, wondering if the prince would be able to see the circle of green around her. There was no sign of him, and she didn't know how far he would have to travel to find a door into the wall and then make it to the part that overlooked them. She looked back over the shimmering grass. Could she turn it into something else?

She took a deep breath and held her hands over the longer

blades of grass beside her. She wanted flowers. As she wished them forward, the grass transformed into thicker stems before thick leaves pushed outwards and bright flowers bloomed at the tips of each stem. Lis chewed her lip to prevent the smile. She wasn't sure if she should be as pleased with herself as she was. She remembered the thick vines the child in her dream had created, and the branches around her transformed again, twisting together to create a mass of knots around her. As she turned, large sharp thorns poked from the vines, creating a fence between her and the rest of the world. Perhaps she could have done this before. She wasn't sure if it was simply that she had never tried or if it was this place. Yet she looked up to the wall again, wondering if a soldier might see what she had done and fire an arrow through her heart.

Movement caught her eye then, and she saw the prince on the wall. She waved her hands, but he didn't appear to see her. He looked over the area near her and then along further. If only she had something bright, other than the dress, to get his attention. She closed her eyes and thought of bright yellow flowers. And when she opened her eyes, they grew large and bright around her.

The prince walked further along the wall as though he searched for something, but there was no indication that he had seen her. Yet he might not want to give that away to anyone who may be there with him. And then there was another man walking towards him. Lis wasn't sure who he was from this distance, but he was clearly a soldier.

They talked for some time, and Lis wondered if she should try to work out how to remove herself from the cage she had built, or whether she should wait for him in case he hadn't seen it. But then she wasn't sure of his reaction either. Despite their recent understanding, she still didn't know what he might do.

She sighed and sat on the ground where she was, hidden amongst the thorns and vines. The ground was quite soft and comfortable, and she ran her hand over the soft grass on which she sat.

She lay back and looked up at the sky above her. Other than the greenery surrounding her, she could see nothing else but sky. She could pretend she wasn't trapped on the Palace Isle. But then, in a way, she had chosen to stay. She could have run away again, despite her promises to the prince. And although she had no connection left with her family, she couldn't bring such dishonour to her father.

She also could have let herself die. She seemed to have the strength within her to prevent Yang's healing magic. But now that the prince had discovered something of his own, there was something else between them.

The gate squealed just enough for her to know someone was coming in. She waited just a moment longer before climbing to her feet, in case, by chance, someone else had discovered them. The prince stood open mouthed, pushing the gate closed behind him and leaning against it.

'I wanted to be sure you could see me,' she whispered, taking in the shock on his face.

'I couldn't.'

'What?' she asked, pushing her hands apart as though walking through a curtain. The plants coiled back away from her to allow her out of her little cage. It was only as she reached the prince, still looking worried, that she knew what she had done. She looked down at her hands, then back at him. 'You couldn't see me at all?'

He shook his head. 'What have you done?'

'I was trying to make the grass grow through the stones, like I saw the girl do in my dream. And then I wanted flowers. And when I thought of what she did, they turned into the vines, and I wanted to be sure you saw me.'

He stepped past her to look over the plants. He walked in a circle around what she had created and then back to her. 'Did this just happen around you?'

She nodded and opened her mouth to tell him more, then stopped.

He was watching her too closely. She sighed.

'I think I could have made the whole courtyard change, but it was…'

He cocked his head.

'Violent. Noisy.' She struggled to find the right word. 'It worried me that it might get away from me, or that others might hear.'

He looked back over the plants. 'You can't control it?'

'I think I can,' she said softly, 'only I'm not sure how.'

'Can you put it back?'

Lis put out her hands, and the flowers closed and disappeared. The vines withered, and the grass disappeared. It felt sad, like she had lost something, and she clutched her hands before her as she looked to the prince.

'Where are the stones?'

She pointed towards where the grass had been and felt the ground move. As she sucked in a breath, the stones popped back out of the earth. She covered her mouth with her hands. She had no idea how she had done that.

'Do you influence plants or the ground?'

'I don't know,' she whispered.

'Try moving the stones,' he directed.

She put her hand out, and a wave travelled along the courtyard, the stones moving up and down as it went.

'I have never heard of such a thing,' he murmured.

'Do you want to try?'

He looked at her as though she had slapped him.

'We can't be seen, can we?'

'It looked dark, misty, as though it wasn't really here. I couldn't see you or your circle of green and yellow.'

'Then why don't you try? I know how you feel about magic, yet you have me working at it, exposing myself in a way. We could learn this together.'

'What if I use it by mistake?'

'Maybe if you know what you can do, you will make sure that you don't.'

He pushed his hand forward, but the ground didn't move.

'Maybe you can only use fire.'

'If only I could make it rain,' he said, holding out his hand. 'Then if I set something alight by accident, I could put it out.' A small cloud formed beside him, and large drops of water intermittently dripped onto the newly emerged pavers at his feet. Lis raised her eyebrows, and he looked from her to his hand. 'I didn't try,' he stammered. 'How is it that this hasn't happened before?'

Lis shook her head. She had no idea of any of this. 'Is it this place?'

'The fire burned in my palace.'

'I don't know,' she said.

'Could it be because of you?' he asked, staring at her too intently.

'That I gave you magic? Do you think you can catch it? Is that why they all had to die?' She hadn't meant to snap, but her voice echoed painfully around the yard.

'I did have your blood on my hands.'

'I'm sure you have had lots of blood on your hands.' She stepped around him, headed for the gate. 'We have only found more questions here.'

'Wait,' he said, reaching out for her. She flinched as his hand closed around her arm, and he released her immediately. 'I'm sorry,' he whispered. 'I would never hurt you. I think we should hide on the way back.'

She nodded, but a fear lingered that he just might hurt her without meaning to, as he had when he had burnt her.

'I know someone who may be able to help us.'

He looked concerned again.

'I need you to give me the opportunity to ask without you. I can't risk them.'

His face hardened. 'Who is he?' he asked.

She sighed before she could stop it. 'Really, you are jealous. That is not the reason I haven't told you of this person, and there may be other people who are impacted by your knowing.'

'Either way,' he started gruffly, 'we must hide to return to your palace, or the soldiers will be wondering what has happened to us both.'

She nodded and held out her hand to him, trying to keep it steady as he reached for her. His hand didn't feel any warmer than it had, or wet for that matter, and she hid them both.

19

Almost as soon as they reappeared in the palace, the prince stepped back, bowed to Lis—which threw her completely—and then left. There was murmuring from the garden as the guards talked with him. Lis sat heavily at the table, pouring water into a cup.

The room was quiet, and she looked around waiting for someone to step forward. When no one did, she stood and looked into the dark spaces of the room. Not that it was very big. But the three of them had been living in the same room for some time.

She pulled a curtain back to reveal a small alcove with a bed and low table. A memorial sat on the table along with a small figure surrounded by incense sticks. 'Wei-Song?' Lis asked the shadows. 'Hello?' she called out, uncertain at being left alone.

One of her guards appeared in the doorway. 'Your Highness,' he said, looking around the quiet palace.

She nodded and tried to smile for the man. 'Where is Wei-Song?'

The man looked her over carefully. 'You sent her out some time ago to get something for you.'

'It has been too long. She should be back,' Lis said. 'I'm worried—can you send someone?'

He bowed and left her.

Why would Wei-Song have left the palace empty? Had she

followed them to see what they were doing? Did she not trust them? Lis wondered if she should trust Wei-Song, but she had helped her so many times. And she was determined to stay; she could be with her mother or back with her school. Lis had hoped that Wei-Song would help her and the prince, but if she was here for her own reasons then she might not.

She was still standing in the same position when Yang appeared beside her. 'What has happened?' he asked. 'Did the prince do something?'

'No,' Lis said quietly, thinking of the flames across his skin and the small cloud that had formed so easily beside him. 'Yes,' she added.

'Has he hurt you?' Yang asked, suddenly taking her shoulders and turning her towards him. The concern made him appear weary, and Lis felt an overwhelming guilt at what she had put her friend through.

'He has more magic than I imagined. But we need help.'

'Help to do what?' Wei-Song asked, appearing beside her and pulling the curtain back across her small space.

'I thought you were to wait for us,' Lis said. 'What if someone had come and found us missing?'

'There was something I needed to do.'

Lis waited, but Wei-Song said nothing further. Lis moved out to the table and poured herself water. She had hoped working with the prince would give her some more clarity, but it had only formed more questions and confirmed for her just how much help she needed—they needed.

Wei-Song sat opposite her at the table, where she poured water into a cup as Yang sat beside her. Lis looked over the two of them. It was hard for them here, and she hadn't made it easier. 'You don't have to remain here,' Lis said. 'You could return to your mother. Yang, you can do as the healers require.'

They both turned on her. Yang looked confused, Wei-Song

angry.

'Why would we leave you?' Wei-Song asked. 'It is my choice to stay. You need us to stay.'

Lis nodded. 'The crown prince and I have found something that relates to the old ways with the hidden princesses. I think they had magic.' They waited for her to continue. 'It is an area hidden from the rest of the island, and we have practiced a little magic there.'

Yang opened his mouth and then closed it.

'What could you do?' Wei-Song asked, an excitement behind her quiet words.

'I made the grass grow, but I could change the plants into anything I wished, and they moved at my command.' Wei-Song continued to stare at her intently. 'I made the ground move.'

'Move?' Yang asked.

'Like a wave on the ocean, only it was the ground that moved. It swallowed the stones and then I pulled them out.'

Yang's eyebrows rose.

'How far did you send the wave?'

'Far,' Lis murmured.

'Could you go further?' Wei-Song asked.

'Perhaps, only I wasn't sure how much of it I was controlling.'

'The prince didn't burn you again?' Yang asked.

She shook her head. 'He made it rain.'

'Rain?' Wei-Song said, standing from the table.

Lis looked up at her. 'I thought such a mix of skills would be unusual. He wished he could make it rain in case he set light to anything by accident, and as he said it, a little cloud formed and rain fell.'

'This changes things,' Wei-Song said, heading for the door.

'Wait,' Lis called after her. 'I need your help. We need your help.'

Lis saw the haze around Wei-Song as she hid, but she could too clearly see the worry on her face.

'I will be a few days,' she said. 'Yang, don't leave her side. And try to keep the prince away.'

'Away?' Lis said. 'Do you realise how long it has taken us to get to this point? We need help—we need training.'

'Stay away from him.' And she was gone.

'I like you in yellow,' Yang said absently, looking at the tabletop.

Lis thumped the table in frustration. 'What are we to do?'

'I could send for another maid. We will need to eat.'

Lis waved her hand over the table, and bowls of rice and meat and vegetables filled the space. The smell made Yang lean forward and salivate.

'I don't think you need any training,' he murmured, pulling a bowl towards himself. 'I wish you had discovered this one some time ago.'

Lis looked at what she had done and then back to her hand. 'I don't understand,' she said.

'You seem to have all sorts of powers. Are you sure you can't make fire?'

Lis looked over her hand and imagined the flames that had danced across the prince's knuckles. Nothing happened. 'Why does she want the prince to stay away?'

He shook his head, his mouth full. 'How can we make him stay away?' He put the chopsticks down and looked up at Lis with real concern. 'The crown prince does exactly what he wants, when he wants. I can't direct him anywhere but where he wants to go.'

Lis sighed, and Yang looked towards the doorway.

Wei-Song moved quickly towards the dock and hoped the man they used was still there. She slowed as she moved through the centre of the island, wondering at the number of people. Usually there were crowds to a degree, if only small ones. And yet, very few moved through the central square. Despite the efforts of the

Empire to assure people the world was safe, the idea of magic had everyone scared. The level of fear had only increased, and with that came more danger.

She rubbed at her eyes as she walked. The world seemed hazy around her, and she tried to contain the sigh in case anyone heard her. She knew Lis had power; it was what they had expected. Having heard what she could do, Wei-Song was even more certain Lis was the hidden princess of the prophecies.

But then Lis was so sure that all the hidden princesses had been magic at some point. That had been long before the war and the segregation of magics. As she considered it, she realised there had always been a segregation. Those with magic couldn't truly explore what power they had or what they could do with it.

An image of the crown prince flickered through her mind, but she pushed it away. She couldn't think about him now, couldn't grasp what he was or how he had managed to live as long as he had without their father wanting him dead. Or had he truly not known what he was?

Wei-Song found the boat, but not the boatman, and she stepped into the boat with a sigh. She wouldn't wait long before looking for an alternative. As she sat down, she saw him across the dock, talking with a small group. She climbed back out of the boat and walked towards him.

As she drew closer, she heard what was being whispered amongst the group, but it didn't make sense. 'Magic', 'war' and other similar words were being used. Had the knowledge of the magics seeped into the general public and worried them? Or had an announcement been made that she had missed?

She wanted to talk to her mother suddenly, desperate to know what she would think if she discovered her son's ability. But then she had to talk to the master first. She had to know if what she thought he might be was true, and what it would mean for them if it was.

She reached the man she had been looking for and carefully

tugged on his sleeve. He turned around and then back to the conversation when he saw no one there. She tugged again and wrapped a hand around his arm.

He nodded and headed towards the boat. She followed as closely as she could, and he stopped to talk with someone else. She stepped onto the boat, but she was only thinking of what she needed to be doing rather than what was going on when she heard the other man ask, 'Do you think it will come to war again?'

'Who can tell? If there was a problem with magics, wouldn't we have heard about it?'

The other man nodded and returned to his work. The boatman stepped into the boat, untethered the rope and pulled the sail tight. It took only moments before they were far from the dock.

'Where to, Your Highness?'

'The school,' she said, allowing herself to reappear before the man. 'What is going on?'

'There is talk of magics and trouble.'

'Do you think there will be fighting again?'

'It is hard to say. No one believes there are any magics left, and if there are only a few, surely the hunters can dispose of them before they become any real threat.'

Wei-Song raised her eyebrows.

'I am just repeating what people are saying.'

She nodded and looked out across the water. If what she feared of the prince was correct, it may be more likely than not. But then, Lis may have more influence than she thought. Wei-Song needed to know just what the hidden princess could do. Other than bringing flowers to bloom, Wei-Song had seen very little skill in Lis. She may not be the hidden princess of the stories after all. And if that was true, then the prince was not what she feared either.

'There have been more boats about in the water,' the man said, and she turned to him. 'Not sure if they are hunters, but they might be looking for anything unusual. I suggest you hide until we get there.'

Wei-Song nodded and hid. He looked through her out to the sea as the Palace Isle disappeared behind them.

The boat knocking against the old pier shook Wei-Song from her thoughts. It had seemed like an age to get from the Palace Isle to here. When she breathed in the scent of the island and the school, she knew she was home. They had remained unknown to the world as the war had raged around them. The people had been hidden. Wei-Song again wondered how her mother had managed to find someone to watch over her. And how her father had remained unknowing. But then, she knew the price she would pay if he discovered her. No matter their connection, no matter what he felt he when he laid eyes on her for the first time.

She did not feel the familial tie to him as she did her mother—nor, she didn't want to admit, to the prince. She could not call him brother, but there was something in him that she had wanted to like. Although that had been before Lis had told her of their work together and what he was capable of.

She looked up into the face of the man waiting for her at the doorway.

'What have you learnt?' Master Yangshing asked before she had even reached him.

'I think we need to sit down.'

'Is she what we thought?'

'I don't know. In some ways I hope not, for I think another story may also be true.'

He waved her inside. She sat at the table in the room when a child appeared in the doorway.

'You called for me?'

He nodded, and she stepped forward and bowed to Wei-Song.

Wei-Song nodded acknowledgement to her, but the child turned to the master.

The girl sat down on the floor with her legs tucked beneath her and closed her eyes. Her hands rested on her knees. She nodded and then shook her head.

'I am sorry,' she said. 'I still see the same thing.'

'You have visions?' Wei-Song asked.

The girl nodded, but she looked sad. 'I have seen the hidden princess and the prince fighting one another. He has great power, and the Empire will be split.'

Wei-Song groaned. 'It is as I feared. He has fire and water.'

'She has so much more, but there is something strange,' the child said. Wei-Song thought she sounded much older than she appeared. 'There is a connection between the two, a force that pulls them together, but it is hidden from them both.'

'They are destined to be together?'

'Or to kill each other and the Empire with them. We must find a way to heal the bond.'

Wei-Song let out a sigh of relief. 'I think they may be doing so already. They have been training together, learning of their skills together.'

'But there are secrets between them,' the child continued. 'Secrets that will damage the bond.'

'Secrets?'

The child looked up at her with deep brown eyes that glowed in the candlelight. 'You are one such secret. One they both keep.'

'He doesn't know who I am.'

The child bowed her head in agreement. Wei-Song found her frustrating.

She had known another child with visions, not so long ago, who had told her of the hidden princess and what she would become. She had claimed that Wei-Song needed to assist her, for it was her Empire as well. Wei-Song had claimed it was everyone's Empire, for she would never be in a position to be a part of the family who had wanted her dead. She had spent much time with the child and still ached at her loss.

'What secret involves me?' she asked, straining to keep her voice level.

The child shook her head in response.

'Who told the magics of the prophecy?'

The child looked up at her with wide eyes.

'Who else may have seen it?'

'There are many,' the child whispered.

'Many who have visions?'

'There are many, and I should be one, but I stay here.'

A sudden chill covered Wei-Song's skin. 'Where?'

A large tear spilled over and down the child's cheek, its sudden movement startling Wei-song. 'They call to me, but they are hidden from me. If I answer the call, I will be accepted by them without question and give up all ties.'

'Do they work with the magics?' Tutor Yangshing asked.

'I don't know. I know nothing of them other than the call.'

'And if you answered the call, could you tell us more then?'

She shook her head. 'I too would become one of the unknown, calling to others for them to join me in the darkness.' Her voice broke and she started to cry, the young woman appearing again as the small child she was.

Wei-Song sat down on the floor with her and pulled her close. Rocking back and forth, she allowed the child to cry. The sobbing slowly eased, and Wei-Song thought the girl might have drifted to sleep in her arms when she murmured, 'Secrets.' Then she was quiet again.

'Where did you find her?' Wei-Song asked in a whisper over the child's head. 'She's not a Hidden.'

'No,' he agreed, squatting down and taking the child easily from her arms. He nodded towards the doorway, and she followed him out. They walked down to the bedrooms, where he pushed a door back and placed the child on a bed. She murmured in her sleep and rolled over. 'She will need some rest,' he said. 'It takes a lot to give us what she does.'

'You still haven't told me where you found her.'

'She found us. She appeared on the end of the pier only a few weeks ago and said that she needed to be here. That she had seen so much.'

Wei-Song nodded slowly as Yangshing pushed the door closed. They walked in silence along the corridor and into another building that housed the classrooms.

'Do others know what she is?'

'Only those of us who should. There are so few who have visions.'

'Not according to the child,' Wei-Song interrupted. 'She said they call to her.'

'She has said this before. It is part of the reason she is here. She heard the call but feared it, and then she had the visions she described to you today. She had visions of you and knew she needed to find you. Her skills led her here.'

'They could have led her to the Palace Isle.'

He shook his head. 'She knew where you were, but she knew you would return.'

Wei-Song let out the breath she was holding. 'The old stories are true.'

He pushed open a door and indicated that she go ahead of him. They were standing on a small paved area that overlooked the sea. A sharp drop before them. 'I never believed them. I thought they were started as rumours during the war to scare those with magic.'

'Where are the magics? They have been determined to kill the hidden princess. Will they try to contact the prince?'

'Do you think they might have already?'

She shook her head. 'He appears determined to kill them, although I think he is coming around to the idea that there are different forms of magic.'

'You said they have trained,' he said, looking at her closely for the first time.

'They haven't told me where; they snuck away. But it has something to do with the hidden princesses of old. Lis is sure they had magic.'

'Another secret of the Empire. So many.' His voice sounded tired. 'Will you stay and see what we can learn from the girl?'

She nodded.

As they looked back over the sea, he asked, 'How is your mother?'

'Better,' she said softly, turning back to him to see the relief on his face. 'How did she know I could come here and be safe?'

'Because I assured her it would be so.'

'You have been very kind to me.'

He reached out and took her hand. 'I have raised you as though you were my own, just as I promised I would, and I have cared for you in the same way.'

'What were you to my mother?'

'A friend,' he said, his voice sad, 'when she needed one the most. I know she would do all she could to return such a friendship. You haven't told the crown prince who you are?'

She shook her head. 'I don't think that is for me to tell. Mother has kept me secret to keep me safe, and she continues to do that for Lis. How can I be a secret of his?' she asked, looking up at the older man.

'I don't know,' he murmured. 'Come and eat, and we can talk some more. When the child has rested, I want you to talk with her, but don't push her to seek out what she would need to search for.'

20

Lis noted the uneasiness in Yang as he watched the door rather than his usual reading. She too felt nervous about Wei-Song's disappearance. Something within Lis's story had unnerved her and caused her to leave them. Lis wondered what she was doing and when she might return.

'The rain,' she murmured.

'It isn't raining,' Yang responded, looking at her briefly before returning his gaze to the door.

'It was the rain the prince made,' she said softly, 'that unnerved Wei-Song.'

'What?' he asked, yet Lis knew he wasn't listening to her.

'What are you looking for?' Lis asked loudly.

'Wei-Song, and the prince,' he added in a whisper.

'Why does he worry you?'

'It is not that he worries me; it is that he worries Wei-Song, and that worries me.'

Lis laughed, and he turned angrily to her.

'When have you seen her worried?' he asked.

'Often,' Lis said. 'She has put herself between me and a number of people far too frequently. She worried about you. She worried about her mother. The woman's life is full of worry and fear. Do you not worry you will be found out?'

'You haven't told him?' he asked, turning his full attention to her.

Lis shook her head. She was trying to work more with the prince—or at least she had been—but there were things she still hadn't told him. She had told herself they were not her secrets to tell, but she knew eventually they would come back to rest on her shoulders. He would see it as a betrayal. As he might also see them not permitting him to enter the palace. Lis was sure Yang was still trying to determine how he would keep the prince out if he were to arrive.

Wei-Song feared what he was. But he wasn't like the other magics. He had water as well as fire, for one thing, and he couldn't be sensed for another. Lis had not paid attention when he had used his magic. They had been too focused on what he could do and what she could do, they hadn't considered whether others could sense him. But no one had pushed through the gate and run them through, so she guessed he was a different form of Hidden.

'I wonder if he can hide?' she asked absently.

'Is he Hidden?'

'He didn't think so, but I don't know what he is.'

Yang continued to watch the door, and Lis tried to focus on the page before her rather than thinking so much of the prince. It hadn't been too long ago that she had been so focused on another man. She felt a stab of regret at having forgotten Peng so quickly. But then, he had moved on as well. There was no chance for them now. That had been another lifetime, another world.

She shook her head and picked up the scroll with the history of the hidden princesses. But it was brief and talked only of numbers, not girls, not names, not where they had come from nor where they went.

'Do we have an image of every empress?' she asked.

It took Yang a moment to look away from the door. 'Why?'

'I just wondered. I am to be Empress one day, if I survive, and I wondered if my face would join the others.'

'There may be something in the library,' he said with a shrug, then turned back to the door.

'How would I get it?'

'You can't leave,' he said quickly, leaping up and turning from his post. 'We could send someone, perhaps. But what if that alerts the prince and he wants to see you?'

'It can wait,' she said, trying to keep the frustration from her voice. There had to be more information somewhere... or had it all been destroyed during the war?

Lis thought about the royal seal and the letter with the strange symbol on it. She had assumed the prince had taken it with him. Yet who could he find to help tell them what it meant? The faces had symbols—could it have been connected to one of them? Although they had all disappeared as well. Lis wondered for the first time if the letter was connected to the disappearance.

She pulled a scrap of paper towards her as she pushed back the books and reports and scrolls. Taking a small brush dipped in the ink, Lis started trying to recreate the symbol she had seen, but it wasn't quite the same. Like the symbol on the faces, it was small and contained within an oval indentation.

She turned the brush around and dragged the end over the paper, pushing a groove into it and slicing through it at one part of the page. The sound drew Yang's attention. He turned to her before turning back to the door, but then looked again.

'What are you doing?'

'Trying to recreate something I saw.'

'Where?'

'Where the hidden princesses were.' She looked over the symbol again and pushed it away. She couldn't remember what she had seen, but it didn't make any sense and didn't look like any symbol she knew.

'I know this,' Yang said, picking up the paper as he looked down on her at the table.

'Where have you seen it?'

'I'm not sure. I thought it was a pattern; it isn't a word.'

Lis sighed. 'Can you try to remember?'

He studied the paper in his hand and closed his eyes. 'Somewhere on the Palace Isle,' he said.

She tried not to groan.

'Can I keep it? Maybe I can have a look when Wei-Song returns and I can go out into the world again.'

'You can go out now if you need to,' she said.

He looked at her as though she were a child not understanding of the ways of the world.

'There are so many soldiers. What could happen?'

'The prince could return. And Wei-Song could kill me.' He sat down next to her. 'I have seen similar,' he said, studying the paper again.

'There were different ones there, but this one I found somewhere separate from the others, so I thought it might mean something else.'

'Did you understand the meaning of the others?'

She shook her head. 'Maybe they marked a family or a group.'

'A group,' he mused. 'I've seen them grouped together.' He squeezed his eyes closed.

Lis watched him for too long before she pulled on his sleeve, and he blinked at her as though surprised she was there. 'Groups,' she said.

'I don't know,' he murmured and looked back at the door.

'Yang, please.'

'Let me think about it and when I get the chance, I might be able to see where they might be.'

'Near the Imperial Healers?'

'I don't think so. I have seen them, but I don't think they are something I have looked at often.'

Lis stood from the table and walked to the bed, where she ran her hand over the carved edging. It was beautiful, but no different from any other carving around the palace. It was square cut at the corners, the narrow wood curving around in an arch above the bed and then straight down at the posts. She pulled the curtain out and looked over the pattern, then back to Yang.

'I think it was in stone,' he murmured.

She released the curtain and moved around the palace. She took her time and covered every surface, running her hands over the wood panelling of the walls, the edging of the screens and the frames that made the doors. She was crawling around studying the wooden floors when Yang made a strange strangled noise, and she lifted her head so quickly she banged it on the table. As she sat back rubbing the back of her head, she wondered if there was anything on the underside the table.

'What are you doing?' the prince asked.

'Looking for something that isn't here,' she said, climbing awkwardly to her feet. He rushed forward and took her hand to help her up. Yang made another noise.

'Is he alright?' the prince asked, leaning in.

She shook her head. 'He was tasked with the impossible, and he has only just realised.'

'Is she so difficult?' the prince asked, turning to the healer, who paled as his eyes fixed on their joined hands.

Lis could feel the heat of them—not burning, but a heat that transferred through her. She remembered Wei-Song and let it drop. 'Is there a book or scroll with all the empresses in it?'

'Their names are listed…'

'No, their images.'

'Images? Do you think…?'

'I'm not sure what I think, but I would like to look. And the faces… what if there were others amongst the faces?'

'There are not that many empresses,' he said, sitting at the table and pouring himself a cup of water.

'Are we sure? We are moving rapidly through hidden princesses. What if an empress or emperor died?'

'The crown has been passed down our family line for so long.

Even if there were many, it is only one empress each generation.'

'There may have been one or two who died during childbirth,' Yang said, standing nervously at the end of the table, his eyes flitting between the door and the prince. 'Sometimes the child died with her. The family line could not end there and the emperor would have taken another.'

'Would they train again? Were there others in reserve?' Lis asked hurriedly.

'I haven't read any such report or history,' the prince said, clearly doubting Yang's words.

'She would have been replaced without the people knowing.'

'How could the people not know?' Lis asked, then sighed as she sat down opposite the prince. 'They wouldn't see her, other than at a distance. What of those within the palace?'

'Servants know how to keep secrets,' Yang whispered.

'I guess they do,' Lis said.

'What is wrong with you?' the prince suddenly asked Yang, and he jumped.

'He was asked to keep you away,' Lis said.

'By whom?' the prince asked slowly.

As Yang opened his mouth to reply she shook her head.

'Who thinks I might do you harm?'

'Many do, and at times I am amongst them.' She reached for the pot, but he poured for her and pushed the cup across the table.

'Still?'

'Only sometimes. There is much we still don't know about each other and the power we have. You may decide I am still too much of a threat; my knowing your secret may be one of those reasons.'

'I may have other secrets, as you do,' he said, focused on his cup. Then he reached up and snatched the paper from Yang's hand, making the man jump. 'Were you sharing one?'

'I just wondered what it was, and Yang thinks he may have seen it.'

'Truly?' the prince asked, and the healer stepped back.

He murmured something under his breath and stepped back again.

'What did you say?' the prince asked angrily, standing suddenly.

'I wish Wei-Song were here.'

Lis cringed inwardly. She didn't want the prince knowing anything of Wei-Song, or even guessing that Yang had magic. For it would put them both at risk, and she wasn't sure she was safe yet.

'She is certainly more determined than you,' the prince said, sitting back at the table. 'She would have found a way to prevent me seeing the princess,' he added quietly, and Lis couldn't quite read the look on his face as he glanced up at her. 'Where is the girl?'

'She had a family matter to deal with,' Lis said.

'How long will she be gone?'

'I don't know. As long as it takes.'

'Did she not give you any indication?'

'Why does it matter? Families can be difficult. She was called away, and it may be that she returns soon; it may be that it takes longer.'

He looked back at the cup.

'Don't you have your own maid to keep you company?' she asked, her voice sharper than she intended. 'Why are you so interested in mine?'

'You will need someone to look after your needs. Do you want me to send...?'

'No, I don't. I was able to look after myself well enough before I became a princess. I'm sure I will manage.'

Yang nodded absently, his focus still on the door.

'Who are you waiting for?' the prince asked him again.

'I need...' He wandered towards the door.

Lis took a step after him, but he didn't turn back. Did he really think Wei-Song would be so angry with him? 'Yang,' she called, and he paused in the doorway. 'You can't leave me alone with the prince.'

'You aren't alone,' he murmured. 'There is a garden full of soldiers.' And he was gone.

'He is not himself,' the prince said. 'Do you think he would share our secret?'

Lis shook her head, looking after the healer and wondering what he intended. Maybe he was looking for the symbols.

'I don't think we should try to train when there is no one here to field questions.'

'No one other than the tutors on their set days would come,' she said. 'I should get used to it.'

'You have Yang and Wei-Song as company,' he said, looking towards the door himself. 'Have you been able to pull anything else forward? Are you growing flowers?' He looked around as she shook her head.

She wasn't sure how to tell him about the food she had summoned. She still wasn't sure how it had been done. Wei-Song had seemed so worried when Lis had told her what he could do. She didn't want to share anything else with him in case he was the danger Wei-Song was so certain he was. Lis missed her, she realised, as bossy as she was. Lis liked her, and she felt her absence when she was gone. Yang's nervousness hadn't helped, and if Wei-Song were to be away for several weeks, Lis imagined it would only get worse.

And they had not managed to do the one thing she had asked. The prince would continue to visit.

'Did you ask your friend?'

'I did, but he is unable to assist us at the moment.'

'Do you think he will?'

'I don't know.' He narrowed his eyes, and she straightened. 'I don't know. This is a difficult thing to ask. It puts my friend at risk as well as us. I can't push...'

True,' he murmured. 'There is no one I can ask. No one can

know what I have.'

Lis nodded. The excitement of what they had created dissipated. He reached across the table and took her hand, holding it tight. In the other he held a small flame that danced above the skin. Lis put her hand beneath his on impulse and wished she could bring her flowers forward so easily. The flame in his hand turned a darker red, the flames leaping and flickering as they took the shape of a flower.

She pulled her hand back, and the flames jumped back to what they had been.

'Try the other way,' he whispered, the flame fading to nothing in his hand. He stood, still holding her hand, and came to sit beside her.

She held her hand palm up and he placed his beneath hers. She could feel the heat of it, and he continued to squeeze her other hand. She willed forth a flower, a single rose. The stem grew up from her palm, the leaves stretched out, small thorns sprouted along its length and the bud formed at the end. When it opened, it was a flame.

The flames appeared to dance within his dark eyes and Lis was lost in his contented smile for a moment. His comfortable heat pulled her closer.

A sharp intake of breath made her pull away from him, and the flower disappeared.

Wei-Song stood in the doorway. 'Have you lost all sense of self-preservation?' she asked in a hoarse whisper. She pushed the door shut and stepped into the room. 'There is a yard full of soldiers poised to run you through, and you work magic so close to them.'

'They can't sense it.'

'Are you sure? You are doing more than you have before. What if it changes? What if he has changed things?'

Lis looked at the prince, who was very focused on Wei-Song. 'What do you think I am?' he asked.

'Trouble,' she said without hesitation, 'and you bring it with you. I suggest you leave now.'

He raised his eyebrows at Lis before standing and bowing to the girl.

'Take your attitude with you,' she snapped, and he straightened slowly.

'You sound like my mother,' he said. 'Am I just a boy to you?'

'You are someone putting my mistress, my charge, in danger, and I won't have it.' Her voice was just as firm, carrying the same edge.

'It was you who ordered me to stay away.'

She ignored him and stepped towards Lis. 'Where is Yang?'

'He has gone in search of something,' she said.

'We need him here.'

'If I see him, I shall send him back.' The prince bowed at the doorway—to her or Wei-Song Lis was unsure—and then he was gone.

'You can't speak to him like that,' Lis said.

'He is not safe, and you can't be playing with magic in this palace. The soldiers could have killed you both. What if the hunter had called to visit?'

'I would have made cake,' Lis said, knowing all too well that she was pushing an already angry barrier. She waved her hand over the table, and it filled with plates of cakes in various shapes and colours.

Wei-Song ignored the table and Lis's satisfied grin. 'Can he hide?'

'I don't think so.'

'How did you get to the place where you trained?'

'I hid him,' Lis said.

'Could he work it out by what you did?'

'I don't know. Do you think he has more power than he says?'

Wei-Song shook her head and then sat at the table. She looked over the spread with a neutral face, then reached for a cake and took a large bite.

'What did you learn?' Lis asked, watching her chew. Wei-Song gave a surprised expression as she looked at the cake, and then she took another bite. Lis tried to wait patiently while the other woman finished the cake and brushed the crumbs from her fingers.

'I can't tell you,' she said, looking over the cakes with more interest.

'Or you won't.'

'It is complicated.'

'My whole life is complicated. Why do you think the prince and I cannot be together?'

'I think it may help you to work on your friendship,' Wei-Song said, selecting another cake.

Lis was tempted to remove them to get her undivided attention. Instead she waited and when Wei-Song looked up, she sighed.

'I can't tell you the details, but I can tell you there is a chance that the prince is a risk not only to you, but to the Empire.'

'The crown prince?'

She nodded. 'There may be a way for you to work together and help instead of harm, but if you don't work together...'

'Don't or won't? You are saying that if we can't find a way, it will all end badly.'

Wei-Song nodded as she bit into another cake.

'You are sure? Without question?'

She nodded again.

'Can you help us?'

'I don't know if it should be me,' she said.

Lis sighed and sat at the table, reaching for a cake herself. Who could help them?

21

Remi tried not to let his frustrations boil over as he passed through the yard and the soldiers. As he walked away from the princess's palace, he saw the hunter in the distance and realised the girl had been right. There was too great a risk of being caught acting as they had been. He felt the tingle of where her skin had touched his and the shared magic that passed between them.

What could they achieve together? What had others tried? He had heard so few stories from the magic war other than the repeated dangers. There were books on the types of magic, but he couldn't remember anything of magics combining their powers.

He had lost so much in the levelling of the residence. There had been too much going on at the time for him to realise just what he had lost. It was the same hollow sensation he had felt when he'd discovered what she was. She may have saved them all, but she was the enemy. Now he was, and it ate at him. He knew there was nothing he could draw upon to understand what he was.

Watching the people move around him, unaware of just what he was, he stopped. He didn't know who he was. He had been so focused on Lis and, despite their recent connection, he still felt she had betrayed him in a way. She certainly kept things from him.

He might have been the reason behind his brother's death. Since he had the skill of fire, could he have hurt his brother without knowing? Could he have forgotten what he'd done, or was he only now experiencing this because of what Lis was?

She had scoffed at the idea that he had caught the magic from her, but what if he had? What if he had developed these skills only because of Lis?

When he was a child, he had found comfort in the temple, looking up at the gods who looked down over him. They had seemed so secure and sure of themselves. They had, after all, selected him as part of the royal family. He had grown believing they would watch over his brother as he grew to be the new emperor.

He walked towards the temple, the white stone glistening in the sunlight. People moved up the steps and disappeared into the cool interior. He stopped again to watch the people wandering in and out. The gods hadn't watched over them as he'd thought they would, and now he was to be Emperor. Remi struggled already with his role as Crown Prince—how would he fill the role of Emperor? This wasn't the life he'd been born for. He was meant to be a hunter, only now he couldn't be.

He noticed Yang walking slowly by the wall of the temple, his hand running over the glistening stone. Was he really so afraid of the maid that he would worry what she might do if Remi got to the princess? He had been so possessive of her before, staying close, making sure she was getting what she needed. He would have put himself between them as he had done before, but this time he had lacked the confidence. Lis must have shared with him what they had. And what did the girl know that she would insist Remi stay away?

Yang reached the door and disappeared inside. Why would Lis tell him what they had done? Did she trust him so much? Or was there something else, as Remi had suspected before? She had promised him that she would remain faithful.

Another face in the crowd caught his eye, and a faint touch of magic reached him. When he stepped forward, the face smiled at him. He was one of the others, one of the magics they had captured before, the only one who would speak. The man tipped his head to the side, indicating the direction he was headed in, then skipped down the steps and along a street leading from the square. Remi picked up his pace and charged after him. But the street was quiet, and there was no sign of the man.

He had a moment's hesitation as he wondered if this was a trap, payback for the prison. But if they wanted him dead, they would kill him. They had only talked of wanting the princess dead, so Remi continued on, wondering what this man knew and what he might be able to offer him.

The magic was faint, but he could sense it. He knew that if a hunter were to come this way, they would sense it also. He moved along the trail of magic as quickly as he could and pushed open the gate it led to without hesitation.

The man stood waiting for him, arms crossed over his chest. 'Close it,' he whispered.

'Other hunters will find you,' Remi said.

'Maybe,' he murmured. 'They haven't found you.'

Remi remained unmoving. *What does this man know or think he knows?*

'Don't want to give yourself away?' he said with a smirk. 'Clever, only I have heard of the visions and prophecies of what you are.'

'Prophecies?'

'You too have been named by the gods as one to change the course of history. One to change the world and bring magic to power.'

'I thought you were trying to kill the hidden princess for that very reason.'

The man shook his head and motioned inside the house. Inside the darkened room, he waved a hand, and the candles sprang to life. Remi wondered if he too could create such a feat. 'She would bring a balance between magics and non-magics. We want control.

You want control. You can give us all what we want.'

'I am not the one to give you what you want,' Remi said firmly.

'From what I have heard, you are. You cannot trust the hidden princess; you cannot allow her the freedom you have given her.'

'She is locked in a palace.'

'She plays with her power.'

The prince waited, staring down the man, unsure just what he thought he would get from Remi.

'She has lied to you to keep herself safe. She is not concerned with the Empire and you. She only wants to be Empress.'

Remi shook his head.

'There are those around her to protect her, to ensure she becomes what she is destined to be. You could stop that. You could be the change.'

'You want me to kill the princess?' he scoffed.

'You will do what you must for the Empire.'

'What do you know of those around her?' Remi asked, ignoring what this man thought he could offer.

'The Order of Huans. The Hidden.'

'Are you saying the healer and the girl are also Hidden?'

The man laughed at him as though he were a boy unable to see what was before him. 'There is much you don't know.'

'And are you willing to tell me?'

'I may. Or I may help you find the answers for yourself.'

'Why should I trust you?' Remi asked. 'How do you know what I am? *I* don't even know what I am.'

'You have been protected your entire life, but there was a skill hidden deep within you. The hidden princess has used her power against us and in doing so has pulled your skills to the surface.'

'Lis is the cause of this?'

'It was always there, but it needed her magic to manifest.'

'Why?'

The man shrugged and sat at the table, pouring rice wine into small cups. 'I only know what I have been told. The two of you are strong, and you stand on opposite sides. You must succeed for the Empire. For if you falter, so will it.'

'Opposite sides? She is destined to be my wife, my Empress. What if we were to work together?'

The man shook his head, and Remi looked over the cups on the table. He could step forward and join this man to see if he could teach him more of who and what he was. But he knew the magics couldn't be trusted. The alternative was to return to Lis, to understand just what power she had and those surrounding her, to see if they could continue to learn together.

This man is trying to use me to get to Lis. Remi rested his hand on his sword and took a deep breath. 'How did you learn what I am?' he asked.

'I was told.'

'By whom?'

'That I cannot tell you. There are many I protect, and I cannot share such secrets until I know you are willing to listen and help us.'

'I can't trust you,' Remi said, backing up.

'I'll be here when you are ready.' The man's grin was unnerving. Remi backed out of the room and headed quickly down the street. He should have just killed the man, but he seemed to be the only one who could tell Remi just what he was.

When he returned to the little palace, the three women sat at the table chatting comfortably—his mother, Lis and the maid, as though she were one of them.

'Who are you?' Remi demanded, drawing his sword.

The healer wasn't present, and Remi wondered if he was still searching the temple for whatever it was he looked for. It hadn't been clear just what Lis had told him earlier, and now Remi wanted to know just what the healer was.

'Remi?' his mother asked, standing as the girl jumped up from the table, her arm protectively across the empress.

'What has happened?' Lis asked, also coming around to stand beside her.

He raised the sword towards the girl, but his mother moved between them. 'You are not what you pretend to be,' he murmured. He was disappointed. There was something about her that he liked, something that drew his respect, and yet she was another who had lied to him, another secret Lis had kept from him.

'Remi, put the sword down,' his mother said, her voice soft and sing-song rather than that of the firm woman he knew. He looked at her for a moment.

'Who is she to you?'

'She is my maid; you know this. I am attached to the girl.'

'She has magic,' he said.

'Can you sense her?' the empress asked, her voice stronger.

He shook his head. 'But I know what she is. She has lied to you, Mother—lied to us all. She is not trustworthy.'

Lis moved, trying to put herself between them as the maid had done for her so many times. But Wei-Song grabbed her arm, preventing her from stepping closer to his sword. She looked uncertain, her eyes on the sword, and he felt a stab of regret. But this wasn't about Lis and her fears. This was about the maid. Ignoring Lis, Remi stepped forward, pushing the tip of the sword closer to the girl.

'Remi, stop,' his mother pleaded, and the girl shook her head.

'I am here to protect the hidden princess. I know what you are,' Wei-Song said softly, and his mother's brow creased. 'I know you are a danger to her.'

'Remi?' the empress asked.

'He's not,' Lis whispered, but Wei-Song kept her arm out, and the princess held back.

'He is,' she said, her eyes not looking away from Remi. 'He has learnt what he is destined to be, and it begins.'

'You have heard the same prophecy?'

She nodded once, and he stepped forward again. The tip of the sword almost touched her throat.

'Where did you hear this?' he asked.

'From one who knows,' she said, her chin held high.

'Wei-Song? What is it?' the empress asked.

'Mother, enough,' he snapped. 'There is much going on here that you do not understand. There is magic in the Empire and…'

'I am well aware of the magic in the Empire,' she said. Her voice carried an edge, as though she was about to slap him. 'I know what happened to your brother. You are the hunter, the greatest we have ever seen, but you may not know all that you think you do. Wei-Song is not a threat to you.'

'The hidden princess is surrounded…'

'By those who care for her,' she finished for him. 'She is your bride. You protected her before.'

'I should have killed her before,' he said. His mother's face paled, as did Lis's, and he only momentarily regretted his harsh words. But if the fire bearer was right and she was not who she claimed, there would forever be secrets between them. 'This maid is not who she says she is; she too protects one who does not deserve our protection.'

Lis pulled Wei-Song back as his mother stepped between them, the sword scratching across her throat. 'She is your sister,' she said as her hand moved to her skin.

'Mother,' Wei-Song cried desperately as his mother collapsed to the floor before him. He stepped back, but the sword was still held high.

'You hid her?' he said, anger heavy in his voice.

'I had to. She was ordered to die by my hand, but I couldn't do it,' she said, her voice soft as she reached for Wei-Song's face.

'Whose child is she?'

'Your father's,' his mother said, pulling herself up. Blood ran from the scratch across her chest, and he was grateful there had been no power behind it. 'As soon as she showed signs of her skill, your father made the decree.'

Remi shook his head. He understood why he had done such a thing when Lis's father had done something very different. 'What would he do to me?' he murmured.

'You are a hunter, a strong hunter, and that is a skill we needed for the Empire.'

'What if I had magic? Would he do the same?'

'Hunting is not the same,' she said as Wei-Song helped her to sit back at the table. Her focus was completely on his mother.

'They haven't told you,' he said. 'If you know what she is, you know of Lis.'

The empress nodded once, and Lis gave her a small smile.

'You are Hidden,' Remi said to Wei-Song, who nodded without looking at him. He felt the loss of her. He hadn't known who she was, but he had felt something and then torn it apart. 'You knew who I was,' he said.

'You are the crown prince of Rei-Een. Everyone in the Empire knows who you are. Yang will come,' she said to his mother—her mother, he reminded himself as she dabbed at the cut across her skin. Blood marked the edges of her clothes.

Yang appeared in the doorway, as though summoned by Wei-Song's need. He rushed forward, pushing the prince out of the way. Only then did Remi realise his sword was still raised. The young healer *tsk*ed the group as though they had all misbehaved and laid his hands directly on the empress's skin. He stepped forward as she sighed with relief. He glanced at Lis, but she hadn't moved, nor had she taken her eyes from him.

'What should they have told me?' his mother asked suddenly, and the healer shushed her. She waved him away and when he lifted his hands, the scratch across her chest was a fine white line.

'You are also one of them. He was right.' Remi turned to Lis. 'You are surrounded by them.'

'Who?' Wei-Song asked, standing and turning to him. Remi could see the resemblance to his mother then, not just in her voice but in her features. And he could see his brother. He gulped down the confusion building in his chest and shook his head.

'Who have you talked with?' she asked again, stepping closer. Lis leaned forward and wrapped her hand around Wei-Song's arm, tugging her back.

'The secrets are out,' Lis said. 'Surely that changes things.'

'It may be too late,' Wei-Song said.

'What did you think they would have told me?' his mother asked again. 'What is it you keep from me?'

'When you have kept so much yourself.' Remi turned then and left them to it. They could keep their secrets and their magic. He wondered if Yang stayed so close to Lis just because he was a Hidden as well, and if that was why Remi hadn't been able to see them the day he had burnt her and the healer had taken her away.

He pushed through the gate and into the street beyond. He walked fast, trying to leave behind all the confusion and mistrust. How could his mother not have told him he had a sister? How long had she kept this to herself, and where had Wei-Song been hidden? Who would willingly take a child with magic from the very man trying to stamp it out?

Remi stopped and looked around. He had lost his brother, but he still had a sibling. And his mother knew of Lis and the skills she had. But then, if she had protected a daughter for so long, she would protect another. He wondered for a moment if she herself had a form of magic that had remained undiscovered. Could she be a Hidden? Could she be the reason Remi had the skills he did?

He was tempted to raise the fire in his hand just to see it. The more he used it, the more grounding he found it. The more he saw himself reflected in the flames. But someone walking by startled him, and he realised it wasn't safe. He thought about the place of the hidden princesses and wondered if he could practice there on his own.

He felt a stab of regret for the words he had used about Lis. She had looked so sure he would run her through, and he realised she'd been living in fear that he would change his mind. But he couldn't justify it now. He couldn't kill her because of the magic she held when he held a power of his own. A power that could rule the Empire.

He looked towards the centre of the island and the little yard he had visited earlier. He would still rule the Empire. He was to be Emperor. And with Lis by his side, they could use their magic for all sorts of good. But the man with magic had implied Remi didn't need her, that he would be better without her. And if he alone ruled a world filled with magic, he would never have to fear a hunter or his father again.

The black gate called to Remi, and he headed for the hidden princesses of old. Many unanswered questions remained in the compound and the papers. There had to be more they hadn't found, and the faces were a worry. Had someone else known they were there? Had the magics found them, watched them? Remi didn't know what power they might have or ability to change the world around them. He had fire and water, but Lis could make anything grow. She had also made the earth move and the stones disappear. What else might she be able to do?

He moved quickly, seeing no one on the way. When he pushed the gate closed behind him, he wondered how he could prevent others following him. He smelt the hot metal before he realised he had melted the latch. He would find another way out if required.

He walked towards the black gate and reached for the writing hidden beneath the paint. This time, it had a different message: 'The way forward is together.'

He rushed forward, looking for any sign that Lis had been there without him.

22

Lis sat slowly at the table beside the empress after the prince had left the little palace. The anger had been like a flame behind his eyes. It had flashed and burned, growing stronger with every word his mother spoke.

The empress ran her fingers over the fine line across her chest, and Yang sighed. 'He didn't mean to,' she murmured.

Lis nodded agreement, but she knew the anger was too much. It would consume him. 'It is too late,' she whispered, looking down at her hands, fearful of the acknowledgement she knew she would see on Wei-Song's face.

'I am sorry he could not embrace you as the sister he needs,' the empress continued, looking up at Wei-Song. 'But then, we knew he couldn't. It is his life to hunt out those with magic, so to find that his own sister is one of them…' She trailed off before turning to Lis and taking her hand. 'He knows what you are?'

Lis nodded, and the empress grew stern.

'He is the one who hurt you, not one of the magics.'

She nodded again, only chancing to glance up at the empress and see the sadness on her face. 'It is who he is,' she said. 'But it wasn't anymore. A hunter with magic of his own. 'He must be very confused,' she murmured.

'I thought I knew all your secrets,' the empress said.

'There are too many secrets and very few of them mine,' Lis answered, pulling her hand from the empress's as she stood.

'What does he think you have told me?' the empress asked, looking between Lis and Wei-Song.

They looked at each other, and Lis indicated with a small tip of her head that Wei-Song be the one to tell, but she shook her head. 'You are his bride. He shared this with you, so you should tell.'

'He should tell,' Lis said with a sigh. 'The crown prince,' she started slowly, unsure of how the empress would respond to such news, 'has magic.'

The empress stared at her for too long. 'His hunting is a form of magic?'

'He holds fire and water,' Lis said quickly.

'When did you discover this?' The empress's voice was calm, calmer than Lis expected.

'Recently. It appears to be connected to me in some way.'

The empress nodded.

'Have you heard this before?' Lis asked.

She shook her head.

Lis opened her mouth to ask more, but the empress turned to Wei-Song and asked, 'Are you angry that he has lived the life you were denied?'

Wei-Song knelt by her mother. 'Of course not. The choice was not yours, and it wasn't mine. The crown prince has only just come to these skills. He is finding his way, finding his skill, finding his place in the world.'

'You are a good child,' the empress said, reaching forward and placing her palm against Wei-Song's face. 'You are better to me than I deserve.'

'Why aren't you surprised by his skills?' Lis asked hurriedly, and a little harshly.

The empress slowly lifted her gaze to Lis. 'I dreamt of it.'

'When?' they asked together. Lis looked across the room at Yang, who remained still, in his usual place on the floor by the bed.

'It started just after the priestess died.'

'Before the next high priestess was raised?' Lis asked.

The empress shrugged then, looking between the two women, the uncertainty and vulnerability clear on her face. 'I have strange dreams of you and Remi with magic, working together, and then it is as though you are shrouded in darkness and he can't see you. He grows angry and hateful, and the world burns around him.' Her fingers worked over the new scar again.

'How often do you have this dream?' Wei-Song asked.

'Most nights,' she murmured.

'You should have told me,' Wei-Song said, reaching for her again.

'I thought it was worry that had caused such an idea to form. But sometimes in my dream you work together in harmony, and the people look so happy. Perhaps it is worry for the two of you, that he cares so much for you that he will not separate your needs from the Empire's.'

'Is that a risk?'

'Maybe not. This Choosing has been so different from any other. The age, the timing, the magic…'

'Others have not always been so easy,' Lis said softly. 'I think there are many stories similar to mine, or where princesses have not survived and have been replaced without the Empire ever discovering. Was your own training so event free?'

The empress looked up but stared past Lis. 'I made some good friends during that time. Friends I can no longer see.'

'Master Yangshing,' Wei-Song whispered, and her mother nodded. 'Was he your tutor?'

'He was far more than that, but it is no longer important. I can never repay the friendship he gave to me.'

'What do you think the crown prince will do with his magic?' Lis asked. 'Will he burn the Empire?'

'He is more driven than that. He has worked all his life to

protect the Empire. He just needs time to adjust.'

Lis wondered about the dream. Wei-Song had talked of someone having a vision and telling her a similar version of what their future might be. She was key, she knew, to keeping them together and keeping him from himself. She had no idea how to do that, and his behaviour had only renewed her fears of what he might do to her if he felt they were on opposing sides.

'There is no connection,' she said to the room. 'There is nothing that keeps us together.'

'You are his chosen.' The empress's fingers played over the scar again.

'Yang, would you be able to see to that?' Lis asked him.

He climbed to his feet and then squatted in front of the empress, this time waiting for her to nod before he put his hands on her skin and closed his eyes. When he opened them, only the faintest red line remained. 'It will fade,' he murmured, staggering a little as he stood.

Lis looped under his arm quickly and guided him back to the bed, where he sat heavily on the floor and leaned back. She sat beside him, leaning on his shoulder, trying to share some of her energy with him. He murmured a noise that could have been thanks and closed his eyes.

'No connection,' she said again.

'He cares for you,' the empress repeated.

'But do I care for him?'

The empress turned to her, and she bit her lip. 'I was chosen, but I didn't have a choice. We have formed a kind of friendship in our magic, but there is a fear of him I'm not sure I can get past.'

'He would not hurt you.'

'He already has,' Lis said, running a finger over her wrist. 'He may not mean to, but there is an anger he has lived with for so long. He may not be able to get past it. And now he has become the very thing he has fought against. He has no one he can share that with other than me. His choices have been taken away.'

'Do not put stock on an old woman's dreams.'

'I have heard too many visions now, or dreams of my future. What if it is something different?'

'What do you think it might be?'

She shook her head. 'I don't know. Right now, I can't guess. I have glimpses of something I think I could live with, and then other times I wonder if I will survive long enough to become the crown princess.'

'Could we help with training, get you working together with support?' the empress asked.

'Who do you propose to help us?' Lis asked, but she was looking at Wei-Song.

The empress turned towards her. 'The master knows the situation.'

Wei-Song shook her head quickly. 'I couldn't put him in such a position, and it would give the order away. I can't expose them.'

'He is your brother.'

'He is the best hunter in the Empire who has just discovered his own power. He could be a danger to us all.'

'You don't trust him,' the empress whispered, her voice heavy with disappointment.

Wei-Song shook her head once and looked at the floor.

'I agree with Wei-Song,' Lis said, watching how hard it was for her to be honest with her mother. 'He is too volatile at the moment.'

'He wouldn't betray you,' the empress said.

'He doesn't know me,' Wei-Song said. 'He owes me nothing. When he lost his temper with the princess, he tried to run her through, and then he burnt her arms. What might he do to a school full of Hidden?'

'I can't believe that,' the empress said. Her voice was soft, but it carried the strength Lis was used to hearing.

'Which is why he must remain as he is until we are sure he can be trusted.'

The empress lifted herself up from the table, clearly exhausted from learning the truth of her son. She rested her hand on Wei-Song's shoulder a moment before continuing outside. Lis listened to the sounds of the gate opening and the guards arranging themselves around her.

'Who told you of the prince and princess?' Yang asked from his position on the floor.

'A child,' Wei-Song said, her shoulders hunching. Lis climbed to her feet, but as she reached out, Wei-Song straightened up. 'A child with visions. They are very rare.'

'And yet we hear of visions all the time,' Lis said.

'The empress,' Yang whispered.

'It is strange that she would have a similar dream so often,' Lis said, still watching Wei-Song.

'I don't know what she is or might have been. It could be that the world is changing now that the two of you are together. Those in the world might be changing along with it.'

'You mean we might be the cause of the magic? We could be the return of magic to Rei-Een?'

'I don't know, not without more time with the child. I fear the world is changing far more than I thought it would. There was a child before who foretold your coming.'

'What does she say now?'

'She died,' Wei-Song whispered. 'And now another child has been found. She says she is called by others, but we have never been able to find them. As things change, as people act to try and change what has been seen, more is seen of the future. I don't know if enough can be changed to stop what has been foretold.'

'You said that if we worked together, it would be fine.'

'That may not be the truth. It may not be the whole story. Even if you manage to save the prince from himself, you may not be able to stop what is to come.'

Lis shivered at the strange sensation that covered her skin.

'We need to know that you will fight for the Empire.'

'Of course,' Lis said. 'I will do everything I can.'

'And fight for the emperor.'

'The man who will kill me for the magic I have?'

'The man who will be your husband,' Wei-Song whispered.

Lis couldn't sleep that night. Once she did drift off, she woke from a dream of the prince with flames in his eyes, hatred burning off him and threatening to engulf her. She found when she woke that she was cold, and she missed the heat of him. How long had it been since he had snuck into her bed in the night and closed his arms around her? It felt like forever, and she wondered what it meant that she missed him.

Yang still remained close, but not as close now that she had healed. There wasn't the need for him to share his energy with her in the night. But as she sat up in the bed, she couldn't see him in the dark room. She longed for the ability to raise flames in her hand as the prince did so she could see the dim room.

In the quiet of the night, she heard whispered voices, and she leaned forward trying to hear what was being said.

'There has to be something on her side for him.'

'And if there isn't?' She thought it was Yang's voice.

'Then it may be that the crown prince will lose his way and darkness will follow.'

'Why don't you refer to him by name?' Yang asked, concern thick in his voice.

'He isn't my brother. No matter who our parents are, I don't know him and he doesn't know me.'

One of them sighed heavily. Silence followed, and Lis wondered if they realised she was awake. She lay back slowly and pulled her knees towards her chest as she curled into a ball and huddled beneath the covers. What would happen if she couldn't connect with the prince?

She thought about his mother, too calm in the revelation that the greatest hunter of the Empire had magic of his own. The dream in itself was not enough. Lis wondered if the woman had more power than she was willing to share, and if she too had an idea of what might happen in their future. It appeared everyone had a better idea of what was to come for Lis than she did herself.

She felt a little lost and again found herself longing for the prince's arms around her. Maybe she did feel something more for him than she was willing to admit. If given a choice, she would have preferred Peng's arms around her, but she knew that was no longer an option for her. There was also no memory to draw from. They had lain together in the field, surrounded by flowers and staring up at the sky, but he had never shared her bed. She felt the loss of him again, the same burning sensation in her heart that she'd felt when the crown prince had knelt before her and announced her as his choice.

In a sense, he had burned her even then. Was that when it had started? Was that when he had first found the fire within? Did he feel a connection to her, some unknown that drew him to her, a prophecy they could do nothing to prevent? The hot tears were a surprise. She knew her lot was set. She had come to terms with that some time ago, and she didn't need to relive it. But the visions had unnerved her.

When she closed her eyes, the magic man who had reached for her through the prison bars sprang at her. She cried out and sat up again to find a shadow standing over the bed. She squealed.

'Lis,' Yang whispered.

'I can't sleep,' she whined.

He ran a smooth hand over her forehead, warm and comforting, brushing her hair back. She lay back down and closed her eyes. He had more power than he realised, she thought as she drifted to sleep.

The dream was vivid. Although she felt as though she was in the hidden princess palace, she knew it was a dream. The stones were neat and level, no weeds growing between them. She waved her hand over the ground, but nothing grew, and her chest tightened with the fear that her magic was gone.

She looked up to find the prince by the black gate. He studied the silver symbols, but from her distance she couldn't see what they were. He stomped his foot. She could feel his anger grow, the heat moving in waves across to her.

'Your Highness,' she called across the gap, but he didn't respond. She wasn't sure if he couldn't hear her or if he was too focused on what he did to look away.

She walked towards him, but she couldn't seem to close the distance.

He murmured and waved his arms.

'Remi,' she called, becoming more desperate. She tried to run, but the gate didn't get any closer. 'Remi, help me.'

'No,' he cried, but he was focused on the gate. The symbols faded and returned, but she still couldn't make out what they were. 'It can't be,' he cried, the anguish clear in his voice.

And then the black gate burst into flames. The crackle hurt her ears. The paint blistered and the wood cried out under the heat of the flames. As it burned, Lis felt her skin blister as well. She felt her own skin disappear as the black door flared to orange. She was surrounded by the flames.

She tried to call out, but her throat burned as the world around her disappeared in the haze of the heat. She tried to raise her arm and felt her skin split, and then the prince turned towards her. She tried to call his name one more time, but there was nothing there.

As the world turned from orange to black, the prince stepped towards her. 'Goodbye, Your Highness,' he said. His grin made her heart stop.

She woke wet, sweat pouring from her and the covers on the floor. She drew a ragged breath, desperate for water. She couldn't see Yang or Wei-Song, but there was someone else in the dim room as she pulled herself from the bed and searched out water. She reached for the candle just as a flame sparked to life.

The prince stood by the table with a small flame cupped in his hand—and the same grin he had worn when she'd burned in the dream.

She screamed.

'Lis,' Wei-Song said softly as she shook her. The morning light slowly focused. 'You were dreaming.'

Lis shook her head and then put a hand to her forehead. It hurt. She felt dry and uncomfortable, sure that her skin had peeled away in the night from the heat of the flames.

'I will get you water,' she said, stepping away, and Lis curled back into a ball, the bed warm around her. 'Here,' she said, but Lis didn't move. 'The tutors come today.'

'I'm not well,' Lis murmured. She pulled the covers up, then pushed them away to take the cup from Wei-Song. 'I'm so dry.'

'You have had such dreams before,' Wei-Song said as Lis gulped the cupful of water.

Lis nodded and held the cup back out to her. 'This was different,' she murmured.

As Wei-Song went to say something else, the door opened and the prince appeared. She scuttled back, and Wei-Song put herself between them again.

'I see we have shared the same dream again,' he said.

'You have had this dream before?' Wei-Song asked, then turned to the prince. 'You have had the same dream.'

He nodded and took the cup from Wei-Song's hand. Moving to the table, he filled it and then handed it back to Lis, who waited too long before putting out her hand to accept it.

'I wouldn't hurt you,' he murmured.

'But you have,' she said. 'And you will again.'

He looked at Wei-Song. 'Can I have a moment with her?'

'What did the gate say?' Lis asked before Wei-Song could answer.

'That I... It doesn't matter.'

'It was enough for you to set me on fire,' Lis said.

'It wasn't you I was aiming the fire at.'

'Who else was there?' she asked, watching Wei-Song disappear into her small alcove.

He shrugged and sat on the edge of the bed, then stood. 'You lied to me. Or at least kept secrets.'

'They weren't mine to tell.'

'Did you tell mine?' He moved uncomfortably from foot to foot.

'She already knew, in a way.'

'Did she?' he asked. 'Would she tell the emperor?'

'No,' Lis said. She reached out to him, but he pulled back.

'No one can know. I need to learn control,' he murmured as he headed for the door.

23

The fire bearer was already waiting for Remi when he pushed open the gate. He had come with good reason, he tried to convince himself as he closed the gate behind him. He needed to learn what skill he had and how he could control it. What if he lost control and exposed himself as a magic in the open? What might the guards do? What might his father do? But then he knew the answer—without question, his father would send someone to kill him.

The emperor might have been the strongest, most feared man in all the Empire, but he had never completed such a deed himself. That was left for Remi to do. Since the emperor couldn't send his son to kill himself, Remi wondered who he might send. *Who would he trust enough to kill the future emperor?*

'Will you tell me what you know of her?' the magic asked, pulling him from his thoughts.

'I am here to learn of myself.'

'She is the reason you are who you are. She is the reason the trouble will come.'

'The prophecy states that she will bring peace between the magics and non-magics. Where is the trouble in that?'

'Their own kind of magics,' the man said. 'The Hidden. They will not include others in that. She has surrounded herself with secrets.'

Remi nodded agreement before he could stop himself. 'How can you teach me? What can you teach me, other than the hidden princess and what she might be?'

'You don't want to work with her?'

'I need to know what I can do.' Remi's voice carried further than he had intended. 'If you can't help me, then I'll find someone who can.'

'And who would help you with such a thing?' the man asked quickly as Remi turned for the gate.

'The hidden princess said she had a friend who could assist…'

'But they weren't able to?'

Remi paused. 'It was a risk to them. I am a hunter, after all.'

'The greatest hunter of the Empire,' the man agreed. 'But I will help you.'

Remi nodded.

'Come,' he said, and Remi followed at a distance through the small house, wondering who would have lived here. Servants perhaps, for very few actually lived on the island. Unless their work required it, such as the healers. His frustration rose at the idea of them. Healer Yang should have been living with the other healers, but he had not only been sent to watch over the hidden princess, he had been living at the end of her bed. Remi wondered if anyone else had queried this move as he had, or whether they assumed a connection with the maid who wasn't a maid. Healers were to remain chaste, but was such a thing truly possible?

The small courtyard opened into a surprisingly large space. 'There is no one living in the neighbouring houses. We are safe here.'

'The hunters may sense your magic,' Remi said.

'But they can't sense yours, can they?'

He shook his head.

'Show me what you can do.'

Remi hesitated and then opened his palm, exposing a small

flame.

'Can you direct it?' the man asked.

Remi let it run over his hand as he moved it around. It crawled along his arm and sat on his shoulder before running down to his outstretched palm again.

'Light that candle,' the man directed, pointing across at a tall candle against the wall, 'without moving.'

Remi reached towards it, but the flame remained on his fingertips, reaching forward for the candle so far away.

'Throw it,' the man said.

Remi flicked his hand, but the flame was attached to him.

The man stepped forward and put a hand on his shoulder. Remi glared at him, but he remained as he was. His voice was kinder as he said, 'Close your eyes. Imagine the candle alight with your flame, as though it has risen in the candle rather than in your hands.

Remi tried to ignore the man's close presence and the fact that he had touched him, which no one had ever done save his mother, or Lis.

She kept creeping into his mind.

'Clear your thoughts. Think only of the fire.'

He took a deep breath, cleared his mind of everything other than the candle and reached towards it, thinking of his fire glowing atop it.

He opened his eyes to find the flames still sticking to the end of his fingers. Closing his fist, he extinguished them in frustration.

'It will come,' the man said, although Remi wasn't sure he believed him. 'You will be very strong, but it will take time for you to become who you need to be. I think we can work well together, Your Highness. My name is Chonglin.'

Remi tipped his head in acknowledgement and took a deep breath. He wished for rain, and a small cloud appeared beside him.

The man nodded slowly. 'Can you make that happen further from your body?'

Remi pushed a hand slowly towards the little cloud, and it floated away from him before drizzle fell from the formation.

He pushed further, but the cloud evaporated and the rain stopped.

'A good start,' Chonglin said.

'It isn't much,' Remi said.

'It is enough to start with. You can't expect to rule the world in a day. You can't expect to magic what you want. Can the girl do that?'

'I don't know,' Remi said. 'Secrets, remember?'

'You have to let her go.'

'It isn't that easy. There is a connection. She is to be my bride, after all, and we have shared dreams.' Remi wasn't sure why he would share so much with this man. But he needed to share with someone and, despite his concerns, Chonglin appeared to be helping him.

'Of what?'

'Hidden princesses,' Remi murmured, still holding back some things.

'We need to know what she can do.'

'I am more concerned about what I can do. And why.'

'I have told you why.'

'How could the prophecy have been unknown before now?' Remi asked.

'The world can change on a single action.'

'If you wanted her dead, why not kill her before she became the hidden princess?'

'Because another would have taken her place. It is destiny that this would occur now. We did not know the impact it would have on you, that it would pull your magic to the surface.'

'Are you saying that everyone has magic of some kind, and it just needs to be triggered?' Remi asked.

'It is an idea, but there is no proof.'

'Unless that is why the girls all had power.'

'What girls?'

Remi shook his head and tried to focus on the candle, still unlit before him. 'I worry that I might hurt her,' he said, unsure why he needed the man to know.

'It is what we hope will come to pass. When you understand the danger she poses to the Empire, you will understand the need to fight against her.'

'What if she is stronger than I am?'

'You will have us on your side, and together we are stronger than you realise.'

'What do you think she could do?'

'My fear is that she will rally the people against you. Tell me honestly what power she has, so that we can fight against her.'

'She makes flowers grow, and she can make the earth move.'

'Move?'

'In a way,' the prince said, remembering the excitement they had shared when the earth moved in a wave across the courtyard.

'I think she is under your skin,' the man said. 'A girl has reduced the greatest hunter to nothing.'

'I am not nothing,' he snapped, the flame growing tall in his hand. Chonglin didn't flinch. Remi looked towards the candle and snapped his fingers. The flame burned bright and tall atop it.

'No, but you can be so much more with us.'

'What else do you think I might learn?' he asked, an excitement growing in his chest at the new ability.

'I think there is much for you to learn. We will find someone with water to assist you as well.'

'I don't think it safe for many to know what I am.'

'We will only include those we can trust.'

'You mean those you can trust.'

The man nodded once with a grin.

'Let us see if you can put the fire into something else.'

'I burnt the hidden princess.'

'Did you?' he asked slowly.

'I didn't mean to. I was very angry and I grabbed her arms, and although I could feel the heat, I didn't understand what I was doing to her.'

'Did she heal herself?'

He shook his head. 'There has been a healer with her since the attack on the residence.'

'Do you know how she stopped us?'

Remi shook his head. She didn't understand herself, and he wondered if she was getting training and support now that she was surrounded by other Hidden, while he had been floundering. He wanted so much to be angry with her, to hate what she was and what she had done to him, but he couldn't direct that at her. He had tried when he'd thought she was running away—but she wasn't running. She was trying to help him, and he didn't know how to deal with his conflicting feelings.

He would stay away. As he should have in the first place. It was the only way. While she was doing whatever it was she did, it was surrounded by soldiers. He could take the time to learn more about his own skills.

He realised then that as his thoughts had returned to Lis, his internal flame had pushed through. He flexed his fingers around the flame in his hand. He tried to imagine the rose she had helped him create, but the flame turned into a ball instead. It floated above his palm.

'Throw it,' the man whispered, and Remi hurled it towards the candle. It burnt through the middle of the candle, causing the top half to fall onto the ground. He stepped forward to study the charred wall on the other side.

'Impressive,' Chonglin said.

Remi straightened and grinned. He formed another flame in his palm and tried to form another ball, which rose easily.

Then he closed his other hand over it, and it vanished.

'I wonder what we can do with smoke,' the other man pondered.

A small spiral of grey smoke appeared in Remi's hand. He tipped it onto the floor at his feet and twirled his finger, making it larger and denser as it moved around him.

'You are a fast learner,' Chonglin said. 'Maybe I can just suggest skills I have seen in others and we'll discover what you can do.'

Remi smiled and, with a click of his fingers, the smoke dissipated.

24

The following morning, Remi stood in the rear courtyard of the little house and wondered why he was there, why he had agreed to work with these men. All he had wanted was some control—and now he stood with the enemy, trusting them to help him. They were still determined that Lis was the danger and that she needed to be stopped. Yet these men might have been behind his brother's death.

'What is it?' Chonglin asked. 'Do you think we can't teach you? Are you too strong for us, or will your lightning never hit the ground?'

Remi scowled at him and then glanced at the other man standing against the wall, his expression far too serious. Chonglin had introduced him as a water magic, but he appeared to trust Remi even less than Remi trusted them, and he wasn't prepared to share his name. He had taken some time to try and explain to Remi the feel of the water in the cloud and how to build the magic within it to form the lightning. Remi could do this to an extent, but he couldn't make it hit the ground.

'You talk of control,' Chonglin continued, 'but what else do you want?'

'I want to know what happened to my brother,' Remi said softly, forming another cloud.

'What makes you think we will tell you?' the water magic asked.

'You know what happened to him, and I need to know. You want my help; you need me to get what you want. And yet I know you killed my brother to get it. I have come to you to learn, yet you might kill me just because I know who you are.'

'We would have killed you already,' Chonglin said. A flame ran over his hand as he watched Remi's little cloud, as though he wasn't even aware of its heat. 'We need you and you know it. Your brother's death is not what you think.'

Remi allowed the cloud to evaporate and turned his full attention to them. They glanced at each other and the water magic shook his head, but Chonglin nodded.

'You know what happened,' Remi repeated.

'I know that the man responsible thought he was helping. That he tried to help,' he said carefully as Remi took a step forward. 'We knew his princess had no power. It was known who your princess was and what she was destined to become the day she was born. The world would be different if your brother had remained the crown prince, married his hidden princess and become the emperor he was meant to be. Your hidden princess would never have been in the position to bring magic together with the rest of the Empire.'

Remi had asked about why Lis hadn't been killed before she reached him, but there was destined to be a hidden princess that would become what she was said to be. 'Would U'shi have been replaced by another?'

'No. Another would have come forward at some point in our future to be what your hidden princess is. In some ways, we didn't want to wait any longer to become what we were meant to be…'

'You killed him to enable Lis to come,' Remi interrupted. 'You helped the prophecy.' Remi wasn't quite sure how he felt about this. He couldn't imagine not knowing Lis—despite the risk she was to him, despite what she had done to him—and yet he missed his brother. If his brother had lived, Remi would never have known she existed.

'The man responsible for his death was trying to save him. He was trying to prevent the prophecy and keep your brother as the crown prince. The moment you moved into the position, the future was set.'

'Not as well set as it was thought to be,' Remi murmured, allowing a flame to run over his hand just as Chonglin had done.

'He wanted to save your brother, or at least prevent a new hidden princess. But the crown prince wouldn't listen. He…'

'He told Ta-Sho why he was there,' Remi finished for him.

Chonglin shook his head. 'He tried to explain to your brother that magic is not all it is thought to be. The crown prince had been looking for something; he had sensed that there was more magic out there and begun looking for a girl. The magic was confused by what your brother was saying. He thought the crown prince was trying to bring the prophesied girl to the Palace Isle. He imagined that act the start of the prophecy. In trying to talk about it, they argued. The magic's anger flared, and the crown prince was dead before he realised what he had done. It was an accident, Your Highness. He was trying to save your brother but killed him instead.'

Remi stood stock still. He didn't know what to say. He wasn't sure Chonglin was telling him the truth, but there was something in his manner Remi trusted. Maybe they hadn't tried to kill his brother. Maybe they had tried to keep him alive—tried to save him.

'Who is the girl he was looking for?'

Chonglin shook his head slowly. 'That I don't know. But if your brother had lived, your hidden princess would not have come to the Palace Isle and you would not have the skills you have.'

Remi nodded slowly, closed his eyes and formed another cloud. As he opened his eyes, he breathed out slowly and the lightning flashed around it. He sighed.

'It will come,' the water magic said.

'You don't regret these skills,' Chonglin said slowly. 'Despite your fears and anger, you enjoy what you have.'

Remi huffed and the cloud disappeared. 'I'm no longer sure of what I should think about magic.' *Or Lis,* he added silently. She was so comfortable with who she was and what she could do. Remi wondered if he could ever be the same. He formed another cloud, larger than the last, which darkened quickly before heavy rain fell to the stones at his feet.

He had wanted to blame them, make them pay for what they had done to Ta-Sho, the pain his death had caused their mother, the way his life had changed. But if it was an accident and they had tried to protect him, they may be better men than Remi had imagined. And they may be able to help him find the control he needed to counter what Lis had done to him.

Remi was still distracted from the magic he had managed to form into lightening the day before, although his frustration remained that he hadn't been able to hit the ground. He almost ran into an advisor as he stepped in front of him. Remi was somewhat overwhelmed by the power he held, and control was still his main focus.

'Your Highness,' the advisor said loudly, and he stopped. 'Is there any response from the reports I left for you?'

'What reports?'

The advisor straightened, and his face clouded. 'You can't ignore your duties.' Remi heard his father in the man's voice. 'There is much to do, much to report on. Have you found any sign of the magics?' he asked in a hushed voice.

Remi shook his head.

'Your father wants you on the Palace Isle, but perhaps you should head out again and see what you can find.'

'Perhaps they aren't interested in coming back,' Remi offered.

'Maybe they are biding their time and making a plan. They

were so determined to kill the hidden princess, and then there was nothing.'

'She is not in any danger,' he said quickly.

'I'm sure you do all you can to keep her safe, Your Highness,' the advisor mumbled. 'She is a clever girl; she will make such a wonderful empress.'

Remi nodded. He only managed to keep her out of his head for a short while before she was somehow dragged back. And he was reminded of the link between them and the shared future they would have.

'Have you seen her of late? I half expect to be told to move your desk to her little palace.'

He shook his head. 'I have business to attend to,' he murmured.

'But the reports... You haven't...'

Remi turned on him. 'I will get to them when I am ready.'

The man took a step back before he bowed low.

When Remi made it to the house they had been practicing at, there was no one there. He spent time strengthening his cloud building, but he couldn't make the lightning strike the ground. After an hour or so of frustrating attempts and no sign of the magics, he gave up and headed back out onto the street. As he rounded the end of the street, a loud scream echoed between the palace walls. He raced towards the sound.

He discovered a small group of people gathered in the street. When one of them saw the prince, they raced forward and bowed. 'The hunter is here,' echoed through the group.

'What has happened?' he asked the group.

'Magics,' someone said.

'On the Palace Isle?' he asked, moving through the crowd to find what they were grouped around.

'The magic has returned,' someone else said. 'I heard stories on other islands, but if it is here, then it is back.'

A child started to cry.

Looking through the crowd, Remi made eye contact with Hui

Te-Sze as he stepped forward. 'What is going on? You have been scouring this island for weeks.'

'As have you,' Te-Sze returned, his scarred face pulling against the words.

'Have we missed something?'

'Something big. Have you talked with the princess?'

He shook his head.

'She might be able to help. She can sense things we cannot,' he whispered to keep the news from the crowd around them, which had started to dissipate now that Remi had arrived.

As the crowd cleared, Remi saw the two men, dead. One of them was the one who had been showing him how to use his water skills. The other was someone he didn't recognise. 'Did you kill them both?'

'This one is magic,' the hunter said, poking the water magic with a foot. 'The other was visiting from another island. A minister or some such, going by his clothing. The group didn't recognise him.'

Remi looked at him more closely. He vaguely remembered the man from court, but he wasn't sure. He looked odd. 'What happened to him?'

'Looks like he drowned.'

Remi looked around. They were far from the docks, and although there were rivulets and ponds that ran through the palace, they weren't near any of them.

'Why would they do this?' he asked. They had appeared as though they had been trying to help him, but actions such as these only showed that they were using him. Remi's frustrations at his lack of lightning increased.

'Because they can,' Hui Te-Sze said. 'There are more of them than we thought. As soon as he used his magic, I sensed him, and I arrived just as the other man died.'

'Are you sure...?'

The man turned on him. 'I can tell the difference,' he snapped.

'I know what I know. They are not Hidden,' he added. 'Perhaps you should talk with her some more. She could help us.'

'You said that. Why don't you ask her?'

'Because she can't come out of that palace without your say so.'

'Then perhaps it is for the best, and her own safety, that she stays where she is.'

'You were so determined to end this, certain they were behind your brother's death, and now you don't care that they are here. Are you so concerned for what she is?'

'Why must she enter every conversation?' Remi muttered. 'I am the hunter.'

'And yet the magic has clearly returned. Like the onlookers said, it is appearing more on the other islands. People are dying; the war is returning to us.'

'I don't believe that,' he said.

'I don't care what you believe. It is true.' Te-Sze stepped closer to him as other soldiers appeared. 'Take them to the healers. I want to know exactly how he died, and anything else they can tell me of the other,' he said to the group. 'Something is going on with you, and I don't like it,' he said to Remi.

'Who are you to tell me what I am to do? It is of no consequence if you approve or not.'

The man bowed stiffly. 'Then I will go to where I can get help.'

Remi shook his head. The hunter could petition the emperor all he liked, but he wouldn't get very far there either. Despite what had been happening in their capital, the emperor still believed the magic had been defeated and any sense of a return had been overturned. 'Do what you think you must,' he said, then headed back through the streets. He wanted to return and talk to the magics he had worked with; but, given the hunter's suspicions, he returned to his palace instead.

Lis was surprised by the visit from the hunter. He didn't pause to talk with the men in the yard as he usually did, coming straight into the palace instead. Wei-Song jumped up from the table and bowed low before disappearing and returning with rice wine. Lis didn't know where she kept it or managed to find it for special visitors, but Hui Te-Sze was grateful and smiled kindly as Wei-Song poured it for him where he sat opposite Lis at the table.

'I have not seen you for some time,' she said. 'How are things on the Palace Isle?'

'Not as they should be,' he said, holding out the cup for Wei-Song to pour again.

'Do you need my help?' she asked.

'Perhaps I come to see if you are behind the trouble,' he said, his eyes on the cup.

'You know I'm not, or you wouldn't visit in this way.'

'True,' he said with a laugh, and Lis tried not to wince at the obvious pain it caused him. He glanced at the healer, who watched him.

'Healer Yang has great skill,' she said.

'I am sure he does, but I don't think there is anything that can be done for me. And it reminds me I need to remain vigilant.'

Lis nodded once, and Yang bowed before taking a step back.

'I have suggested your services to the prince, but he feels you would be safer here.'

Lis chewed on her lip and waited. She hadn't seen the prince in some time, and she wondered if he would ever return after learning what he had of his mother.

'Magic has very clearly returned to the Empire and the Palace Isle. The reports grow daily of brazen attacks. They seem to be targeted, but it is still a risk since we can sense them as soon as the magic is used. I managed to kill a water bearer today.' Lis gulped down the fear rising in her chest. 'He was not near here. I think there would be enough soldiers to protect you here, if they knew where you were.'

'I don't think I am as well hidden as you think I am,' she said, 'but I appreciate the men protecting me.'

'You don't fear them?'

'Not like I did,' she said. 'They may have been placed here to stop me escaping, but I understand how they keep me safe.'

'I have asked the prince if I can use you for your sensing skills, but he won't allow it.'

'He doesn't want me to leave,' she said quietly. 'Healer Yang has similar skills in sensing,' she said quickly, looking up at him, and the hunter sat his cup down carefully on the table.

'How similar?' he asked.

'We were both able to sense things you could not.'

'Are you a Hidden?' he asked Yang openly, and Lis held her breath. She didn't want their secrets exposed to this man, but she had to trust him in some way because of the trust he held for her.

'I am,' Yang said, his voice surprisingly strong. 'I could also reduce some of your pain.'

There was a clear hesitation before the hunter nodded once. 'I need a scar to remain,' he said.

Yang bowed before he knelt beside him and held up his hand. Te-Sze nodded once, and then Yang placed a hand over the mark on his face. After a moment, Te-Sze sighed with relief, and although Lis could see that the skin didn't pull in the same way, the scar looked to be the same.

Te-Sze gave Lis a small smile. Then, taking a deep breath, he turned to the healer and pointed to his shoulder. 'Would you mind?'

Yang bowed his head again. 'You will need to remove your armour.'

The man looked at Lis before he unbuckled and slipped the metal from his shoulders. Yang then helped him to remove the leather beneath it, and Lis chewed on her lip to prevent her surprise escaping. The man was well built beneath the armour, clearly a soldier who worked hard, but the skin was red and tight and deeply marked across the left side of his body.

'Not as pretty as you imagined,' he said with a laugh.

Lis smiled with him. 'Not quite what I imagined,' she said, thinking that he did indeed look quite pretty. Despite the redness.

Yang slowly moved his hands over the mark, and the redness faded. The skin didn't look quite so puckered now. The man sighed with the relief. 'If only all the healers could work like this,' he murmured, his eyes closed.

'Cake,' Wei-Song whispered. Lis waved her hand over the table, producing a small plate of cakes.

'That sounds nice,' the hunter said, opening his eyes and looking at the plate before him. 'Just what I need.'

Lis indicated the plate, and he helped himself as Yang continued to work. As Te-Sze rolled his shoulders, Lis was tempted to lean across the table and touch him.

'You will have some work to do to bring the condition back to your muscles, but they will be able to handle it now,' Yang said.

Te-Sze nodded slowly and shrugged his leathers back on. 'Thank you,' he said, reaching for another cake.

'Would you like to stay for dinner?' Lis asked. 'I am sure we have enough.' She looked to Wei-Song, who nodded once.

'I would not like to be a bother.'

Lis shook her head. 'I would like the chance to talk with you,' she said. 'Tell me, have you seen much of the crown prince? He doesn't visit as he did, and I worry that things are not as they should be.'

'We have talked of the increased magic, but the prince doesn't seem to see the same issue as he once would have. I thought that may be because of you, but I think it is something else.'

'He does seem a little different,' Yang said, looking at Lis.

'He is struggling with what I am,' she said, 'and how that will fit with his future. I would like to be of help, but he isn't going to let me.'

'He might allow Yang to be of assistance,' Te-Sze said.

'I'm not keen to leave the princess,' Yang said quickly.

'She is surrounded by soldiers.'

'Who know what she is and may kill her.'

The hunter nodded slowly. 'But I could use your help…'

'I will see what is taking Wei-Song so long,' Lis said.

Beyond the curtain, she magicked up a large meal. Wei-Song started to carry it out to the table. 'Will you let him go?' she asked Lis when she returned for more plates.

'I think we need to, but I understand why he won't.'

'I think you are better able to defend yourself,' Wei-Song said.

'Am I? I can grow flowers.'

'You can move the earth—perhaps you could swallow them whole.'

'Not if they were throwing fire at me. It is up to Yang,' she said, then returned to the main room carrying a bowl of vegetables.

The hunter looked up from the food and smiled. 'If this is a usual meal, I may have to visit more often.'

'You are always welcome.'

'And if I could borrow Yang, perhaps I could leave another hunter to watch over you…'

Lis nodded slowly, looking at Yang, who didn't seem happy at the idea.

'If it could stop the war we fear is coming, it would be better for you to go,' Lis said.

He nodded slowly. 'As you wish, Your Highness.'

He hadn't been so formal with her in a long time. And it tugged at her heart. 'As long as you return.'

He bowed, his smile bright, and she sat back to watch them eat.

25

Remi walked quickly towards the house where he had been working with Chonglin. He had managed to lose the advisor again this morning, but there was something going on with Mu-Phi. She watched him far too closely, and it was unnerving. After the death of the water magic, he had been unable to find Chonglin for several days, but he had returned to the house to practice what he could on his own.

The fire burned quickly whenever he called it, but he was having very little luck with the cloud and rain. He struggled to make it any larger, and the lightning still flashed within the small grey structure rather than hit the ground. Now, with the water magic gone, he doubted he would find anyone else to assist him; and with Chonglin missing, he wondered just what control he could muster on his own.

His temper seemed harder to maintain, he thought as he pushed open the gate. In some ways, he considered returning to the hidden princess compound and using the open space there to see just what he could do. But his dreams of the gate had unsettled him, and there was always the risk of running into Lis.

He stopped in the doorway and sighed. The image of their rose came to mind as he wondered just what they could achieve together. If they worked together, they might actually be able to convince his father and the Empire that there was a way forward. A way to a world like they'd had before the magic war. He missed her, more painfully than he would have expected, and yet the uncertainty of what she was and what she had done to him put a distance between them he wasn't sure how to cross.

Had he put himself in that danger? he wondered, still standing in the doorway. All those nights he had lain against her as the black sickness leached from her… Could that have been the cause of all of this? But then, that had been his fault. That had been him pushing his hatred onto her.

It wasn't hatred she felt; it was fear. After the dream of the gate, she really thought he would burn her to dust. Maybe he would. Maybe he could if he needed to, to save the Empire or himself. He walked unseeing through the small house and out into the rear courtyard. As much as he wanted to be the altruistic prince and sacrifice himself for the Empire, as his brother had done, Remi knew deep down he wanted to live more than he wanted the Empire to succeed.

It was a disappointing revelation. He took a deep breath. The flames danced over his skin and he felt the relief of it, as though keeping the flames from the world caused him pain. He shook his head. The flames threatened for a moment to engulf him completely, but he pulled them back to his hand. He couldn't let his ideas of what Lis should or could be into his mind; it twisted him, and he was struggling enough.

'Your Highness,' a soft voice greeted him. He looked up with surprise to find Chonglin sitting against the wall of the house. A small flame worked its way across his fingers.

'Where have you been?' Remi asked. He wanted to think it was concern, but it was more for himself and his lack of training. His selfishness was more evident in his voice than he would have wished.

'Hiding,' Chonglin said with a strange laugh.

'Hiding?'

'The hunter knows we are here. You saw Li-Ze, his blood spilled out across the street.'

'The water bearer?' Remi sat slowly on a stool that rested against the back of the house. 'Why did he kill the minister?'

'He was to work with us, help us, but he changed his mind.'

'Perhaps he knew just how expendable he was. Killing such a man in the middle of the Palace Isle does you no favours.'

'We are not trying to impress anyone. We don't need to,' Chonglin said, lifting his dark eyes from his hands and staring with the same intensity across at Remi. 'When we rule the Empire, no one will dictate to us how we should behave.'

'Will you kill the common people in the same way?'

'We will do what we must to survive. Your princess is helping the hunter.'

Remi shook his head. He had told Te-Sze that he couldn't use her.

'Your instructions mean nothing. She does what she wants. She might not leave the palace—trying to maintain an image of observing the traditions, perhaps. Yet whatever her reasons, she allowed the healer to go out with the hunter.'

'He can sense the Hidden. It doesn't mean he can sense you or your kind.'

'Your kind,' the man snapped back, and Remi felt the heat rise across his skin. 'You are one of us.'

'The hunters can't sense me; they never could. I don't know what I am, but I am something different from you. And you need me. I am the way you will rule this world.'

'So it is,' the man said, his voice softer, yet Remi sensed something behind his eyes. They might need Remi to be what they wanted, to get what they wanted, but they might not be willing to bow down to him as Emperor once they got it.

'Why should I help you?' Remi asked, standing slowly, the flames still burning in his hand. If only the rain came so easily. 'Why should I turn my back on my family and my bride for the likes of you?'

'Because it is the only way you will be free,' Chonglin said, climbing to his feet. 'You will never be free with her.'

'We could be free together.'

Chonglin shook his head. 'You must see the danger she is to you.'

Remi was more confused than he had been. He wanted so desperately to hate her for what she was, but he was the same. He wanted to blame her for making him what he was. But in his heart, he knew that wasn't true.

'You can't do this without me,' he said.

The man laughed, a high and screechy sound that echoed off the walls. 'We have been doing this a long time without you. We don't need you to win this. But the visions tell us that we can't do this against you. I don't care what you do, but they care. The Empire cares what you are, and they will never accept you as magic.'

'My mother knows what I am.'

'Yes, as she knew what her daughter was. And yet she did all she could to save her from your father. Would she do the same for you?'

'She keeps the secret now.'

'Does she? There are more who know your secret than you would want. Any one of them could tell your father.'

'I can stand up to him.'

'Can you? Can you stand up to Hui Te-Sze as well? How many men might he bring to your little palace of a night, if he knew the truth?'

Remi bit down on his lip. He had told the hunter what he was, in a way. He didn't think the man had believed him. But he doubted Remi and his actions. That had been clear when they had come across the magic. The hunter knew he wasn't acting as he should. Remi wasn't sure who he was fighting any more.

'And the maid, your brother's lover—there is a hatred deep in her. She is willing to kill your bride, no matter what you ask of her or what friendship you think you have.' Remi nodded slowly. 'She might kill you quickly, at least, if she has any love for you left.'

Mu-Phi knew something was different about him. He had hoped it was her frustrations at his protecting Lis, but he knew Chonglin was right.

'You are one of us,' the man continued. 'Whether you are the same or something else. You are magic; you are a threat to the Empire, and the people will not love you for it. You can run back to your little princess, try to mend the hurt between you. But you will always be the magic hunter, the man whose life has been a lie. They won't trust you. They won't forgive you.'

Remi's flame burned brighter, hotter. Again, he feared it would take over his soul and burn him away.

'She doesn't love you, if that was ever important to you. That is not what marriage is. That is not what royalty do. She was just a girl you chose from a small group of girls. It would not have been any different had you chosen another. Whatever you think you have with this girl is an illusion. This was not her choice, but yours and your mother's. Where would she be now if you had chosen another?'

Peng came to mind, the skinny boy he had met on the pier. Lis would consider herself content with that boy, and Remi knew there were still moments when she would rather be there than with him.

Chonglin pushed himself up from the wall. He was right, Remi knew. What he was telling him now, Remi had been telling himself since she had arrived, long before he had known what she was, what he was. This was not the life she wanted. He was not what she wanted.

'You must do what you were meant to do. You must prepare to be Emperor.'

Remi could feel the fire burning. It didn't glow or dance above his skin, but he felt somewhat more in control, despite the fact it burned within him. The cloud formed quickly above him, and as the fire burned hotter, lightning flashed beside him, scorching the flagstones.

'Forget her,' Chonglin whispered. 'Be what you were destined to be.'

26

'The tutors have been told not to travel,' Wei-Song said, entering the palace.

'Travel to where?' Lis asked.

'There are posters up around the island discouraging any movement that isn't necessary,' Yang said.

'When did they go up?' Lis asked.

'Have you not noticed how quiet it has been over the last few days?'

'No quieter than usual. The guards still fill the garden, and I wouldn't be allowed out no matter what posters are around the Palace Isle.'

'The prince isn't going to turn up and take you to your secret training ground,' Yang said. 'No matter what you wish for.'

'It isn't that secret,' she replied, but it was still a place she had kept from them. She didn't fully understand the hidden princess compound, and the last time she had visited had been during a dream in which the prince had tried to kill her again.

'It isn't somewhere we can visit either,' he replied. She tried not to stare at him. She understood his frustrations, but there was nothing she could do to ease them. Nothing she could do to ease her own uncertainty, which she had felt growing over the past few weeks. There were more rumours of magics in the centre of the capital, and she had no idea what the prince had in mind. Nor what he was doing. He hadn't visited again, not since he had discovered his sister living beneath her roof. And Lis couldn't ask the empress about him, for she hadn't seen her either.

'How is your mother?' she asked Wei-Song.

She shook her head. 'I can't get close. As soon as I am seen in the street, I am sent back or the guards want to travel with me.'

Lis studied the woman for a moment.

'I can't hide, not when there is so much uncertainty about magics out there. If I were discovered, it would do more harm for all of us.'

Yang at least had spent some time away from the small palace, searching with the hunter Te-Sze. Although they hadn't found anything of use either. The stories of magics had increased, so Lis was thankful for the visits from the hunter. She thought he visited to see Yang and his healing hands more than to converse with her. She tried to ask after the crown prince as much as she could without sounding desperate, but the longer he stayed away, the more she understood that the prophecy might be right. They weren't working together and would therefore work in opposition.

'Do you think I will survive to become Empress, or will he kill me first?' she asked.

Yang half growled at her before he cleared his throat. 'Why do you always consider the worst scenario before you look for the hope?'

'I haven't much hope left. I don't have the chance to learn what I can do, what I might be capable of. I thought we would learn together, combine our skills.'

'Like you did with the flower?' Wei-Song asked.

'In a way. I would rather we work together, and without seeing him I don't get that chance to build on what we had—the excitement of the magic working together. Instead I am living in fear that we will be facing each other and I'll be trying to meet his fireballs with a rose.'

'You must have more skill than that,' Wei-Song said. 'Maybe you can change what he directs at you. The connection might be more than you think.'

Lis shook her head. As soon as she felt that there was a connection and they might be able to work together for a better future, it all fell apart. 'I don't know what we have or had, but I think it has gone. Can't you find out more? Can you talk with the child and see if the visions have changed?'

Wei-Song shook her head. 'I can't leave you.'

'What of your mother?' Lis asked softly. 'She had dreams of something more.'

'If you want to consider such things, then you have had enough dreams of your own.'

'I need to get out,' Lis cried, desperation overwhelming her. 'I can't spend another day surrounded by soldiers.'

'The hunter calls too often. And he may not be as forgiving as you think if he were to see you throwing your magic around.'

'I hardly throw it,' she said.

'Your cakes might not agree.'

Lis sighed, overwhelmed by the frustration and the unknown of what was to come.

'There will come a time when you can to do more than you think you are capable of,' Wei-Song reassured her. 'It has been seen.'

'But when will that be? If I can't practice and explore what magic I have, then I'll never know what I will be able to do.'

'You have your barrier,' Wei-Song said.

'But I don't know how I did that. I was so busy just trying to protect myself, to keep my magic hidden.'

'And yet you were Hidden all along. How did your father discover your skills?'

'I opened a jade flower on the end of a pin. We talked about this.'

'Tell me more of the dreams with the prince,' Wei-Song

pushed.

Lis shrugged. 'He is exploring, and then he sees me and turns his magic on me.'

'Exploring?' Yang asked.

'The place of the hidden princesses. The black gate,'

'The black gate?' Wei-Song said, standing up.

'You have heard of it?'

'The girl, she told me something of the black gate.'

'What exactly did she tell you? The gate seems to hold answers to something, but then it never gives us what we want to see.'

Wei-Song looked at her closely.

'It has silver symbols on it. But they are sometimes hidden. The prince drew them forward, but they never show the same message. Sometimes I can't understand it at all. In the last dream with the prince, he didn't like the message, and although I couldn't see it, I knew I made him angry—enough that he aimed his anger at me and burnt me to nothing.'

'Then what happened?'

'I woke and found him here, grinning at me with the same hatred, although he wasn't really here. I don't know any more.'

'I think we need to visit this place.'

'What if the prince is waiting for us?' Lis was sure she sounded as scared as she felt. She wanted this to work, yet she was too afraid to test it. 'How can we get there? You have already told me we can't go out.'

'Yang can keep watch.'

'Can I?' he asked.

'People listen to healers,' Wei-Song said.

'That hunter may not.'

'He likes you,' Lis offered.

'And what will you two be doing?'

'Heading for the hidden princesses, to discover what this hidden princess can do to save us,' Wei-Song said quickly.

Lis sighed, and the two of them hid at the same time, heading out carefully through the yard. The stool that had rested against the wall was gone, and Lis wondered if the prince had ordered it moved. She stepped back as the gate suddenly opened and the hunter appeared. She could almost hear Yang groan from the doorway. As he stepped inside, Lis slipped through quickly, Wei-Song only a step behind.

'I'm sorry,' Yang said as the gate closed. 'She isn't well today. Could you call again another time?'

The gate opened again and the hunter appeared, looking disappointed. He sighed before he walked slowly back towards the centre of the island. Lis and Wei-Song headed in the opposite direction, but it wasn't long before they realised he was following them. Wei-Song pulled Lis against a wall, and she held her breath. Te-Sze paused before continuing on, and Lis wondered if he was becoming attuned to what they were. All that time sitting at her table, he might have worked out that he could sense them in a way.

They followed him for a moment before he stopped and turned back, striding towards the main square. Lis held her breath as they waited for his steps to die away before the two of them continued towards the hidden princesses. They walked in silence, in case there was someone else nearby that they couldn't see. Lis still had no idea what was on the other side of the walls around them.

When they reached the hidden princess gate, Lis wondered again what was on the other side of it. Wei-Song stopped and looked over it, her hand on the latch. The gate screeched, but it didn't move. Lis tugged at her and indicated further along the wall. But when they reached the gate she had been using to get in, she found that the latch wouldn't work at all.

Maybe the crown prince had been there and was trying to stop her getting back in. Her hand pulled away from the latch. What if he was here and she was putting Wei-Song in danger as well as herself?

Wei-Song took her hand and pulled her back down the laneway towards the first gate. 'It won't work,' Lis whispered.

Wei-Song took a deep breath and held her hand over the latch. She closed her eyes, and Lis heard the sound of metal scraping against metal. She slowly moved her head to the left, and the gate swung open with a small click.

Lis stepped forward and looked around to ensure no one was near.

Wei-Song pushed it open a little further and then disappeared inside. After what seemed like too long, she reappeared and waved Lis inside.

'How did you do that?' Lis asked when she stood facing the princess inside the compound.

'I am good with metals,' Wei-Song said with a shrug

'You could have done that with the other gate,' Lis whispered, but then she wasn't sure if the prince had been on the other side. She shivered and refocused on the woman before her.

'It was too damaged to move, and this one has been used recently.'

Lis wondered what other skills Wei-Song might have, what else they could do if they had the opportunity to really learn and practice. 'You have more skills than I was aware of,' she said softly, unsure what she felt.

'I have had the chance to learn,' Wei-Song said, turning away from her.

Lis focused then on the world around them. They had entered not far from the quarters of the tutors, if that was what they were. She turned back and looked at the gate, which seemed like the entrance to any other palace on the island. She wondered why she hadn't been able to find this side of it before, but then she had been distracted by the contents of the rooms ahead of her.

As Wei-Song looked around the space, Lis pushed ahead of her towards the end room. She opened the door slowly, worried she might disturb someone on the other side. She paused as the faces stared back at her. Stepping forward, she ran a hand over one of them. She didn't recognise any of them from her dreams. If only she had managed to get paintings of the empresses, she might have been able to learn more.

These faces could have been anyone. Lis gently ran a finger across the mark on the bottom of the tile. She hadn't got anywhere with that either. She couldn't decipher them, and although Yang was sure he had seen something similar, he hadn't been able to remember where. Lis wondered if they were still in existence.

'I thought you said they had gone,' Wei-Song said from the doorway.

'They had,' Lis whispered, scared she would frighten them away. 'I think they only want certain people to see them. Maybe they hid from the prince once he started developing his magic.'

'Maybe someone made them disappear,' Wei-Song suggested.

Lis looked over the walls and ran her hand along another face. There was something familiar about it, but she couldn't place it. But then there were so many faces; it could be that one of them would end up looking like someone else she knew. She gently touched the symbol in the bottom corner, different from the other one she had run her finger over but then similar to others. 'I still don't know what it means.'

'Not a word. Maybe a spell,' Wei-Song said, looking closer.

'A spell?'

'Maybe they link their magic in some way. All those with this symbol have a type of magic like fire or water, something to do with the earth, like yours.'

'But they are all Hidden.'

'Are they?'

'I don't know,' Lis admitted. 'There is so much I don't know, so much I don't understand.'

'Where were you training?'

'Through the black gate,' Lis said, turning from the faces and heading out into the muted sunshine. Although it was still midday, it was the darkest it had been for a long time. Lis wondered if the sun was hiding from the fight that was to come.

Lis paused when they moved past the sleeping quarters, thinking that Wei-Song wanted to go in and look around, but she continued past the building and along the indistinct path. As they rounded the corner, she stopped.

'The black gate?'

Lis nodded. There were no silver symbols visible. She wondered if she would be able to bring anything forward with Wei-Song present, or if it was something only for her and the prince.

Wei-Song ran her hand over it, but it didn't change. 'I can't feel anything within it,' she said.

'Maybe it is only for the prince and I to find,' Lis said.

'You don't call him by name,' Wei-Song said, catching her off guard.

She shrugged and moved into the open space beyond the black gate. She could see the scorch marks on the other gate from this distance, but she wasn't prepared to get closer. The prince had been here and had tried to prevent her entering. She wondered if he would return.

'I'm not sure about this,' she said, turning back to Wei-Song, who stared across the expanse and then up at the wall.

'Is this safe?'

'They can't see us.'

'You are sure?'

Lis nodded. 'We tested it. But I wonder if the prince might return.'

'It might be a chance to find some common ground. There was a connection, so we might be able to connect to you again.'

'It might be too late for that,' Lis said, holding her hand out over the dry earth and summoning a plant up to meet her. She longed for the fire to greet her as it opened its petals, but then she wasn't sure she wanted to see flames.

She sucked in a deep breath, closed her eyes and asked the flower to open.

'There must be more that you can do,' Wei-Song said, and Lis opened her eyes to look at the bright flower before her. She snapped her fingers and it withered to dust. 'Other than food and cakes and plants. You can draw forward what was not really there, but…'

She stopped as Lis waved her hand across the courtyard and the ground shook. A wave of dust moved across the ground, the stones disappearing in its wake.

'That is impressive,' Wei-Song said softly.

'What good would it do?'

'You could unsettle an army,' she said.

Lis shrugged. She moved her hand in a spiral, and a small hole opened in the ground by her feet. When she spiralled faster, the hole grew and the dirt disappeared from beneath it. Lis snapped her fingers and it stopped, then began to fill with water.

'Where did the water come from?' Wei-Song asked.

Lis shrugged again. 'I am just trying things.'

'What about your barrier?' Wei-Song asked.

'I don't know what I did with that,' she said. 'I just knew I had to protect everyone.'

'Can you create a plant that looks like a man?'

'I could try,' Lis said. She held her hand out, and a plant sprouted up before her. Its vines thickened and twisted together, and then the tan-coloured flower opened, looking like a face.

Wei-Song started to laugh.

'You asked for it,' Lis said.

'It is so lifelike,' she said. 'Take a step back and imagine that the flower man is trying to hurt you.'

Lis took several steps back and studied the flower man she had created. She tried to remember the barrier she had made to protect herself from the magics, and to hide her own magic. There had to be a way to keep her safe. But looking at the flower man, she couldn't quite muster it.

'He is trying to kill you,' Wei-Song said.

'But he isn't,' Lis said. She tried again to muster the same feeling, but she couldn't.

'If they find you, they will kill you.'

'I'm Hidden; the same level of fear is not there.'

'If they discover you, they will discover us all, and that will put the prince in greater danger than what he already is.'

Lis shook her head. She imagined him being discovered by his father and the hunter who ate so frequently in her little palace. She could imagine him driving a sharp sword through the prince's chest, causing the same fizzle sound as the magic man who had died in the baths. He might hate her—he might want to kill her himself—but there was something there she had to protect because in protecting him, she protected herself. They fit together.

She heard the crack of the vines before she realised what she had done.

'I knew there was something there,' Wei-Song whispered.

'But I can't do that on demand. I'm still not sure where it comes from.'

'We need to find out,' Wei-Song said, walking over to the remains of the plant. 'Maybe you could create an army,' she mused.

'I don't think that I can get them moving. I make flowers grow.'

'There is more that you can do.'

'I don't know if that is true.'

'Think of the cakes,' Wei-Song offered.

'I don't know how I do that, either. I just want. I think of what I want, which is usually flowers, and then they appear.'

'Even at the end of a jade pin?'

Lis turned and looked over the pond she had created. With a wave of her hand, she moved the earth back. Although the ground was damp, the pond was gone and the flat stones back in place.

'Could you hide the soldiers in the yard?'

She shook her head. 'There are too many who visit. There are too many variables. What if I do something that changes the visions you have—changes what has been seen?'

'I don't see it,' Wei-Song said. 'The child is the one with the visions.'

'Who else has visions?'

'That is an important question,' she said, 'but not one I can answer. There are too many things we don't know. And if you are going to fight the prince, we need to be sure of what you can do and who will work with us.'

'What of the other Hidden? The school?' she asked.

'I can't risk them just yet.'

'But you will risk me?'

'You are destined for this. My family isn't.'

'Your family is a part of this. They are buried in it. And if your brother doesn't kill me, then I will be your family too.'

Wei-Song threw her arms around Lis, scaring her for a moment as she pulled her close. 'You are already my family; you are Hidden. I have a mother, but I don't have a family here. There isn't a brother, there isn't a father and, despite some calling me Princess, I'm not.'

'You are. You are the hidden princess. More so than I am.'

'You, Long Lisabet, are Hidden Princess of Rei-Een. You will carry all the hopes of the world on your shoulders. The Empire looks to you.'

Lis felt her heart stop. 'I can't perform with such pressure, and I can't fight the prince. No matter what he thinks of me.'

'You care for him.' The relief was evident on Wei-Song's face.

'You need me to, I know that. Maybe there is a connection, but I don't know what it is. And there will always be someone else in my heart.'

27

Remi tried not to fidget as he watched General Long walk into the throne room. His father had summoned him without explanation, and Remi wanted to be anywhere but here at this point. The sight of the general was not only a surprise, but it scared him. The man looked older than he had the last time he had visited, more of his hair peppered with silver threads. The two people walking behind him only made him more uncomfortable.

They all bowed low to the emperor, then turned and bowed to Remi. The general gave him a friendly smile, but he couldn't return it. He didn't know what he had heard or what he could say. Remi had promised to watch over his daughter, yet he had nearly killed her; and the more time he spent learning who he truly was, the more he thought he should have.

'It is good to see you again, old friend,' the emperor said, indicating that they rise. 'Your daughter is as beautiful as her mother.'

Remi thought she wasn't nearly as beautiful as her sister, but he pushed the thought quickly from his mind. It no longer mattered what he had thought he felt for the hidden princess. What she represented now was far more important.

'This is your husband?' he asked.

'My new son, Wu Peng,' General Long said.

Remi made the strangled noise before he realised what he had done. The group looked towards him. 'You were to marry the hidden princess,' he said, trying to bring himself to the conversation. The man's face flushed, and the sister fidgeted.

'Peng has been a part of our family for some time,' the general admitted.

'What brings you to the Palace Isle?' the emperor asked, barely looking at Remi as he drew the group's attention back to himself.

The general glanced at Remi before he cleared his throat, and Remi felt his own throat closing. *What did he know?*

'I have heard worrying rumours, Your Eminence, and although she is no longer my daughter, I felt the need to check on my… the hidden princess.'

'What rumours?' the emperor asked.

'That magic has returned to the Empire and it is openly used in the streets.'

'Have you really heard such things so far out on your little island?'

The general nodded and looked again at Remi.

The emperor followed his gaze. 'What have you done to stop this?'

'What am I trying to stop? You have been so sure that magic can't have returned to the Empire.' The emperor glared, but it only increased the fire burning inside Remi, and it took all he had not to release it in the room. 'It is not that it has returned.'

The general opened his mouth and then closed it again.

'It never left. It was never defeated.' Remi stood taller, felt warmer. 'Magics killed my brother, Ta-Sho; they have been hiding and waiting.'

'The Order of Huans,' General Long murmured.

Remi turned and stared at the man. Could he tell him his own daughter was one of the Order?

'I can't believe that,' the emperor said.

'You never have. Not when I warned you, and not when my

brother died. You think you won the war, but you lost.'

The emperor turned white with rage and stood slowly from the throne. The general and his family subtly moved back a step. When Peng moved between the emperor and his wife, Remi decided he was a fickle man. How could he love Lis so completely and then her sister?

Remi stepped forward to meet his father. He could take him now before these people without a thought, and with little effort. He clenched his fists.

'What can you do to stop it?' his father asked, his voice softer, more desperate than Remi expected.

'I may not want to stop it,' Remi admitted.

'You are the Empire's greatest hunter,' the general said, pulling his attention from the emperor.

'I should take you to your daughter.' Eyeing Peng, he walked through the room and out the door. It took a few moments before the Long family followed him.

'What has happened?' General Long asked, racing to catch up with him.

'I will let the hidden princess explain.'

'Is Lis…?' Peng asked.

Remi stopped and turned to the man, who stopped suddenly and took a step back. Remi grinned despite himself, then turned back and moved quickly towards the palace.

'This is not the way,' the general murmured, looking over where the residence used to be.

'She had to be moved for her own protection.'

'From whom?' the general asked, looking him over carefully.

'She'll tell you, I'm sure.'

They continued to walk in silence through the streets and into the quiet corner of the Empire where he had hidden the princess. He pushed open the gate, and the general sucked in a breath.

'What has happened here?' he demanded, taking in the number of soldiers that still filled the small yard of the little palace.

'She wasn't safe,' Remi said, heading for the door.

'She isn't safe,' one of the soldiers muttered, clearly unaware of who he was in the company of. Remi glared at the man, and he snapped back to attention.

Inside the door, he met Hui Te-Sze. 'We need to talk,' he said, bowing.

Remi nodded absently. He had other plans.

'It is nice to see you again,' the general said.

'General Long, how good to see you. Your daughter is always full of fun stories of your little island. I must come and visit with you some time.'

The general smiled kindly and bowed his head. 'We would be honoured,' he said.

'She is very special,' Te-Sze said quietly as he passed the general, but Remi heard him quite clearly and hid his scowl.

The general pushed ahead of him then. Lis looked up from her reading and jumped to her feet, rushing forward. She threw her arms around his neck, and he closed his arms around her.

'Father,' she whispered. 'Why are you here?' She looked over at Remi, her eyes hard. 'It isn't safe.'

'It is not safe for you,' he whispered.

'We already know what she is,' Remi said loudly, stepping into the room, and the general let her go and turned to him. Healer Yang, forever in her company, stepped forward.

'General Long, it is an honour to meet you,' he said, bowing low. Lis stepped out of her father's arms to take Yang by the arm and pull him forward.

'I would like to present Healer Yang, the best healer in the Empire.'

'Don't make up stories,' he chastised her.

'Ting,' Lis said, looking up and noticing her sister. She stepped forward and then stopped. 'Peng?'

He bowed. 'Your Highness,' he said stiffly, and she stepped forward and threw her arms around him.

He looked uncomfortable, but she held tight, and something inside Remi snapped. The fire leapt in his hands before he could stop it, but Lis moved quickly, releasing the man and pushing him back.

The general reached for a sword he no longer carried. Lis had somehow moved between him and her family too quickly, and the flame danced over her arm, catching her dress. Remi stood stunned and watched the material burn as she patted at it.

'Stop,' she said loudly, her voice carrying. He heard the soldiers moving towards the door and extinguished his flame. He shook his head and stepped back. Again, she was protecting him, trying to contain him, and the heat flared again beneath his skin.

'Enough,' she snapped as the soldier stepped inside.

'A minor disagreement,' Remi said, his voice clipped as he waved the man away. He waited while the soldier disappeared. He could hear so much more, as though the air carried the voices to him.

In the silence that followed, Ting started to cry.

'Go,' Lis said.

He shook his head.

'Please. This will only make things worse.'

He grinned at her concern.

'Go!' she said firmly, and he turned and walked to the door.

He turned back, and she maintained her firm stance. The general looked scarier than he imagined, and he understood the fear the magics had felt when they had tried to hide around the Empire.

'I will return for you,' he said.

She only shook her head.

She needed to understand what he knew to be true. She could deny it all she wanted, but they would face each other, the Hidden would be exposed and he would rule the world.

Lis turned back to take her father's arm as he made to go after the prince. He looked at her, then pulled her into his arms. 'I was so worried for you,' he said into her hair.

'I didn't think you could visit anymore,' she murmured into his chest.

'You are no longer my daughter, and yet you always will be.'

She pulled back from him and bowed before him. 'Thank you,' she said softly. 'But it is not safe for them here. Why would you bring Ting?'

'I needed to see that you were safe,' Ting said, but her hand moved across her body. Lis looked to Yang, who nodded once. Her sister had everything Lis had ever wanted and, despite her love for her, it hurt.

'He will kill you,' her father murmured, looking towards the door. 'And all those guards won't stop it.'

'There are less of them than there were. And despite their fears of me, they watch over me. No one knows what the crown prince is,' she said, taking his hand. 'We are surrounded by secrets, but you cannot tell what he is.'

'And what is he exactly?'

'Destiny,' Yang said, indicating the table for her sister as he waved Wei-Song forward. 'Find the wine,' he whispered.

Lis waved her hand over the table, and it filled with bowls of food and rice.

'Cakes,' Wei-Song murmured, and Lis added cakes with a flick of her wrist. She reached for one and Lis smiled, 'Wei-Song, wait for our guests.'

'Wei-Song?' her father said, turning quickly to look over the woman as she pushed a cake into her mouth. 'I...' But he shook his head. 'How can you all be so calm?' he boomed, and Lis worried that the soldiers would be racing back through the door.

'We have had longer to live with this,' she said. 'Much has happened since I came to the Palace Isle.'

'You told me of the man with magic, but the prince killed him.'

Lis indicated the table to her father, who sat beside Peng and looked over the food. 'How long have you been able to do this?'

'A little while. I discovered it by accident, as I have with so much.'

'So many rumours have reached us,' Ting said.

'That surprises me,' Wei-Song said. 'For we have all been very careful. What have you heard?'

'That the princess was living with the royal family and the prince had broken with tradition.'

'I did for a while, until there was an attack on the residence, and then I was moved here. The idea being that less people would know where I was.'

'Did he break with tradition?' Ting pushed.

'I was to be isolated until my training finished, but he spent a lot of time with me.'

'Has that changed?'

'Yes,' Lis said, unsure what else she could add to that.

'How did you feel about him being here?'

'Ting,' her father chastised. 'You shouldn't ask a princess such questions.'

'I am asking my sister such questions. He is to be her husband. Would it not be better to know him?' She looked across at her own husband, but Peng watched Lis.

'It is complicated,' she said. 'Please eat. The food is hot. He was not happy when he discovered what I am.' Lis's hand rested on her father's shoulder. 'But he grew to accept me, in a way. Until his own magic formed. He blames me, and he is right to.'

Wei-Song scoffed, and the general watched her. Lis knew he had some understanding of who she was, but she was grateful he didn't say anything.

'There are many secrets,' Yang said quietly. 'Between us and around us. But the world is changing, and I'm not sure what will happen when everyone knows.'

'He has become what he has been raised to fear,' Lis said. 'We are linked in this, and if we could have found a way to work together… But the time has passed.'

'If the emperor were told…' Peng started.

'The line would end,' Lis said.

'There may be another way,' her father added, looking at Wei-Song.

'The only way is magic,' Wei-Song said, giving him a nod. 'I fear if the Hidden are not involved in ruling our Empire, there will be no Empire left to rule.'

'When will it no longer be a secret?' Ting asked.

Yang smiled. 'A clever question.' He looked to Wei-Song for the answer, but she shook her head.

'We know what will happen, but we have the chance to change it,' Lis said.

'You have found someone with visions?' her father asked, standing quickly from the table. 'Beware the priestess.'

'We are aware of the risk the priestess posed, but she is gone. Replaced by one we think we can trust. Wei-Song found a child,' Lis added.

'She found us, but she wanted to talk with me. She knows my connection to you. She found what she saw so distressing,' she murmured.

'What did she tell you, exactly?' her father asked, and Lis felt the strength behind the words. It reminded her of when she'd gotten in trouble as a child.

Wei-Song looked to Lis and waited for her approval before she answered. 'She saw that the prince and princess are connected, that they must work together to bring magic back to the Empire.'

'How is that possible?' Peng interrupted.

Wei-Song scowled and continued. 'There are secrets between them that may push them apart. If they cannot work together, the prince will rule the Empire alone, and it will be destroyed by the magic he tries to rule.'

General Long blew out a long breath. 'You have worked together?'

Lis nodded.

'But he no longer wants to work with you?'

'It is hard. He discovered some truths that had been kept from him,' Lis said quietly, glancing at Wei-Song. Her father nodded, although Ting screwed up her face in confusion. 'He is certain he can do this on his own.'

'We must stop him,' Peng said.

'How do you propose we do that?' Lis asked, her frustrations at his outbursts causing her own harsh words. 'Do you not think I have tried everything I can with him?'

'Including feeding him your magic and flashing a leg?'

'Peng!' Ting cried. 'Why would you say that? She is his chosen bride. She is the hidden princess. There are rules and traditions she must adhere to as she tries to help the prince. As I helped you.'

He looked down at the table then, and Lis took a deep breath.

'You chose to send me back to him,' she said, surprised at the calm she maintained. 'On that return, I chose to remain here with him. This is what we have, and no matter what I want, it is my fault this has happened to him.'

'It is destiny,' Yang said. 'It is how it was meant to be, and I think we have already established how the traditions have changed over time.'

Her father looked at her then.

'We found where the hidden princesses used to train and live together. That they were all trained until the choice was made. It isn't clear if they killed each other or were killed as they failed tests,' Lis said.

'Where?' he asked.

'In the far northern corner of the island.'

'There is no such place.'

'It is well hidden, for I think they were all Hidden.'

'Hidden?'

'The Order of Huans,' Wei-Song said softly.

Lis's father looked between the two of them, his hand again

reaching for a sword he didn't have, and Lis wondered why he wouldn't have it with him. 'You know of them.'

'I am one of them,' Wei-Song said.

'As am I,' Lis added, bowing her head and disappearing before her father.

He was on his feet in an instant. 'Where did she go?'

'I am right here,' she said, reappearing. 'It is one of the skills of the Hidden. We can hide in plain sight. It also means the hunters can't sense us, and it has kept us safe to a degree.'

'So the hunter I saw coming in…?'

'Hui Te-Sze knows what I am,' Lis said. 'He was keen to have me killed not so long ago, but now he knows I am not a threat to him. He is starting to see that the Order of Huans might be able to help him.'

'His face? The prince?' he asked.

She shook her head. 'They tried to capture some magics, to question them, but they burned their way out.'

'You must be careful,' her father said, stepping forward. 'They can burn right through you.'

'I have seen what they can do,' she said quietly, 'and heard. My maid, U'shi died by fire magic.'

'Were they trying to attack you?'

'They were planning to, but they used her to send a message. Silly girl,' she murmured.

'Why silly?' Ting asked.

'She did something she knew better than to do, and it put her in a place of danger. She always wanted what she couldn't have.'

'What can we do to help?' her father asked.

'There is nothing. A fight is coming, and I can only hope the crown prince and I are on the same side when it comes.'

'And if you are not? How can you defend yourself from a prince with fire?' her father asked in a hushed, frantic voice.

'I can protect myself,' she said.

He shook his head. She closed her eyes and took a deep breath.

'Try to hit me,' she said.

'Lis,' he scolded.

'Try to touch me, at least,' she said, indicating that Yang step further away. She pushed out her barrier just a little as her father stepped forward, grateful they had worked on her skill when she had the chance. He reached forward and frowned.

'Father?' Ting asked.

He grinned and pushed against the barrier again. 'Come and try, Ting.'

As Ting rose slowly from her seat, Lis realised just how much extra weight she carried. She joined her father and then reached out a hand.

'How are you doing that?'

Lis shrugged and expanded it just a little further, pushing against them. They took a step back, and Ting stumbled. Lis reached for her, but Peng was up with his arm around her before she made the distance.

'Does he know you can do that?' Peng asked as he helped Ting back down to the table.

Lis nodded.

'Then he could find a way through it. He could burn his way through.'

'The others couldn't,' she said quickly.

'A couple of magics might be easy compared to the prince,' he muttered.

'Twenty of them certainly tried, but they were no match for our princess,' Yang said. His light voice didn't give away the tension Lis knew he felt. 'She managed to save us all, not just herself.'

Peng looked back at Ting, who tried to push him away. 'I'm fine,' she murmured.

'I worry,' he said softly, and Lis felt the pang of loss at his concern for someone else.

'About her,' Ting whispered. 'It will always be her.'

'You should rest,' Yang said.

She nodded and then flinched, clutching at her side.

Yang knelt beside her, his hand on her arm. Lis smiled at his caring nature. 'Does it hurt often?' he asked.

She shook her head.

As he reached out a hand, he cocked his head to the side. 'Very healthy,' he murmured, and Lis stepped forward.

'Don't tell me,' Ting said quickly. Yang drew his hand back.

'What don't you want me to tell you?' he asked gently. 'You know more than you would say.'

Ting blew out a shaky breath. 'So many try to guess the gender, but I don't want him to be disappointed.'

Yang looked up at Peng, who stepped forward, but Lis's father put a hand out to stop him.

'There is something else,' Yang said, looking at Lis. She had known the moment her sister had entered the palace that she was with child, but she wasn't keen to accept it. It meant so much more now that she had something Lis did not. She had Peng, who should have been hers. Lis didn't even know if she would end up married to the prince, let alone whether they could have children. It hadn't been so long ago that she had considered such a thing, but now she couldn't.

'Magic,' Lis whispered.

The healer nodded. 'It is faint, but there is a sense of it.'

'Could you take it away?' Ting asked. 'Could you heal the baby?'

'There is nothing to heal.'

'We can't have a child with magic in this world. He wouldn't survive beyond birth,' Peng said, the strain and anger evident in his voice. 'It would mean death.'

'It might not,' Lis said.

'The world is changing,' Wei-Song added.

'Until your prince and his magic change it in his favour, and he kills you and all your kind.'

Lis stepped back at his words. Did Peng really think so little of her? What had happened to his wonder and joy at her tricks not so long ago? And he had been happy enough to eat her food.

'This child could be something very special,' she said, stepping up to him. 'This child could be like me, Hidden.'

'Even if you survive to become Empress, it will be many years before you are. What power do you expect to really have?'

'I'm not looking for power. I'm looking to help the crown prince find equality for those with magic, like it used to be.'

'It can never be like that,' Peng said. 'It should never have been like that.'

'Would you rather see the child die?' Ting asked amidst the murmuring.

The pause was too long before he slowly shook his head.

'Guard,' Lis shouted, making her sister jump. A soldier appeared in the doorway, looking a little uncertain. 'My brother wishes to visit the temple. Would you show him the way?'

The man bowed and waited while Lis stared Peng down, and with a scowl he relented and left with the soldier.

'I didn't know he thought like that,' Ting whispered.

'Perhaps you should stay here with your sister. It will be safer for you and the child.' Their father cleared his throat. 'You would have the healers on hand—the best one on hand,' he added, looking to Yang, who bowed low before him.

28

Wei-Song wasn't quite sure how Lis had convinced her this was a good idea. She had been too aware of the risks to even visit with her mother, and now she was dragging a pregnant woman through the unsafe streets of the Palace Isle. It certainly wasn't safe for her to remain with Lis, and the crown prince came to mind.

What might he do? she wondered. There was a real hatred in his eyes when he looked at her, and Wei-Song wondered what could have changed his heart so quickly. Despite what he was and what Lis was, and despite him continuing to cause her pain… Wei-Song knew that he cared for Lis, that he didn't want to hurt her.

She had told him that herself. Called him on his empty promises. And maybe there was more to it than that. Maybe he didn't care. Maybe his concern was in keeping her hidden away until he could work out what to do with her.

Ting pulled her to a stop, and she focused on the world around her. The girl opened her mouth to say something, but Wei-Song held up a finger. Ting nodded in the direction they were headed instead.

Wei-Song tightened her grip on Ting's hand. There seemed too many people ahead of them, as well as not enough. The usual number of visitors to the Palace Isle was never high, but there were even less people moving around the island now. She was sure the

241

restrictions had something to do with that, but there was something else. A fear, perhaps. Yet there also appeared to be far more soldiers than Wei-Song had seen before.

Was this due to the increased threat from the magics? Or was there something else? She gave Ting a gentle tug, and they moved towards the dock. She knew the boatman would be waiting. The master had given instructions that no matter whom he carried to or from the island, he was to be ready for her.

He was just where she expected him to be. As she helped Ting climb into the boat and followed her in without releasing her hand, she saw Hui Te-Sze across the dock looking over another small boat. Without pause, the boatman raised the sail and they moved quickly into deeper water. Still holding tight to Ting, Wei-Song turned back to look over the soldiers and wondered if she would be able to return as soon as she wanted to.

They sailed in silence, still hidden, to the island school, where she was met again by Master Yangshing as they climbed from the boat. She bowed before him but said nothing as she followed him inside, leading the princess's sister by the arm.

'Rest,' she said, showing Ting into a room. 'I will return with tea.'

She slid the door closed behind her and turned to Yangshing.

'What is this?' he asked.

'The princess wants her and her child kept safe. The war we feared is coming. The crown prince won't work with her.'

'Do you think anything could bring them together?'

Wei-Song shook her head. The flames had leapt dangerously in his eyes when he had confronted the general. 'I think it is too late. He has allowed the magics to roam the streets. They killed Minister Xi in broad daylight. It was only when the other hunter was nearby that the magic was discovered.'

'Can you trust Hui Te-Sze?'

'I don't know,' she admitted, pulling the older man away from the door.

'The princess trusts him?'

'She does, but I think she is clutching at people to trust. She is scared of what is to come.'

'Did you learn more of the hidden princesses?'

She nodded. 'Let us sit, and I will tell you as much as I can before I need to return.'

'You aren't staying?'

'I am needed on the Palace Isle.'

'I don't want you caught in the fighting. What can you do?'

'I can try to keep them from killing each other.'

He raised his eyebrows and, with a small smile, walked with her towards his own room.

The child pushed the door open and stared at the woman sleeping in the little room. She had been waiting days for her to arrive. Another one who thought she could change things. She would only put more distance between the prince and princess when they needed to be working together.

'Hello?' the woman asked in a sleepy voice.

'Why are you not at home with your husband?'

'He isn't able to provide for me at the moment,' the woman said, rolling towards her.

'Your sister shouldn't have sent you here,' the girl said. 'It puts us all in danger and will not help your child.'

'What do you know of my child?' Her hand moved protectively over her stomach as she sat up.

'You need to leave,' the little girl said.

The woman shook her head.

'I am sorry,' the girl continued, 'but your child will die. It is better that she dies on your island rather than mine.'

The screaming was unexpected. When Wei-Song appeared in the room, she threw herself at the woman. They wanted the girl's knowledge, wanted to know what she saw, yet they didn't want the truth of it.

'There is a chance,' she said, hiding her face in Wei-Song's skirt.

'Ting, please,' Wei-Song said as the other woman continued to carry on.

'You are not your sister,' the girl said quickly. 'You can do nothing to change the fates.'

'She said the baby would die,' the woman blubbed.

Wei-Song knelt before the child, her hands on her shoulders. 'What did you see?'

'The prince is willing to risk it all, including the princess. If this child is born here, she will bring the wrath of the prince on us. If she is born on her island, we will remain hidden for another generation.'

Wei-Song looked at the woman.

'You can't send me away,' she murmured.

'You told her the baby would die?' Wei-Song asked.

The girl nodded. It would take the mother with her, but she didn't share that. No healer could stop what was to come. 'If the child is born here, the princess will not help us. If the child is born on her island, there is a chance.'

'Peng?' the woman asked.

'He will not hurt you,' the child said. He had already killed her by planting the child in her belly. It was his loss of the princess that had caused his heart to harden, even though he knew he could never have her. She sighed. She wished she didn't know so much of the wishes and thoughts of others. But it was the prince the princess should be thinking of. 'If only she could love him,' she mused. 'If she could see what he is, what he means to her, there may be a chance.'

'Peng?' the woman asked again, rubbing the back of her hand across her cheek.

'The emperor,' the child said, rubbing at her eyes. 'I want to sleep,' she said, taking Wei-Song's hand. 'She needs to leave now.'

Wei-Song watched the small boat sail out into the ocean. Yangshing had used his skill to take Ting's memory of the island away, and Wei-Song wondered if Lis would forgive her. She headed back inside and stood over the sleeping child, always restless. She murmured in her sleep. Wei-Song wondered if there was ever a time the girl wasn't plagued with visions, and if there was some way to help her.

As Wei-Song tried to sneak from the room, the child sat up. 'She will die,' she said. 'The sister—the child will take her on her way to the gods. If she died here, the princess would blame us.'

'She would understand.'

'No, she would not. She would channel her hatred towards the prince instead of working with him, and we would all die.'

'Did you just learn this?'

The girl shook her head. 'I have known for days that this was coming. I could only hope I would have the chance to set it right.'

'Will her family stay away?'

'Wu Peng will take up the sword against her. She represents all that he has lost. And she will lose more than she knew she could. As will you.'

29

Lis sat at the table and watched Wei-Song eat her cakes. 'Tell me again what she said,' she demanded.

Yang paced behind her, clearly unnerved, but his movement annoyed her. She glared at him.

Wei-Song put the cake down. Lis was sure something else had happened that she wasn't saying. But her focus needed to be on the prince.

'You have to find your connection to him,' Wei-Song said, brushing the crumbs from her fingertips.

'I already know there is a connection, from the other stories, and I know we can work together.'

'Although he isn't really willing to work that way now,' Yang said. 'He won't visit, and the last time he came…' He shivered.

Lis remembered the dark and fiery look he had given her. She closed her eyes, and he grinned at her in the darkness. The fire had leapt so quickly into his hands. And she had felt her father's fear. 'He won't work with me,' she whispered. 'But he has been working with someone,' she added.

'Who?' Yang asked sharply, and she looked up at his serious face.

'Magics,' she and Wei-Song said at the same time.

'You have to talk to him,' Yang said, and Lis raised her

eyebrows. 'I know it seems like a strange idea, and I would rather keep you as far from him as possible, but he may listen to you. You could explain the dangers, let him know just what might happen.'

'I think he has a very good idea of what might happen. Something he hopes for.'

'You think he wants the power?'

'I think he is lost. He doesn't know what he has or what to do with it, and then there is the fear from what his father will do when he is discovered. If I were him, I would be trying to find strength to ensure I would stay alive.'

'But it is corrupting him,' Wei-Song said, nodding slowly. 'I think Yang is right. The child is sure you must work together. He cares for you; you could convince him, and maybe we can help each other.'

Lis blinked at her for a moment. 'I don't think he cares for me as he might have done. It is my fault that he is what he is,' she whispered.

'No,' Wei-Song said, leaning across the table and taking her hand.

'I need to see the Imperial Healer,' Yang said loudly. Lis looked at him confused for a moment as he nodded towards the door.

She shook her head, but he glared at her before taking another step towards the door. With a sigh, Lis hid and followed him from the little palace across the garden. As the gate was closed behind Yang, he bowed to her and nodded towards the prince's palace, then headed towards the Imperial Healer's.

Lis walked slowly towards the prince, unsure just what she could say to him if she managed to find him at home at all. She had no idea of his movements, or if Mu-Phi was still present. Had he told her what was going on? Had he shared with her what he wouldn't share with Lis? She knew it was his brother who Mu-Phi still cared for. And again, she wondered what the girl had been doing when he'd died. Why hadn't she been watching over him as closely as she appeared to watch over this prince?

Lis entered the small palace with surprising ease and found the prince pacing back and forth across the small room. Energy buzzed around him, almost sparking. Lis wondered if it was fuelled by his fear of what he was and what he could do. She stood for a long while, watching him, growing more fearful by the minute of what he might do to her, and then she took a deep breath. It was his fear fuelling her own.

She unhid as he paced away from her. When he turned, he continued forward at the fast pace and then stopped suddenly, looking her over. She felt a stab of sadness before his anger filled the room.

As the power of his anger pressed on her, she wondered what other skills he might have. 'I would like to talk,' she said softly, trying not to step back and press herself into the wall.

Mu-Phi appeared beside him, a sword held towards Lis, but he pushed her out of the way and put himself between them. He grunted as the sword sliced through his arm. Lis reached forward as Mu-Phi dropped to her knees.

The prince grabbed Lis by the wrist and dragged her out of the house into the yard. With a quick glance behind him, he let her go. 'What do you want from me?' he asked.

'Nothing,' she said quickly. 'I only want to talk. So much has happened; I am worried for what is to come.'

'What else have you heard? What else do you think I could give you?'

Lis shook her head, unsure how to ask him what she needed to ask. Unsure how to convince him of the importance of the child's words. 'Wei-Song has heard more from someone with visions.'

He scoffed then and turned his back. Lis bit her lip.

'You can't trust what she says,' he murmured.

'The child or Wei-Song?'

He turned, the anger flaring behind his eyes, and she took a step back.

'I don't want you to become what they say you will,' she said quickly.

He drew his sword, surprising her, holding out the sharp point towards her. The rain started to spit.

Lis drew a deep breath. 'We must work together.'

'Must we?' he asked, the grin making her skin crawl.

'If we don't, you will destroy it all.'

'The magic?'

'The Empire,' she whispered.

The rain started to fall more heavily, pushing its way into her clothing, running down her cheeks.

He shook his head. The small tendrils of hair that had escaped their tie stuck to his face, and she wondered why it wasn't as perfectly smooth as it usually was. Even after sleep, he always appeared so perfect.

'If we don't do this together, you will destroy the world,' she said, stepping forward closer to the end of the sword.

He shook his head again. 'I don't need you to be the emperor I am meant to be.' But there was an uncertainty about him, as though he wasn't sure it was the right answer. The wind started to blow about them.

'The magics only want you for the power you will give them.'

'It is you who wants power.'

'No,' she called above the noise of the weather. 'That isn't what I want. We can do this together. They are using you.'

'I can do this,' he screamed above the noise as the wind tried to push against her, the rain almost hiding him from her. 'You will only stop what needs to be done.' But he lowered the sword. 'I know you don't want to be here. I know this is not your choice.'

'I chose to be with you,' she said, hoping he could hear her words above the increasing wind. She tried to shield her eyes from the pelting rain.

'You lie,' he said. The energy was gone from his voice, yet his words reached her with his overwhelming pain. He sheathed his sword and swung around, leaving her alone in the garden.

She headed into the street. He wasn't going to help her. He wasn't going to consider working together. And despite what they had all suggested, she was certain he didn't care for her. Although it hurt that he thought her words were a lie.

The rain continued to push against her, and then an arm closed around her shoulders and she stifled a scream. She looked up at Hui Te-Sze, who nodded and guided her back to her own palace, the wind and rain lessening as they moved away from the prince.

Lis sucked in a sob as they neared her palace, and the hunter's arm closed tighter around her before he stopped. 'It is not safe,' he said.

She nodded slowly, wiping her fingers across her face. She wasn't sure if it was rain or tears, but the world appeared blurry around her. When she looked up, she blinked into the sunlight. She tried to twist back towards the prince's palace, but the hunter held her tight.

'He needs us,' she said.

'There may not be much I can do to help him. He is not what he was.'

Lis shook her head slowly as the tears started to flow again. *What did I think I could do? What difference did I think I could make to the fates?*

Te-Sze sighed and continued towards her palace.

'Do you want me to hide?'

He shook his head but kept them moving quickly forward. It was only as they reached her gate that he released her and bowed before her. 'I am sorry, Your Highness, for my forceful ways.'

She pushed at the gate, and the few soldiers who were present in the yard turned and bowed to her. She feared she would cry again. One man opened his mouth to ask something of the hunter, but he didn't.

'Where are the others?' she asked.

Wei-Song raced from the house, then stopped and bowed.

'Come inside and change, Your Highness,' she said.

Lis looked over the men and then back to the hunter, and she tried not to shiver. She was soaked through. Thunder rumbled in the distance.

'They had more important work to do,' he said.

She raised her eyebrows, and he laughed. 'You are offended now that they don't need to watch over you. That there is a bigger threat to the Empire than a girl who can hide.'

She wanted to laugh with him, but she knew the truth of it—and she didn't know what she could do or how she could face him. She covered her mouth to stifle the sob that threatened to erupt as the tears flowed too freely down her cheeks. The hunter stepped forward, but she put her hand up. 'I am crying for myself,' she said. 'It is my fault we are here, and there is nothing I can do to prevent it. And selfishly, I don't know how I will face it.'

'Come inside,' he said kindly, taking her arm and guiding her past Wei-Song into the house. 'You need to change before you catch your death.'

She turned slowly on the spot and his eyes widened. She was dry, but she shivered. 'I can't reach him,' she murmured.

'I don't think anyone can,' Te-Sze said, staring at her.

'I am sorry,' she said.

'What else?'

She waved her hand at the table, and it filled with cakes. Then she moved back to the door, looking out at a grey sky. 'Where did they go?' she asked, turning back to the hunter.

'There are more magics on the streets. They seem to hold no fear, and I worry that this will escalate beyond what we can fight.'

'Yang went to the healers.' Lis strode towards the gate, and a young soldier stepped into her path. She turned back to the hunter to plead her case when the young man bowed low before her.

'I shall go, Your Highness,' he said. 'Hui Te-Sze is correct. The fighting will soon be upon us, and you should not be in the streets.'

'I may be the only one to prevent this.'

She could feel the doubt radiate from the young man before he bowed again and disappeared through the gate. This was happening much faster than she had expected. In her vain attempt to fix things, she may have made them worse. She looked up at the sky, the clouds thick and dark and low as they moved towards her.

'What can I do?' she asked the hunter, heading back inside. 'He won't work with me. I have only made things worse.'

Wei-Song shook her head. 'He cares for you,' she repeated.

'It isn't enough. I don't care for him in the same way. I care more for stopping this.'

Wei-Song looked down, and the hunter glanced at her. 'What do you know?' he asked.

'We have heard various prophecies and visions that all lead to the crown prince and the hidden princess,' Wei-Song said.

'That they will work against us with their magic?'

'No,' she said sharply. 'That they must work together to save the Empire. If they don't, the crown prince will destroy it.'

The man ran a hand over his scarred face. 'He won't work with you.'

'Not now,' Lis agreed. 'I fear that I am the reason he is what he is, and he cannot forgive me.'

'Mu-Phi cannot know the truth, or she would have come to me.'

'She cares for the prince. I don't know what she might do if she were to discover the truth of him. He is strong, and I fear he is stronger than anything I can do.'

'Then we must ensure you are strong enough to help us save the Empire.'

'Do you propose to tell the emperor?' Lis asked.

Te-Sze stared beyond her.

'He should know,' she answered for him.

Yang stumbled in, the soldier beneath his arm, and Lis raced forward.

'There are magics in the streets,' he said.

'Stay here,' the hunter said, heading for the door.

'The crown prince is with them,' Yang said, his voice barely audible above the loud beat of her heart.

'I'm not ready,' Lis said.

'I'm not sure any of us are,' the hunter agreed.

'It will not be safe anywhere if they have started this. The only way to end it is for us to face each other.'

30

General Zho-Hou stared at Lis across the table as though she had lost her mind completely, then turned to the hunter, Te-Sze. 'You cannot seriously consider this.'

Hui Te-Sze looked to Lis before he nodded. 'It might be the only way. Being able to hunt them out is not enough. They have already brought this to the streets.'

'The emperor will not like this turn of events,' the general said. 'I have already had to explain to him that his son has appeared amongst the enemy.'

'How did he take the news?' Lis asked carefully.

The general shook his head. 'He thinks the prince is trying to infiltrate them in some way.'

Lis nodded slowly. 'If we are able to turn things around, if I could gain his trust, then he would not have to face his father's anger when all of this is over.'

'You said yourself that the connection is missing, that he will fight you.' Te-Sze said.

'We can't unleash the armies of the Empire on the crown prince,' she said.

'We can't face an army of magics with the hidden princess at the front of ours,' the general returned.

'I may be able to prevent this. I may be able to protect

everyone.'

'And if you can't?' Yang asked.

Lis laced her fingers together and studied them rather than the four looking over her.

'What if she were towards the back? Out of sight, but helping in some way?' Te-Sze asked.

'You are talking of using magic to fight magic,' the general boomed. 'I can't believe we are even discussing this. I can't believe you have let her live this long.'

The hunter moved so quickly that the table shifted, and Lis was knocked back. He put himself between them.

'I wouldn't hurt her,' the general snapped. 'I have known her father longer than she has lived. This would destroy him.'

'He knows what I am,' she murmured.

'But does he know you plan to run into battle against we don't know what? Does he know the risk we face?'

She shook her head.

'Perhaps the princess's skills will help end this sooner.'

The general sighed and stepped back from the table. 'Show me this barrier,' he demanded.

Lis held her hand out and he raced forward, then bounced back as he hit her invisible wall. The hunter wasn't quick enough when the general drew a sword and pushed forward, but it too was deflected.

He sheathed the sword, and the hunter gaped at him. 'What if it hadn't held?'

'Then we would know it would do nothing to protect her when faced with whatever we might face out there.' He pointed out beyond the palace, where Lis noticed the dark clouds still hung over the Palace Isle, growing darker with every moment. Was that the prince's doing? Had she upset him by trying to talk to him? Could she be the true cause of all of this?

A soldier ran into the house, startling Lis.

'Magics are gathering in the main square,' he said. 'The soldiers keep a close watch, but the storm seems far worse there.'

Lis nodded. He bowed towards her, then turned expectantly to the general.

'Tell me you can do more than grow flowers,' he murmured.

Lis nodded once, but she wasn't sure just what she could do, particularly when faced with the fear of so many, and the prince across from her. She didn't know what he might be able to do with his fire. As she watched the dark clouds swirl and lightning flash, she was even more certain the storm was caused by him.

'What if he twists what I have?' she asked Wei-Song, who had remained silent at the back of the room.

Wei-Song shook her head once.

'Could that happen?' the general asked.

'We worked together briefly. He changed what I made, and I did the same. What if we can still influence each other?'

'If that were the case, you may have been able to reach him before we got to this point. Is there any sign of the emperor?' he asked the man who had entered.

He shook his head.

'He will let us deal with this,' Te-Sze said softly. 'We might all be dead by the end of the day.' He looked directly at Lis. 'Or you may be able to save us after all. We have no choice but to take you with us.'

'I will come too,' Wei-Song said quietly.

'I think you would be best served here.'

Wei-Song held out her hand, and the temperature in the room dropped dramatically. The steam disappeared from the kettle, and the coals died. Lis shivered as she noticed the general's face pale.

'What can you do?' the general asked Yang sharply.

'Other than heal others quite quickly, not much. But that may be useful with so many swords around.'

Lis shook her head.

'We are all a part of this,' he said.

She was scared of what they might find, and she wasn't sure she would be able to do anything in the face of the prince with his fire.

They had barely made it out of the gate when the first fireball sailed towards them and a scream went up from the nearest soldier. Lis threw her shield forward. It deflected the fireball, but the barrier disappeared around them as another fireball skimmed the general's shoulder. She tried again to push out her barrier, but it wasn't working like it had before. She couldn't hold it in place—it moved in a wave and disappeared. She wasn't sure she could maintain it.

She sucked in a deep breath as a man strode forward and lightning struck the ground before him. Lis pushed her hand slowly forward, focused on the ground, and it moved in a wave beneath the men growing closer. Some fell while some only stumbled, but continued towards them. The rain started, not as heavy as she had experienced before, but it was cold and sharp.

Yang shivered beside Lis, and she wondered if the cold rain would affect the fire bearers. But the flames continued to burn in the hands of the man before her. He hadn't lost his footing enough to fall, and he was focused on her.

She made the earth move again, but instead of just moving the stones, she pushed them into the earth until his feet disappeared beneath the surface with them. He growled, and the flame grew higher in his hand. Lis hoped she could maintain the barrier if he threw it, but his face screwed in concentration as the flame flickered in his hand.

He opened his other hand, revealing another bright fire. That too started to splutter, and Lis allowed her hand to drop as she watched it.

'What are you doing?' Wei-Song cried, and Lis looked across at the woman with her hand outstretched towards the fire bearer. 'He is not the only threat.'

As his flames died down to nearly nothing, Lis willed the ground to open and pull him deeper. He forgot the fire and struggled to release himself as he sank deeper into the road. Another man near him faltered, and Lis caught him in the same way.

Lightning struck the ground just before her. She jumped, losing her focus on the ground, but the two men appeared to be stuck fast. Another lightning bolt struck behind her, and she turned just as the young soldier went down.

'Yang,' she cried, but he was already at the soldier's side. He shook his head.

This time, the lightning wasn't just taking them out of the fight, as with the emperor when they were attacked in the throne room. This time, they were taking them out of the fight for good. Lis tried not to cry. This was far more than she'd expected—this wasn't playing games with the prince in the courtyard of the hidden princesses.

'You knew this would be the risk,' the general said, too close to her, and she startled. 'Find a way to be what you need to be.'

She nodded slowly, then took a deep breath and pulled the barrier close around her. She held in everything she had. 'When I say the word, you must drop to the ground.'

She closed her eyes, hoping that this would work as it had before and not kill those with her. She blew out a soft breath, pushing her barrier out a little, and it maintained its integrity. 'Now,' she shouted as she pushed with everything she had.

The men around her dropped, pulling others with them, and she heard the fizzle of dying magic and the crack of breaking bones. She wanted to close her eyes again at the idea of what she had done and what her actions made her. But she didn't. She held out her hand to the general and he took it, his grip strong and his grin broad as he climbed to his feet.

'I am impressed, Your Highness.'

'I'm not sure that I am,' she said.

'Battle is bloody,' he said, clapping her on the shoulder. 'And we have not seen the beginning of it yet.'

Lis swallowed down the rising bile as she looked over the remains of the magics spread across the street around them. They had only lost one soldier, but the sky above them was still dark and, in the distance, rain fell in the main square. The usually bright spire of the temple was dull and grey, reflecting the sky.

31

Their travel to the main square of the Palace Isle was hampered by other magics, and Lis wondered where they could have all come from. When five men appeared, blocking the street, she pushed her barrier forward without pausing, knocking them to the ground. One had thrown a fireball, but it died as it hit her barrier.

The general cocked his head to the side and then turned to her seriously. 'Are you getting stronger?' he asked.

'Why?' she returned, coming to a stop.

'The fire wouldn't have died like that. He was still strong behind it.'

She shrugged.

'Do you feel different?'

'I have just killed men. Magic or not, I feel different for it,' she snapped, stepping forward. He grabbed her arm, pulling her to a stop. 'I have allowed myself to let my magic be what it needs to be,' she admitted. 'I have spent my whole life in hiding. Whether my father thought me safe on the island or not, I never tested what I could truly become. There is no need to hold back now,' she said, turning again, and he released his hold. She still wore the flowing silk she would have worn in her palace. Now, with only a thought, she changed into something far more suitable for battle.

'Can you add armour to that?' the general asked behind her. She

260

turned to find the group standing still, watching her closely, some of the soldiers with a hint of awe.

'I have my shield,' she said. 'This small group is not going to be able to defeat whatever we might find in the centre of the island. Can I suggest we try to meet with more of our allies before we get there?'

Hui Te-Sze smiled and bowed low. He nodded once as he straightened and took the lead of the group. Around the next corner, two magics stood across the narrow street. Lis was waiting for the fire to start in their hands when she dropped to her knees, coughing up water.

She was drowning. She could feel the water filling her lungs, and there was nothing she could do. She tried pushing out her shield, but it faltered, and although it gave her a moment to suck in a deep breath, the water soon returned.

The rain had returned and fell heavier around them. She tried to focus on those around her, but the world appeared blurry, as though she were underwater.

She shivered as the rain pushed into her clothes, and she wondered absently if armour would have prevented it. She could feel the world slipping around her as she knelt on her hands and knees in the street. She pushed into the earth, trying to push the water filling her away from her. A crack appeared, and the street opened up directly in front of her before running towards the two men standing before her. They tried to move out of the way, but as one slipped into the fissure, it started to fill with water. Lis wasn't sure if she had pulled the water from her drowning lungs or if she pulled it from beneath the street.

As he fell into the widening river, he sank quickly into the water and Lis sucked in a ragged breath. The other man turned his focus on her, but she raised her hand and the ground beneath his feet gave way. He too disappeared into the water. Lis stood slowly. Her chest burned as the air tried to fill her lungs, and she coughed. She waved her hand over the rough river that had grown through the street. It disappeared, the road returning to what it was.

She sighed and stumbled forward as the general put his arm around her. 'Your armour might not be enough,' he said softly.

She nodded and continued with him supporting her as her breathing returned to normal and the burning sensation in her chest died down. As they rounded the next corner, they discovered more soldiers, and Lis realised that Yang walked beside her, his hand on her shoulder.

'Thank you,' she murmured, pushing him off. 'You need to keep some of that strength.'

He smiled and bowed. 'I am sure you will put yourself in far more danger before this day is out.'

A soldier she didn't recognise moved forward and bowed to the general. Then he focused on her and stammered, 'Why would you bring the princess into this?'

'She can help us,' the general admitted. 'Without her, we might not have made it from her palace to here.'

'The prince...' he started, but he clearly didn't know how to explain any of what he had seen.

'We know,' she said kindly. 'Where is he?'

He indicated over his shoulder. 'They surround the temple and have tried to destroy several buildings, but as yet they haven't been able to breach the throne room.'

'You think they would try to reach the emperor?'

'He has called for his father repeatedly, but he will not come. Several others have tried to reach the emperor, but so far we have managed to push them back.'

Lis walked past him to the end of the street, which looked out over the main square. So many men and soldiers filled the space. Where could they have all come from? The soldiers outnumbered the magics, but given their various skills she feared the soldiers were more likely outmatched.

The prince sat idly on the steps. He looked towards the throne room from time to time, but otherwise he was focused on his hand.

Lis stepped forward, and the soldier pulled her back.

'He has called for you as well,' he said softly. 'I don't know what he thinks he can get from you, but the flames dance over his skin when he speaks of you, and they seem to glow brighter.'

Lis chewed on her lip. What did he hope would come of their meeting in such a way? Did he simply hope he could force her out of hiding and end this?

More soldiers moved into the end of the street, blocking her access to the prince and his to her. A soldier amongst the group growled, and she turned to find Mu-Phi looking out into the square. She hadn't known what he was then, but Lis wondered if the girl now blamed the prince for her lover's death.

She turned and met Lis's eyes, then lunged forward only to be blocked by another strong arm.

'She is on our side,' Hui Te-Sze said.

'How can she be? She has magic,' she spat.

Silence descended on the square behind her, and Lis stepped forward to look through the gaps in the soldiers to see what had happened.

'No matter what happens,' Te-Sze said, 'you are our last line. You must wait.'

She nodded, but she was focused on the prince. He stood on the steps, the fire burning bright in his hand. 'Will you not come out to see what you have created?' he shouted into the silence, and Lis looked towards the steps to the throne room. There was no sign of his father. The fire flared in his hand and then he held out the other, which also contained a flame. When his hands came together, she tried not to call out as the fire grew into a fireball between them. With seemingly little effort, he lobbed it towards the throne room. It burst apart on the stone steps, doing little damage. Lis wondered what he could destroy if he was determined enough.

'He wants the throne,' someone whispered nearby, and she sighed.

'What does he think his father can give him?' Lis asked no one in particular.

'He sees nothing as he did,' Mu-Phi spat.

The dark cloud above them started to rain again, and Lis shivered as the sharp, needle-like droplets hit her skin. Then, almost as quickly, they stopped. Lis looked up at the dark cloud and then around the square as snow drifted down around them. She turned and found Wei-Song with her arms stretched above her, her eyes closed and a look of concentration etched into her features.

It was beautiful. Lis turned back to the prince as he stepped forward, formed another fireball and threw it up into the cloud. It petered out before reaching it. The prince scowled, and Lis could feel his anger flow across the square, hot and hard. Lightning flashed through the cloud before the deep rumble of thunder made her shiver.

Mu-Phi was suddenly running across the square, and Lis wondered how she had made it between the soldiers. Several others ran out to join her from other streets and alleys that edged the square, and some of the soldiers who had stood silently watching them moved forward.

The world descended into chaos, and Lis could do nothing but watch as the men blocked her path.

'Last resort,' the general murmured.

Despite the maid's hatred for her, Lis couldn't let Mu-Phi run to her death. The prince remained on the steps, but the other men around him rushed forward to meet the small force racing towards them. The snow continued to fall, and it melted as it reached the stones, making them shiny and, Lis guessed, slippery. Then it turned to steam as the fire moved around the square, the world almost warming around her. Mu-Phi was still making a straight line for the prince. Lis couldn't look away, too scared of what the woman might do when she reached him.

The sword Mu-Phi carried stretched out towards the prince. Lis was too far away to see if she had struck him or not, but he glided away from her, and Lis could feel his anger swell. Mu-Phi turned to follow the prince, but she dropped suddenly to her knees as a magic reached out and put a hand to her shoulder.

Lis closed her eyes. She turned back to the square quickly at the sound of the fizzle of magic, but there appeared to be more of the soldiers down than those with magic. She shook her head. This would be a slow slaughter if she allowed it to continue. Even if they sent every man they had out to meet them, the magics were too strong. They needed more; they needed a decoy.

Lis looked back at Wei-Song, who was still trying hard to pull the heat from the air. Lis reached out between the soldiers and blew out a slow breath. The ground creaked and split as plants pushed their way through the rocky surface. They formed quickly into thick vines, taking the shape of men and reaching forward. The magics turned their attention on them, while the soldiers still standing didn't know whether to get out of the way or attack. The ground bubbled and moved as her plant soldiers pushed forward. A fireball hit one, and it burst into flames. Lis was tempted to pull her hand away, feeling the heat of the prince's anger in the flames. She blew out another soft, long breath, and the plant soldiers grew taller, thicker, broader. The five of them closed in on the temple before one was struck with lightning.

Another suddenly reached out with thick tendrils and grabbed a magic close to it. It pulled him close and wound tightly around him, keeping him locked against the chest of the plant-man that continued to move forward. Lis could hear the fizzle of his dying magic. Although she felt sick, she pushed on.

'Do you want to destroy me?' the prince's voice called out amongst the noise. 'I thought you wanted to work together?'

The plant men stopped, but the noise of the square continued.

Lis pushed her way out between the soldiers to stand within the square. The prince continued to look around for a sign of her. He stepped slowly down the steps of the temple.

'Where is my hidden princess?' he called.

Lis flicked her hand and pushed a wave across the surface of the island. The movement unsettled many of the magics and some of the soldiers. She had tried to slow it around them, but she wasn't quite sure she knew what she was doing. She pushed a plant up to steady a soldier as a magic rushed him, and the fizzle echoed through the now-silent square.

'You can end this,' she called to the prince, now staring her down across the distance.

'You will have to end this, by destroying me or dying.'

'I don't want to hurt you,' she returned. 'I know what you can be.'

'I know what I am. And when I am Emperor, this world will be a very different place.' The flames danced over his skin, along his sleeves. They danced in the dim light of the storm clouds, where the lightning still flashed and the thunder rumbled a little less loudly. At another time, in another place, Lis thought it would have looked beautiful. As though a fire beast lived within him and if he asked, it would help him rather than burn with his fury as it did now.

Lis sent a small wave through the ground to meet him, but he quickly directed his fire into the ground at his feet and the wave stopped. He grinned at Lis across the expanse, and she could see the fire dancing in his eyes. They would never be able to work together. He was determined now, no matter the secrets, that there was nothing for them.

Lis pushed the barrier forward, wondering what would happen to her when she was no longer a hidden princess. Would there be a world left where she could return to her father and the island home she had loved so much?

The prince met her with more fire than she realised he could muster. It licked over the barrier, and she felt the heat of it push against her skin despite the distance between them. Then it started to cool, and Lis glanced at Wei-Song standing beside her, her hand outstretched.

The world erupted into chaos around them. Magics raced forward to meet soldiers with nothing more than sharp swords and shields. Flames danced around Lis while rain and snow continued to fall. The wind picked up, blowing debris around them, and Lis could do nothing but push back against the prince.

She tried to create another plant soldier to distract him, but he burnt the shoots before they could grow to anything of use. If only she could contain him.

She tried again, willing a small shoot from between the stones behind him. His fire seemed to intensify as her barrier thinned a little while she tried to use her magic for something else. She stepped forward slowly. He did the same. The push became more intense, the flames hotter, and again she thought she could see something else around him. Something separate from him and part of him at the same time. She closed her eyes and could see the whole world burning as it had in her dreams not so long ago, although it felt like another lifetime. When she too had burned along with the prince. Every building burned, as did those in the square around them. And she faltered, unsure if it was real or her dream.

She pushed forward suddenly, knocking him from his feet, and she used the distraction to pull the plant from the ground and create a solid cage around him. His eyes flashed with anger again. As Lis took another step forward, the cage burst into flames and disintegrated to nothing. She didn't have the skills to create anything that would contain him. And then she wondered about her barrier.

If they could be inside it together, he wouldn't be able to burn anything around him. But she was sure he would destroy her at the same time, and then the shield would fail and he would go back to destroying the world. She wondered, as she stepped closer and flicked the shield at him to deflect the fireball he threw, if she could wrap it around him.

32

Yang was focused on Lis's back, worried she was getting far too close. He knew she still felt there was a chance, that something was there for the prince that would allow him to want to connect and save them all from another war.

But Yang knew there was nothing now. The crown prince almost glowed with the fire. Then Lis did something different with her hands—he wasn't sure what, but the following explosion was enough to knock everyone in the square to the ground.

He staggered forward. The snow fell heavily across the square, soldiers and magics alike lying unmoving or slowly climbing to their feet. The dark clouds still hung thick above them. If the magics had been stopped, he had thought their magic would dissipate. But it hadn't, and the lightning flashed.

Yang pulled himself to his feet and headed towards Wei-Song, who was kneeling in the snow. He couldn't see Lis, but he was sure they were together. As he staggered towards them, the men on the ground starting to move. Magic flared in the air and a soldier cried out.

He couldn't see her.

Wei-Song looked around, but when she locked eyes on Yang, she shook her head. Panic roiled in his stomach as he continued towards her. 'Where is she?' he asked.

'I don't know,' she cried, surprising him by throwing herself into his arms as he dropped to his knees beside her.

'What did she do?'

'I think she was trying to slow him down, but he was too strong,' she said.

Fire and lightning flared across the square, and Yang reluctantly pulled back from Wei-Song to help her to her feet. There wasn't the same power behind the magic as there had been, and when he looked around he couldn't see the prince.

Something dark and charred caught his eye. Despite the movement around him, Yang pushed forward, dragging Wei-Song behind him.

Could it be that they had killed each other? he wondered as he stood over the dark mass on the stones. The world was unnaturally quiet around him; maybe others had the same thought. Wei-Song squeezed his hand, and pain overwhelmed his senses.

'Yang,' Wei-Song's voice echoed through the fog filling his mind. 'She's there,' she whispered.

Hope filled his chest, pushing out the fear as he turned to look where Wei-Song pointed. They raced together towards the edge of the square.

At the entrance to a small street, he looked over Lis's bruised and battered body. He leaned forward and grabbed clumsily at her wrist. She made no movement to resist him, and her hand hung limp. He closed his eyes and took a deep breath, feeling the slow ebb of life running through her. He looked back over his shoulder towards where the magics had gone.

The magics had disappeared from the square. As some soldiers looked warily in their direction, the general and the hunter strode towards them. Lis remained unmoving.

'Get her off the island,' the general whispered hoarsely. 'Take her home to her father to hide.'

'Or bury,' the hunter said, the tear clear on his cheek. Yang could feel the sadness pushing across the square.

Yang pulled her into his arms and staggered to his feet. Wei-Song put her hand to his elbow, and he felt the flow of magic give him strength. He bowed to the general and hurried through the soldiers who moved closer, worried they may realise she was not as dead as they believed. He didn't know how they would react. They all knew what she was, but could they consider working with the Hidden as the general and the hunter had? Once the emperor had his say, Yang was sure the Hidden would be in just as much danger as the others.

He didn't know what was to come as he held her close, allowing the tears of his fear to flow freely, letting those around him think she was gone. It might be the only way to keep her safe.

33

In the distant room of the temple, the priestesses sat in silence. The magic of the white stone kept the space protected from the noise of the battle going on around them. They had no idea if the fighting continued or had ended. The high priestess fought to keep her eyes closed and her mind focused on the visions the gods provided as she wondered at what the prince and princess might have done to each other.

When the fighting had started, there were some amongst them who feared it would come to them, working its way inside the temple and discovering what they were. The magics knew far too well just what power the priestesses had, and the high priestess wondered who had shared their secret.

She knew they were safe from both the fighting and discovery; she was more distressed by the visions she had been granted. The future before her was changing, fuzzy. She wasn't sure if that was because of the decisions being made on the battlefield or if the decisions of importance were yet to come. Each moment changed the vision; every step a soldier took, or magical power used, what she saw of the future was altered.

The magic was strong, as was the prince. She had expected him to lead the magics to victory over the Empire's soldiers with little effort. Yet it had not happened as she had hoped, and the visions showed her that many more than expected had followed the princess into battle. The general and the hunter amongst them, men she hadn't expected to stand against the prince, no matter what magic he had.

Why didn't I see that before? Surely the gods would have realised these men would follow the girl.

The visions faded as her frustrations increased. She looked over the room, where the other priestesses also appeared to be struggling to see what was to come. Some sat rather than knelt, looking down at their hands instead of keeping their eyes closed. Those who remained in their prayer positions wore pained or frustrated expressions.

The high priestess climbed slowly to her feet. Several of the priestesses looked up at her, but no one questioned why she no longer tried to pray. *When the world is clear, we should return to the Sacred Isle*, she thought, looking over the group. Perhaps when they were all together with others of their kind in such a place, the future would become clearer. She knew there were others headed to the Sacred Isle already. Young girls with the skill of visions who had heard the call, who knew it was the place they were meant to be.

There was one who fought the call. The high priestess wasn't surprised; there was one in every generation, one who thought she was better placed to tell others of what she saw. But then there had been such a girl already. The high priestess had seen her sharing the visions, but she had been sickly and had seen little. This other child was very strong. She saw far more than the high priestess would have expected for one of her age. She appeared to have a strong link to the gods, and she had impressed upon the little princess Wei-Song just what the crown prince and hidden princess could be together.

The high priestess looked over the mess that was the meditation room and headed out through the temple. She glanced over the gods and their offerings as she made her way towards the door, but she didn't pause or pray before any. Standing at the base of the stairs, she could hear no sound of fighting, and she wondered if it had ended. She closed her eyes as she emerged from the doorway of the temple. She wanted to see what the gods would show her before she looked over the world before her.

The visions that formed were fuzzy, and when she searched for the prince in them, she couldn't find him. She knew she should allow the visions to come in without pushing for something. But she was becoming desperate. She sucked in a deep breath and opened her eyes. The main square of the Palace Isle was not what she expected.

The smooth stone surface of the square had been ripped open; mud and blood and plant debris littered the space. Soldiers and magics lay dead, unevenly spaced throughout the area, swords abandoned. A faint mist hung just above the fallen. It appeared as though neither side had won.

She took a step forward. There was no sign of the princess or the prince. *Could they have run away together? Or have they killed each other?* She didn't know which she hoped was true.

They needed him to bring the magic back, but his betrayal of his father might be enough to shift the balance of power and put them where they needed to be. Surely the Empire couldn't believe in the royal family now that the magic war had returned, and to the very centre of Rei-Een.

The residue of magic was thick in the air, but there was no one nearby. It appeared that even the soldiers had disappeared, but then she saw the general. He moved slowly through the dead, directing the men behind him. The high priestess focused on the man and could feel the sadness emanating from him. But she wasn't sure if it was because of the situation or the dead.

She took another step forward and closed her eyes. An image of the princess came to her, lying lifeless in the arms of the healer with tears tracking down his cheeks. Uncertainty and fear in those around them.

She opened her eyes, unable to contain her smile. *She is gone.* But had the magics been killed, or had they escaped?

'General Zho-Hou,' she said softly, walking towards him through the dead. The low mist was becoming thicker to fill the square, and she wondered if it was a remnant of the magic or the weather. She glanced up at a dark sky that warned of a coming storm. But then it might be that the storm was still clearing.

He bowed his head to her and then pointed at the man on the ground at his feet. Several of the men behind him moved forward, picked him up and disappeared. 'It appears to be over,' he said softly, walking past her to another man, whom he tapped with his foot before moving on.

'Are not all the dead worthy of your time?' she asked.

'Not all are dead,' he answered without looking back at her. 'Once we have those who are injured safely with the healers, we shall return for the dead. They will all be burned here. Ours and theirs alike. I apologise for the stench that will fill your temple.'

She screwed up her nose. 'I have decided to send the remaining priestesses to the Sacred Isle. I fear it is not safe enough for them here.'

'Everyone else is leaving, and there would be no one for you to advise if you were to remain.'

'Surely the royal family would need our council.'

He laughed, the sound disappearing oddly into the mist that surrounded them. 'There is little you could offer them. Their princess is lost, their prince an unknown.'

'He lives?' she asked.

'I cannot say. I fear they have killed each other. But there are no bodies to confirm my theory. If he lives, he is a threat to the Empire. An enemy of the throne and crown. Are you to go with your priestesses?'

She wondered just where the magics had withdrawn to. 'I cannot stay. This is not the place for me now,' she said, turning back to the temple. She tried not to look at those who littered the ground around her. The mist clung to their bodies. As the general had already been this way, she could only assume they were dead.

She looked out across the square through the thickening mist and felt the magic surrounding them. Whether it was the prince or not, it was angry magic. The mist grew thicker, until the she could no longer see the general or his men moving amongst the dead. Dark clouds hung low in the sky; there was the crackle of lightning and the rumble of thunder.

The magics were still strong in the Empire, and close. She would send the others away to ensure they were safe and that the priestesses' secret remained hidden. She would scour the island and find the magics. She might be able to sense them better than any hunter. With her decision made, her mind cleared and she felt calmer. The image of a black gate appeared to her, and she knew where they were. All she had to do was find the gate.

ACKNOWLEDGMENTS

Darja and Kim at Deranged Doctor Designs (DDD) for facilitating absolutely brilliant cover design work and all the marketing extras. Thank you for your support and clear emails around what was needed from me to make the magic happen.

TWG members: Melissa, Matthew J Morrison, John Hargreaves, Sue Larsen, Nicholas Jansen and Chantelle Griffith for listening and support in all things writing related. Special thanks to Yasmin and Belinda for taking the time to read what I thought was a finished draft and making the story stronger.

Allison E Wright for wonderful editing work. Despite my Aussieness sneaking in, she carefully smooths out my words.

My parents, Francine and Ken Smith. Amazing, supportive people who I don't thank often enough. Thanks for keeping me grounded and being the best grandparents ever.

As always, Temwa for being my biggest supporter.

ABOUT THE AUTHOR

Georgina Makalani survives life as a servant of the public by hiding in her office at lunch time with dragons, witches, a laptop and a little bit of magic.

For more about Georgina and her books visit her website: www.theflowofink.com

www.ingramcontent.com/pod-product-compliance
Lightning Source LLC
Chambersburg PA
CBHW032002130726
47903CB00012B/536